EVERYTHING OLD

Lindsey Brunette

*To nine-year-old Lindsey who knew this
was her future. You did it!*

We must be willing to let go of the life we planned so as to have the life that is waiting for us.

JOSEPH CAMPBELL

1.

Nurses go rushing past me in a frenzy down the sterile white hallway, nearly knocking the paper cup of hot tea all over my work uniform. I don't mind, my American brain can't quite wrap my head around the idea of tea instead of coffee but the coffee in the breakroom looks more like motor oil than a beverage and I desperately need my caffeine fix.

"We've got an emergency in the tower!" someone calls out. I've only worked at London's private Greenfield Care Home for a few days, and this is already the fourth such emergency. Such is the life of an elder care worker, I suppose. Believe it or not, I do love what I do, it's the only thing that I feel sure of anymore: this is who I am. But sometimes, it can be downright sad.

"That'll be Mary, I expect," says Linda, one of our most vivacious residents. Everywhere I've been since I started on Monday, Linda has been there, too. She doesn't seem like the type to waste away in her room the way some of the others do, she's always front and center to the action.

"You always expect it's Mary, you old coot," comes the reply from Jane, Linda's constant companion. They laugh and laugh, giggling more like schoolgirls than like women in their nineties. I like to imagine that they've been friends for their whole lives and have come to the home together in their old age. I hope to find that someday, a friendship like the one that Linda and Jane share; the kind of friendship where we go to the home to terrorize the other residents together.

Right now, that idea feels daunting. I moved across the ocean without knowing a soul here because Greenfield Care offered me a job and the pathway to a visa. I was so desperate to get away from my life back home that I hadn't stopped to consider things like friends. I just packed up and boarded a plane. I want to make it on my own, that's part of why I came in the first place. But it wasn't until I landed that I realized that making it on my own means being totally alone until that happens.

"Alright, everyone, listen up," my boss, Sheila, announces to the recreation room. It is only about half full of residents, because many are not like Linda and do want to spend most of their time in their rooms. "We've got a new activities director who's come all the way from America. She's been with us for a couple of days now, hasn't she? You've seen her around, and now she's ready to get to know all of you and take over the social calendar. So, without further ado, let's give a warm Greenfield Care welcome to Molly!"

I give a small wave, this is the fourth home I've worked in during my career and the second where I've had the title of activities director, so I've come to expect very little excitement surrounding my arrival. The welcome I receive today is even less enthusiastic than I might have anticipated, but that's okay. It just means I have my work cut out for me. Where some people might see that as an impossible obstacle, I see it as the very thing that makes my job fun and exciting. It's both challenging and rewarding to get these ladies and gentlemen excited about life again.

"What did you come all the way from America to work here for?" a grumpy old man near the back of the room calls out.

"Oh," I start, taken aback by receiving a question in light of the unfriendly welcome. "I... I wanted a fresh start in a new place." I try to smile but they're all staring at me like I've got a unicorn horn growing out of the middle of my forehead. I promise, I really do love my job.

"Well, I want to spend some time getting to know you and learning what types of things you enjoy so that we can work together on building a fun calendar!" I conclude. I don't usually mind being the center of attention in a work setting like this, but the way everyone is staring at me makes me feel extremely anxious and uncomfortable so I'm eager to excuse myself from the front of the room.

I make a beeline for the table where Linda and Jane are sitting and playing cards because I feel like I already know and understand them and that they're the kind of women I'd like for my friends – even if they are at least sixty years older than I am.

"Good morning, ladies," I say cheerfully. "I'm Molly, it's nice to meet you."

At first neither of them speaks, instead, Linda turns her head fully to the side to stare at me as she babbles something incoherent. Jane taps her hand softly and Linda pulls herself together, but I still can't tell whether she was joking or not. That's one of the tricky parts about this business, it's sometimes hard to tell when someone's age has taken control of their mind, to put it nicely.

"Never mind her, dear, we've got to find a way to liven things up in here while we can," Jane says then, excusing her friend's behavior as a joke, though I'm still not sure if I'm supposed to believe it. Jane is exactly the way I'd always imagined a British grandmother and I kind of wish I could claim her instead of my own Grandma Betty back in the States. Grandma Betty had always seen me as more of a nuisance than a blessing. I'm not sure what I had done or why she felt this way, but she had made it clear that I was the black sheep of the family and that there was nothing I could do to change that story. I had a feeling, though, that Jane never would have treated her grandchildren that way.

"I'd like to help with that, too," I explain. "What sorts of things would you enjoy? Maybe a dance to all the classics?"

Jane looks around dismissively. "I don't think many here would be up for dancing," she acknowledges. I can see what she means. Most of the people in the recreation room, aside from Linda, Jane, and a few others, are in wheelchairs and have probably been brought here by their families against their will. She pats my hand reassuringly, not unlike she'd just done to

Linda a moment ago, and it almost makes me feel like I'm a part of their little circle.

"You'll find something, you seem to genuinely want to try," she says reassuringly. Linda still stares at me without speaking, which I find odd since I have observed her over the last few days to be one of the most talkative residents here.

"I should introduce you to my grandson," she interjects finally. I smile thoughtfully, this is probably the number one comment I receive from my residents. Everyone seems to have a cute grandson who would be just my type. Spoiler alert: they never are.

"Linda, back off the poor girl, she's just arrived," Jane chastens. "What brings you to London, dear? Don't tell me it's the work." It is the work, literally. The work is the reason I am in London and not, say, Chicago or Sydney. But if you want to get into the reasons why I needed to be someplace else, then that gets a little more complicated.

"Like I said, I wanted a fresh start," I repeat. It's easier than providing an explanation, I've found. It worked especially well back home when people would ask me why I was moving. And it wasn't a lie, I was desperate for a new beginning in a place where nobody knew what had happened to me, it was just an omission of all of the additional details.

"She's been jilted," Linda says. "I've a keen sense about these things."

"Well," Jane jumps to my defense, "if she has been then it's no place of yours to pry."

"It's complicated," I answer.

"Jilted, and for her best friend, too! Shame," Linda continues. Jane scolds her again. Instead of feeling bothered, I'm kind of impressed. It's amazing, really, that she's been able to identify my situation so precisely without knowing the first thing about me.

Truth be told, I did have a best friend like Jane once. At least I thought that I did. Becca and I had been best friends since the first day of kindergarten back in Ohio, where I'm from. We had been inseparable all the way through high school and college, and we'd even shared an apartment in Cleveland after we'd graduated. Becca was like my sister, to the point that I'd chosen her over my actual sister to be the maid-of-honor in my wedding to Jake. Everything was going perfectly, she was right by my side through every element of the planning process; every fitting, every tasting, Becca was right there next to me. And then on the night before our wedding, Jake stood up to give a speech at our rehearsal dinner and admitted that he couldn't go through with marrying me because he was in love with someone else. Becca. I was completely blindsided.

That was six months ago, and I haven't spoken to either of them since. Whenever someone brings them up, I change the subject. But just ignoring them wasn't enough. I mean, it was at first, but Cleveland can feel like a small town sometimes, especially when you're trying to hide from the two people you thought that you could trust the most in the world. So when I received a call from someone at Greenfield Care who wanted to speak to me about my resume, I packed up and moved as far away from Cleveland as it made sense to do at the time. And now, here I am in London, starting my new job and my new life where I sublet an apartment that I keep forgetting to call a flat and drink tea instead of coffee. And I am all alone.

"Where are you living?" Jane turns her attention back to me, changing the subject.

"I'm renting a... flat. In Lisson Grove. Right on the... High Street above a... shop. I sublet it from someone I found on the internet and have never met or seen in person," I reply, stuttering over the words that aren't yet a part of my American English vernacular and providing way more information than either woman asked for.

I'd rented it sight unseen, at the time I'd agreed to sublet I didn't care where in London I lived because I didn't know anything about the city before I'd arrived. It comes out to just over a thousand US dollars a month and it's near a tube stop. Plus, the internet had informed me that it wasn't far from the private care home where I had accepted the job just a few days prior. I've already lived in it for a week and a half and it's comfortable, though the furniture left behind in the sublet is not to my taste. The woman I'd rented it from was subletting on behalf of her mother who hadn't updated the décor since at least 1985. The apartment itself has just the one room with an attached bathroom and features the nonstop musical stylings of my next-door neighbor, an elderly Chinese woman who sings to herself what seems like 24/7. But it will be fine for a while, I'll get to know the area better and figure out exactly where I want to end up.

I thought that the move would be easy. There was nothing left for me back home. But I'd chosen to move 3,700 miles away, to a city that I'd never been to and one where I knew no one. I guess maybe I'd been a little overly dramatic, but when I'd gotten the job offer here it seemed like the perfect opportunity to start over. The fact that they found me and helped arrange my work visa had made it seem like an easy way to begin again. And those parts of it had been easy. They'd been the only easy part. I feel like I don't know who I am anymore, now that everything is broken, but being able to jump right into a job with which I am so familiar has helped some. I just didn't expect it to feel so lonely.

"Linda, didn't you date that boy from Lisson Grove?" Jane asks, then turns her attention back to me. "Back in the fifties, Linda was quite the tart."

I smile, so I'd been right about them having been friends for years and coming here together. It made me love them all the more.

"What? Oh, yes, Georgie. He was a sweet boy. Handsome face, tiny prick," Linda says, almost as if she's not thinking about it. I stifle a laugh as Jane rolls her eyes.

I feel like I could stay and talk to Linda and Jane for hours but I know my job is to spread my time around to all of the residents and so I make to stand. As I do, Linda grabs my hand.

"You should meet my grandson," she repeats with earnest. I smile graciously and move onto the next table where the man who had heckled me about my arrival is gnawing on a digestive biscuit (another new vocabulary word!). The mashed pieces of the biscuit stick to his hands and his cheek.

"What do you want?" he mumbles as soon as he sees me. I try to smile, just like I'd done when he made his previous remarks.

"I just wanted to come and introduce myself since I'm new here. I'm Molly," I say. I don't offer my hand given the situation with the biscuit. He grunts in response and continues gnawing away at his snack. A cup of tea sits in front of him on the table, but he doesn't seem interested in it until a nurse breezes by and places it into his other, non-biscuity hand.

"Alright then, Angus?" the nurse, a girl I think is named Lily, asks him. He grumbles at her too, but happily takes a sip of the tea.

"Never mind Angus, you've actually caught him on a good day," she smiles at me warmly. I smile back, happy to talk to someone who isn't over the age of seventy. With the exception of Sheila, this is the first time it has happened since I started this job.

"We're glad to have you here, it'll liven the place up a bit," she continues. "It's been a while since there has been anything going on here to keep them busy. Most of them stay in their rooms and watch the telly all day. Can't tell you what day it is, but they can tell you about every plotline on *EastEnders*."

Just then another resident demands her attention and she makes her way across the room, leaving me alone with Angus and his soggy biscuit.

"Angus," I try again now that I know his name. "What sorts of things do you like to do for fun?"

He grunts again and keeps munching on his cookie, but this time something in his manner is different, like he's trying to think about something to say. "Football," he says finally, after painstakingly swallowing his bite of biscuit.

"You like football? Did you used to play?"

"Ah, here and there. More of a spectator, myself. Use to go watch those Eagles play every match when I was a younger man."

I smile and nod, though I have no idea who the Eagles are. I'd tried to study up on soccer before I made my move, but it had never been my sport and my research into the many different teams hadn't been very fruitful. Still, watching sports games gives Angus and me something to talk about at the very least.

"I'm sure you miss that. Do you ever watch them play on television?"

"Sometimes, but it's not the same. The roar of the crowd, a pint in your hand, the camaraderie... nothing compares to a live match!" He makes a noise with his mouth then that sounds a lot like a cheering crowd, whispering to himself as if he's providing the play-by-play report.

When people ask me what it's like to work with seniors, I often tell them it's like teaching grade school. One minute you're having an intelligent, thoughtful conversation and the next minute they're off. Sure some, like Jane, are sprightly and with it, but even they can have their moments... just like a child. You just do your best to capture their attention before you're forced to move on.

That's been the theme of my life the last few months, someone forcing me to move on. I never had a say in any of it, it wasn't like I'd wanted to be jilted right before my wedding day. If it had been up to me, I'd be married right now, living a quiet newlywed life in Cleveland, Ohio. The only choice I'd made for myself in any of this was the one to take this job and move over here. Even now, the reminders of being forced to move on come at me in ways I don't expect. I'd promised myself that it wouldn't get in the way of my work, but sometimes it can't be helped. You'd think that after six months I'd be doing pretty well. At least that's how I feel, like if it happened to anybody else, they'd be living their best life by now... but me? I'm still really struggling. I keep wondering when I'm going to wake up and feel differently, if I ever will at all.

2.

I go back and forth between feeling homesick and forgetting that anything is different. The latter sometimes seems impossible, but then there are things, like talking to my sister on the phone after work, that happen the same way here as they happened back home and it's a lot easier to forget than I would have thought.

"So, how's the first week going so far? I can't believe you're living in London! It sounds so glamorous! Tell me everything!" It's the middle of the afternoon back home in Cleveland, but my sister Mindy is a stay-at-home mom, so she's found time to chat in her SUV while her son is at baseball practice.

The small talk about my apartment and the sightseeing I've managed to squeeze in so far is nice; it feels familiar, like my sister is just on the other side of town and not over three thousand miles away. No one in my family had understood why I felt like I needed to pick up everything and move to another part of the world. In their opinions, Columbus or Cincinnati would have been plenty far enough for me to begin again. Mindy was no different in that regard but talking to her still helps give me the feeling of home that I've been missing so much since I arrived here.

Mindy is older by four years, but based on the trajectory of our lives, it might as well be forty years. She's always been so much more settled than I have been. She married her husband, Greg, right out of college and she'd worked for a few years at a law office until they'd had their son, Teddy, and she'd quit her job to stay home with him. Teddy is nine now, and he's seriously the coolest kid I've ever met. Mindy's never regretted quitting to be with him, and she's never struggled to find her place in the world. She knows exactly who she is, she always has. That's part of what makes us so different.

Unlike Mindy, I've bounced all over the place. Our parents split up when I was sixteen and I'd spent the last two years of my teens going back and forth between the house I'd grown up in and my dad's new condo in the city. I didn't have it easy in college the way Mindy had seemed to either. I didn't meet the love of my life or graduate with a job that instantly allowed me to live the life my sister had had and that made it tough for me. It's always been hard not to compare myself to my sister because literally everyone else always has. I was born in Mindy's shadow, and no one has ever let me forget it. Except for Mindy. She is about the only person on the planet that has ever seen me as Molly and not just as Mindy Walton's baby sister.

"I keep thinking I can just invite you over for lunch on Sunday, and then I remember." I roll my eyes. She's always had a flair for the dramatic.

"God, Min, it's not like I'm dead!" I laugh.

"I know that, it's just… it feels so far away. Couldn't you have stayed closer to home?" she asks, renewing the argument that my family has been making ever since I'd told them about my decision to move in the first place.

"I guess, but this is where I got the job offer. Besides, it's kind of fun don't you think? This new adventure? You said yourself that it sounds so glamorous." I try to sound upbeat whenever I talk to Mindy because the last thing I need is someone in my family trying to convince me to move back. I'm afraid that if she started asking, I'd cave immediately and be on the next flight back to Cleveland before the dot even landed at the bottom of the question mark.

The truth is, in the week and a half I've lived in London, I've only had conversations with my coworkers, the residents, and a checkout girl at the market on the street level below my flat who had tried to quiz me all about my American accent. I've tried to walk around and explore my new city some, but since I wasn't working until just a few days ago, I was doing my best to conserve my resources and didn't make it very far. The first three days I was here, I watched the changing of the guard at Buckingham Palace each day, because it was the only thing I knew was free. It's been a much harder transition than I had anticipated and it's only now that work has started that I have any hope that that might change.

"I know, it's just weird is all," she admits. I survey the room as I wait for one of us to think of something else to say, the lady who rents me this apartment has a strange collection of spoons from all over the world in a curio cabinet next to the table and they make for a good distraction when I need them to. Apparently, she's been everywhere: spoons from Copenhagen, Las Vegas, and Johannesburg are displayed right next to those from Dubrovnik, Buenos Aires, and Hong Kong. The spoons have no purpose except for being reminders of vacations past, but they are strangely fascinating, and I find myself getting lost in the wonder of who this woman was that she traveled to see both the Statue of Liberty and Christ the Redeemer before her daughter was forced to sublease this flat.

"So, have you heard from Becca or Jake at all?" Mindy asks suddenly. It's out of the blue and enough to bring me back to the dismal reality that is my life. My whole body tenses at the sound of their names.

"No," I snap.

"Have you thought about call…" she begins before I cut her off.

"No, Mindy. Just… no," I say. I can't believe she's even bringing this up right now. The whole point of me moving so far away, the thing that doesn't make any sense to her, was to get away from them. Having to hear their names is not something I want to make a part of my London life.

"Well, I just thought that…" she starts again.

"Mindy, I can't talk about this. You should know that better than anyone. You were there," I cut her off again. She sighs deeply and drops the subject. Maybe it's immature of me, but I don't see why I should have to discuss my ex-fiancé and my former best friend and their new budding relationship, which from the state of social media (that I have definitely stalked) is all rainbows and butterflies. Whether it's immature or not, I'm angry at Mindy for bringing them up and for reminding me of how my whole life fell apart. I end our conversation quickly because I can't deal with her or this anymore. I know I'll have to talk about it eventually, but right now I still can't. Every time I try, I'm reminded of the betrayal, and it fills me with rage.

*   *   *

I'm still angry the next day when I make my way into work. It's the kind of thing where I wish that I had a friend at work (or at all) that I could vent to about these kinds of things, but I haven't found anyone yet. I don't even know where to start with making friends. I'd never had to think about it before because I'd had Becca for so long and that relationship had formed naturally when we were five. I have a feeling that making friends is a little bit different now that it's not just asking someone to play on the monkey bars with you at recess.

On top of not knowing how to make friends in general, I feel like it's especially hard to do here. It's not really a problem with the city so much as it is that the people seem different somehow. Everything I've ever known about human interaction doesn't seem to work for me here the way it might have in Ohio, and I know that's probably not a thing and the problem is my own insecurity with trying to meet people. But it makes for a good excuse at any rate. A lot of the nurses and assistants seem to be about my age, but they're chummy with one another and I've never been great at inserting myself into existing friendships. That's why what Becca and I had was always so great, we had been friends for so long that we didn't even have to try. It makes me miss her for just half a second before I remember and get angry all over again.

"Morning, Angel Face," one of the male assistants greets me as I'm in the staff room placing my belongings into a locker. I'm already angry so I know immediately that this interaction won't end well for him.

"Does that line usually work for you?" I snap bitterly. He looks at me like he doesn't know what I mean. "Like, does a woman ever hear you call her angel face and demand that you must take her to bed immediately?"

He looks back at me thoughtfully. "Your knickers a little tight today, love?" I roll my eyes so hard that I feel like they might get stuck in the back of my head.

"Sorry, rough night," I respond finally. It's not this sexist assistant's fault that I'm angry. He nods in acceptance of my apology, which I find to be a strange gesture, but it's fine with me because I don't want to continue our conversation any further.

"Jimmy!" someone else greets him as they walk into the room, saving me from having to speak anymore. I'm sure that Jimmy now probably thinks I'm just a crazy American with no place here. That's what everyone else seems to have been thinking ever since I arrived. Or maybe it's just the way I think everyone is thinking, there's no way to be sure since I don't have anyone to ask. *I* feel like I'm just a crazy American with no place here. Maybe that's it.

It's hard not to eavesdrop on the conversation Jimmy is having with the nurse, whose name I remember is Cat, especially since they're having it right in the doorway preventing me from being able to make an angry, albeit quiet, escape.

"She's been getting worse lately," they're saying. "Even Jane isn't able to help her anymore, at least not like she could when they first arrived."

My mind wanders to Linda and Jane, that must be who they're talking about. Who else could they mean? There's only one Jane in the whole place.

"Well, her family is adamant that she not be moved to Memory Care just yet. They want her life to be as normal as possible," they continue.

"It's that blasted grandson of hers. *Sam.* He's a real self-righteous twat, that one."

"He means well, how'd you feel if your Nan was laid up in a place like this?"

"I just don't see how Jane is doing her any good. She could hardly keep her on track when they first got here – now it's like a toddler trying to wrangle a monkey," Jimmy says. I can feel more rage rising in my cheeks. I've only met them once, but I've already taken a special liking to Linda and Jane, I feel a certain sense of loyalty to them. And I don't like the way Jimmy is talking. Still, they're blocking the door and I have nowhere to go. I look down at a stack of magazines on a table, they're all tabloids and I don't recognize anyone on the covers, but it gives me a way to avert my eyes.

"Not our place, we just do what the families want," Cat replies. Then it's like she notices me for the first time.

"Hey, new girl, a couple of us are going out for a drink after our shift tonight. You should come," she says. I look up then, pretending to be startled by her notice, like I haven't been listening to their entire conversation, and agree. Even though I'm in a bad mood, this might be the only chance I ever have for friendship in this new city, and I can't afford to turn it down.

Friends! Imagine that! Everyone at work has been nice enough. Other than Jimmy's bizarre pickup line, I've been treated with kindness and respect ever since I started here. But kindness and friendship are two very different things and I'm excited for the prospect of seeing what friendship with these people is all about.

My loneliness in the last several months has made it glaringly obvious that I used Becca as a crutch for too many years. While I haven't made any new friends here, I also didn't do a very good job of maintaining the ones I'd had back in Ohio. I don't know if I was too embarrassed by what had happened or if I was certain that they'd all side with Becca over me, as so many people had done throughout our lives, but I'd let things fall by the wayside and I'd allowed my loneliness to overtake me. Thanks to the offer of drinks with my co-workers, an occasion that feels special even though it's one that I've celebrated dozens of times in my life, I might finally be on my way.

As Cat and Jimmy finally unblock the door, I am left to run through everything they've just said about Linda, and though it's not a totally shocking revelation, it makes me sad. I think about how every time there is an emergency call, she expects it will be Mary – though I've learned there's no Mary who lives here. But no matter what, Jane is by her side. I miss that, what I used to have with Becca, that friend who is there no matter the circumstances. We'd always joked about how they'd have to send us to the home together and that we'd be in our walkers terrorizing the other residents up and down the halls. In fact, once in high school they'd done an "old people" spirit day where we'd done just that. We'd outfitted ourselves in long cotton nightgowns and Velcro curlers and large plastic framed glasses with the lenses popped out and then we'd pushed walkers we'd purchased at a drug store up and down the halls of school, yelling for kids to get off our lawns. Remembering it now brings a smile to my face, especially since it's exactly the kind of thing I can see Linda and Jane doing.

The happiness of the memory fades quickly. I've had a lot of that these last several months. The memory of a good time I shared with Becca will come up and make me smile, and then I remember how she ruined any chance we ever could have had of making more memories and I get angry again. Not having anyone else to talk to about it hasn't helped, other than Mindy there hasn't been anyone to commiserate with me about just how awful Becca was in the end. And sometimes not even Mindy is willing to do that. Maybe tonight after work that will change. Maybe I'll be able to meet my new Becca – my Jane. My friend forever, until the end.

3.

Making friends is supposed to be the easy part. That's the reason I hadn't given it any consideration before I jumped at the chance to move someplace new. I'm friendly, I'm likable, I'd want to be friends with me. I'd always had plenty of friends back home, though now I could count the ones I still think about on one hand. I had ended almost all of my friendships, mostly by accident, after what happened - partly out of shame and partly out of being so busy trying to survive that I forgot to keep in touch. Now I'm here, in my new city and my new life, trying to figure out how I'm supposed to make friends at this stage in my life. Drinks after work with my co-workers seems like a good place to start, it's certainly something that's worked in the past.

I've heard a lot of stories about English pubs, mostly from books and movies, so I have certain expectations when I walk into the one that's just down the street from our facility. Because of these, it's a little disappointing to find that it's just like so many of the bars I had visited in Ohio. Still, I try to follow the lead of my co-workers as they order at the bar and settle into a table by the front door. You know, just in case there is some kind of strange pub etiquette of which I'm not aware.

It's weird that I'm struggling so much with culture shock here. Part of the reason I'd been responsive when Greenfield Care had reached out was because I thought that it wouldn't be all that different in London. After all, we already speak the same language, I didn't think there would be much more to it than that. But even something as simple as ordering at a bar with co-workers, something I've done hundreds of times in my life, feels foreign. Just the other day when I was trying to buy some groceries, I asked about ranch dressing and the clerk looked at me like I had three heads. There are so many things that I didn't even know I was taking for granted back in the states. Not to mention that the way of life here is different: I'm too loud when I talk; apparently, I write the date wrong, and the time, too; also, my tone is too positive, which is strange considering that I can't think of anything that I have to be positive about. These are just some of the things I've learned in my first week and a half in town. Stand by for a more comprehensive list to come.

"So, what's your story?" Lily asks me once we've all settled in with our drinks. Everyone turns their attention toward me and there's nothing I can do about it.

"Well, I was looking for a new adventure, something to get me out of Ohio. And I heard about this job and thought 'why not?' and now here I am," I reply.

"There must be more to it than that, this is a big move. Did something happen to make you want to set out looking for adventure?" Lily presses. I take a long drink of my beer and think about how I want to answer.

Over the last six months I've gone through a wide array of answers. At first, I was always completely honest with anyone willing to listen, and even some people who weren't. In fact, I'd often lead with the story of how Jake had left me for Becca the night before our wedding, just to get it out of the way so that no one could find out on their own and start asking questions. Then I began to learn how to craft the story to make me seem less pathetic, if that's even possible. I mean, even I must admit that it sounds pretty pathetic. If it was someone else telling the story, I'd have so many questions: How did you not know this was happening? Didn't you see any signs at all? But the answer, for me, was no. I had been completely blindsided. Maybe I'd been too busy planning the wedding to notice. I remember being happy that Becca and Jake were friends because I felt that made my life so much easier. I never, in a million years, would have imagined that their relationship was anything more. I'd never needed to. But eventually, telling their part of the story got to be too much for me to handle. Around the time my visa came through, I started telling my current story: that I needed a change and decided that moving to a different country made for a great adventure. I don't know what version of the story to tell today.

"It's pretty complicated and I don't want to bore you with my sob story," I begin finally. "I've just gone through a lot of changes in my life in the last six months or so. I thought that everything was going to be one way and it turned out to be something else entirely and I felt like it was a good catalyst for making a new life. So, here I am."

It's hardly an answer, but the group seems satisfied, and they quickly begin other conversations. It's easiest, I find, to give this vague answer to those who have never met me before because they don't ask any follow up questions. When someone is a stranger, you're more prone to believe that they genuinely just needed a change of scenery than that there must be some hidden motive underneath it all. By the time I'd begun to tell this version of the story back home, there was hardly anyone in my life who knew any better. This version isn't a lie. I absolutely decided that I needed a change and while adventure isn't my usual forte, I had been looking forward to the excitement that would come with living somewhere new. It's not the entire truth either. If I wanted people to know the truth, there was nothing stopping me from telling them... except for my own shame.

It's hard not to feel like an outsider with this group, they've clearly been friends for a while, and it shows. The four of them, I learn quickly, started around the same time and started making a point of going out for drinks after work as a way of blowing off steam. Besides Lily, Jimmy, and Cat, there's also Tom who I'm told works in the kitchen, which explains why I've never seen him in my life before tonight. They're all nice enough, and they seem to be trying to make me feel included. It's just hard to readjust to hanging out with people my own age after the last week of socializing only with our elderly residents.

"Where do you live?" Cat asks after a while, turning the conversation back to me. I smile as I tell them about my subleased flat with the weird spoon collection and how everything about my life currently feels borrowed. They laugh and smile and return to their own conversations, and that's when I notice him out of the corner of my eye for the first time – the man sitting at the bar who seems to be keeping an eye on our table. He's one of the most attractive men I've ever seen in my life: dark brown hair perfectly coiffed over chiseled facial features and just the right amount of stubble. He's wearing a suit, though he's removed the jacket and has loosened the tie, and he's nursing a scotch at the bar while he throws sidelong glances in the direction of our table. I can't help but blush knowing that his eyes are on me.

I haven't noticed men since Jake. Not because I don't eventually want to meet someone else, it's just hard to think about meeting someone else after you've been hurt so badly. So, the fact that I can even look at a man and notice he's attractive is kind of a big deal for me, at least it's a bit of progress. Jimmy follows my gaze, and when he reaches the end of it he swears under his breath which only draws the attention of the rest of our group.

"Sam," Jimmy says with contempt. "What's he doing here?"

"I'm going to go out on a limb here and say: having a drink, same as us. Aye?" Tom jokes.

"It's a public place," Lily chimes in. "He probably needs a drink for the same reason we all do. Imagine if Linda was *your* grandmother?"

Wait, THIS is Linda's grandson? The one she keeps telling me that I should meet? If I'd known that he looked like that, I would have agreed right away instead of putting her off like it's always been my habit to do with residents in the past. I've never met anyone with a grandson like Sam before. I wish I hadn't been so quick to dismiss her when she'd mentioned him, not that anything would ever come of it. Like Linda, a woman with dementia, would ever follow through on introducing me to her grandson.

"Well, we shouldn't just sit around here talking about him. We don't want our *lack of propriety* reported back to Sheila," Cat says with similar contempt. Though I haven't worked with them long enough to know what the problem with Sam is, it's clear my co-workers are not fans of Linda's grandson. But until I know their reasons, I'm content to keep a snapshot of his face in my mind. It's too nice of a face to be spoiled by their opinions after all. Finally, Cat offers a wave, to which Sam nods in acknowledgment before he swallows the dregs of his drink and heads for the door.

"Tell me about America, I'm dying to go," Lily says then. It keeps me from being able to watch Sam leave, which is a little annoying, but I don't say anything, instead turning my attention back to where it belongs.

"I don't know what to tell. I mean, if you're planning on visiting your experience is going to be different wherever you go. I can tell you about Cleveland, but if you're planning on going to New York or L.A. or Florida… those are going to be nothing like Cleveland. It's like if someone heard you were from London and asked you to tell them about Europe because they've always wanted to visit Berlin," I say, feeling a bit more confident to speak up with a beer in my hand.

"You've got to be more specific, Lil," Jimmy jumps to the defense of one of us, though whether it's of Lily or me I'm not sure. "Like, what's the deal with American football?"

I laugh, it is a particular obsession but not one I've ever understood. "That is a question I can't answer. At least not from an athletic perspective. But it's fun to go to games. Everyone wears team colors, and you sit and cheer while you eat hot dogs and fries… er, chips and drink beer; I never pay attention to what's happening on the field. Not that I could tell you what's happening if I did pay attention, it's not my sport," I reply. Jimmy seems satisfied and looks around the table to see who is going to ask me the next question.

"I've got one then," Tom says with a laugh. I've been watching him tonight, since he's the only person I hadn't met before, and I'm expecting his question to be a joke before he's even asked it. I'm not disappointed. "Why do you all wear clothes made out of your flag?"

The whole group laughs and for a second, I feel like it's at my expense, but when the laughter finally stops, I find that Tom genuinely wants an answer. "I guess some people think it's patriotic, that it represents national pride with their clothes. I don't personally own any flag themed clothing," I say. "There are some people there who think Ginger Spice's Union Jack dress signifies a similar trend from this side of the pond," I add before they can start laughing at me again. And this time when they laugh, I feel much more like they're laughing with me.

"Honestly, though," I say after a few minutes. "I thought that moving to London would be a breeze. We speak the same language, but that is sometimes all that feels similar. I wasn't expecting such a culture shock. It's been quite the struggle."

When they ask, I begin to tell them about the things that make me feel like I stick out like a sore thumb. There's nothing they can do to fix any of these things, they're just things that are going to come with adjustment. My experiences don't ring true for any of them either. All four of my new friends are born and raised Londoners and have only ever known the one way of life. Up until a few weeks ago, if any of them had picked up and moved to Cleveland, we'd be having the exact same conversation in reverse.

"The one thing I am grateful for is that the work is the same," I add finally, when I'm afraid that things are starting to sound a little bit too 'woe is me.'

"Really? You're grateful for that place?" Cat asks, as if she genuinely can't believe it.

"Well, I like the work. And since it's what I've done for years back in Ohio, I feel confident in being able to go to work and not totally feel like an outsider. Plus, I love meeting new people and hearing their stories. I always hope that I'm able to make the end of their lives a little brighter," I respond.

They all look at me like they're trying to figure me out. It makes me a little uncomfortable to have every single pair of eyes trained on me all at once. I've never been particularly fond of being at the receiving end of an interrogation, even a friendly one like this; I think it comes from the time after my parents' divorce when I'd go from one house to the other and have to sit on the couch and explain what happened at the other house as if I was putting on a one woman show. It always made me feel like I was sneaking around and betraying the other parent, so I finally just stopped doing it. Having all the eyes at the table on me now reminds me of so many of those old feelings, only this time I feel like I'm betraying myself. I can feel the color rise in my cheeks the longer they look my way, which feels like it's been close to ten minutes at this point, though I know that it hasn't.

"Well, I think that's cool," Jimmy says, finally breaking the trance of endless stares at my bright red face.

"Cool?" Tom asks, poking fun at Jimmy's word choice.

"Sure," Jimmy says then, unfazed by the criticism. "It's good to like your work and to feel like you're making a difference in people's lives. Without that, what have we got? It's just a boring existence, day in and day out. So yeah, I think it's cool that you like the work, Molly."

With Jimmy's comment out in the air, everyone seems to shrug off my opinions and move onto other things. He gives me a wink from across the table and I smile gratefully. To be honest, I don't know where I stand with these people. One minute it seems like everything is going well and then the next they're judging me because I say that I do enjoy my work. I can't tell if I have any chance of ever being friends with them or not. But at least I'm not sitting alone in my flat eating buttered noodles for the fifth straight night in a row while I try not to think about what time it is in Ohio and what I'd be doing at that time if I were there. Being out with people who may or may not become my friends is definitely better than that.

4.

I guess that when I decided to pack up my life and move halfway around the world, I thought it would somehow distract me from the reality of my tragic tale instead of serving as a constant reminder of everything that happened when my life fell apart. In my fantasy life, which I'm afraid to admit has grown very active over the last six months, I would land in London and my life would instantly resemble a romantic movie in which I was the adorkable heroine for whom everyone is rooting. Something about London had contributed to that fantasy, but honestly, I didn't have time to think it through. I was so desperate to escape my life back home that I would have gone just about anywhere. And now, it's Saturday morning and I'm sitting home alone in my 1980s subleased flat, flipping through channels on the TV and finding absolutely nothing comforting or familiar.

Things were okay at work after the pub. It's hard to truly be friends with your co-workers during work in our field because we all have staggered schedules and an array of responsibilities. But at least I no longer feel like a stranger to them and that makes things a lot easier. Still, it isn't the kind of thing where I know any of them well enough to ask about or try to tag along for Saturday plans, at least not yet. I have spent a good deal of time wondering what Sam is up to, though. It's a fun distraction: imagining him at the gym in a sweaty t-shirt, sipping coffee and reading a book at a cozy cafe (weirdly still in his sweaty t-shirt), catching a movie with his friends (really wearing the heck out of that t-shirt...) It's harmless, it's just a lot better than thinking about Jake and Becca all the time.

To add to my boredom, it's four o'clock in the morning back in Cleveland, so I can't even call Mindy to help me pass the time. She's the only member of my family with whom I'm currently on speaking terms. Things had never been great between me and either of my parents after they'd split up, but those relationships have only become more strained as I've gotten older. Everything seemed to be going well with my mom when we were planning the wedding together, but after Jake's announcement everything changed. She blamed me for the wedding being called off and for her losing out on all of the deposits. As for my dad, there's not any real reason that we don't talk – other than the fact that he got busy with his new family about ten years ago. I guess he's trying to not be an absentee father this time around, which is great for my half-sister but doesn't do much for Mindy or me. Her name is Mallory because Dad said he wanted to keep all of the names consistent. She's eight, which is weird considering that my dad was having a baby around the same time as his oldest daughter, but she seems to be a pretty cool kid, from the little time I've spent with her.

The knock at the door startles me and pulls me out of my thoughts. I've been so caught up in them that I've almost forgotten that there is a world outside of these walls. Self-centered Molly, per usual.

"Oh, hello," I greet my neighbor. I'd been told by my landlord that her name is Mrs. Wang, but that's all I know about her. She smiles at me but doesn't speak.

"Can I help you with something?" I ask. She seems sweet and harmless, the type of older woman that I work with every day. And just like so many of those women, too, she seems to be totally alone. In the time that I've lived here, I haven't seen anyone coming or going from her flat. The only thing I have noticed about her at all is the constant singing. Today though, she is silent.

"Yes," she says after a moment, as if it's taken her a few extra seconds to process my question. I wait for her to elaborate, to tell me how I might be able to help her, but she doesn't speak. Instead, she turns and begins walking slowly back toward her own door.

"Guòlái," she adds. She motions with her hand that I should follow her.

"Um, English?" I ask awkwardly as I close my own front door behind me. She shakes her head slightly and I can only imagine what life must be like for her in a world where she doesn't speak the same language as her neighbors and is totally alone. It makes me a little sad just to think about it. I may also be totally alone here, but at least I can understand and communicate with everyone around me.

Inside her flat, which is laid out in the mirror image of my own, it is dark and heavily furnished. There's hardly room to walk, but I can tell that each piece is precious and meaningful to her by the way she gingerly rubs a hand over each as we pass by. I don't know what I'm thinking, going into a stranger's home without knowing the first thing about them. But something about Mrs. Wang puts me at ease. If I'd had relationships with my own grandparents, I think that being here could easily make me feel homesick. Instead, I have Grandma Betty, and so far, I haven't missed her at all.

Grandma Betty is my mother's mother and we've never particularly gotten along. I don't know why exactly, I never did. But I don't have any memories, even my earliest childhood ones, where Grandma Betty seemed to like me. To hear her tell it, I was no Mindy. I would never measure up to the, apparently, incredibly high bar that my sister had set simply by being born first and there was nothing I could even do to try. To Grandma Betty, I always fell short. I wasn't as tall as Mindy or as pretty as Mindy or as smart as Mindy or as successful as Mindy. You'd think that this attitude would have pitted me against my sister, but instead it just made me resent my grandmother. I stopped trying to impress her when I was about thirteen and I've never regretted it.

"Oh, thank you," I respond as Mrs. Wang hands me a

steaming cup of tea that I did not ask for. If we didn't have a massive language barrier between us, maybe I could better surmise whether she was just looking for a friend, or if she did, in fact, need my help with something. Although the tea is delicious and I had so far done nothing all day, nor did I have any plans to, standing in her kitchen without knowing why feels like a major inconvenience on my day.

Mrs. Wang and I drink our tea in silence, which is the only way we can drink it without any ability to speak to each other. Somehow, though, it doesn't feel awkward. It feels like I am having coffee and a chat with a girlfriend. Maybe I'm lonelier than I had originally thought. Still, it's nice to sit with a companion and not feel like you have to fill every inch of your time together with words.

"Jiā," she points to China on a globe that she's retrieved on one of the seven bookshelves which line the walls of her cramped living space. I smile, though inside I can't help but think 'yeah, I could have told you that.' She turns the globe slightly and then points to England and makes a disdainful noise in her throat. Then she hands me the globe and I understand that she wants me to show her where I come from. So, I turn it a little more and hover over the United States before I place my finger down right along the shore of Lake Erie where I had spent my entire life until a couple of weeks ago. She smiles and repeats "jiā." I make a mental note to look up this word when I get back to my flat, though I have a pretty good idea that it probably means "home."

Now that we've found a way to communicate with each other, Mrs. Wang seems beyond thrilled. I watch as she pulls framed photos down off the shelves and hurries over to show them to me. First, it's a black and white wedding photo of a beautiful couple dressed in traditional Chinese dress. Then it's a photo of the same couple with a little boy, then the family at what is presumably the same little boy's graduation ceremony. These are followed by a picture of another wedding; the groom is the same young man from the previous photo. Next is Mrs. Wang sitting next to the young man, cradling a baby in her arms, but this time, Mrs. Wang's husband is not pictured. And then a photo of the young man's family, the baby now about four years old, standing with Mrs. Wang in front of Big Ben. It's amazing how these photos give me such a complete picture of her life without words needing to be said at all.

I pull my cell phone out of my back pocket and open my photo gallery, attempting to give her the same kind of glimpse of my life. There's not a lot I can show her, though. In a fit of rage on what would have been my wedding night, I deleted every image that I had ever saved of either Becca or Jake. I hadn't regretted it until now, because now I have no way to show Mrs. Wang how I came to be her neighbor. She's the only person I've met so far in London that I've actually wanted to tell. Instead, I show her pictures of me with my sister and nephew and with my dad's replacement family. Even though they're not much, Mrs. Wang smiles and laughs and claps her hands at each photo. I get the sense that she feels much the way that I do about being here in this strange city all alone. We're both so hungry for human connection.

I've almost forgotten why I'm there when Mrs. Wang grabs a box of crackers off the counter and thrusts them in front of me. "M. T," she says. It sounds more like she's saying the two English letters than a word.

"Empty? Do you want some more?" I ask.

"Yes. More," she answers, nodding her head vigorously. I want to ask what that has to do with me, but I've been listening to Mrs. Wang try to communicate with me and I can only imagine how difficult it must be for her to try to navigate an English-speaking world with her limited skills.

"Would you like me to pick some up for you?" I continue. She seems to understand more than she can speak, so I know that I have to lead the conversation. She nods and claps again, I know her joy is less over the crackers and more that she has found someone with whom to communicate, but it's easy to confuse the two. She pushes way too much money into my hand, but rather than protest I decide it will be easier to bring it back as change than to try to help her count out the accurate amount.

"Alright, I can go down later today, would that be okay?" I ask. She nods and claps again. To be honest, I'm feeling a bit elated myself.

I think I finally have a friend in London.

5.

B Fourteen! Bee One Four!" I shout. I quickly write the number in large print on the dry erase board I've set up next to the number bowl. I've had a slow start in my role as activities director, it's been hard to get people excited about much of anything when the people who have held my role in the past have let it fall by the wayside. But today I've finally found something that works: the recreation room is packed full of residents, some I've never met before, who are the most excited I've ever seen them about playing bingo. I don't know what it is about the elderly and bingo, but it's always something I can count on to draw them in no matter what and no matter where in the world I find myself. It also requires next to no effort on my part since I've done it so often. Maybe that's laziness, but it's nice to have those fallbacks at work that you can always count on.

"Next number... O Forty-Two! Oh Four Two!" I exclaim, erasing the first number and replacing it with the second.

"Bingo!" comes a voice in the back.

"You can't have got a Bingo yet, she's only called two numbers, Angus!" comes another.

"But I have got. I've got the O Forty-Two," Angus answers matter-of-factly. And so, I explain the rules of bingo again.

Over the years I've talked to quite a few people who find my job to be boring or they'll apologize and ask what it is that I want to do. I guess I can see why they'd think that, when I'm explaining the rules of bingo to a group of geriatrics for the third time in fifteen minutes. But I've never seen it that way. I've always felt like you have the most patience for the group of people with whom you're meant to spend your time; and for me, that's always been these folks. And when Angus calls "Bingo!" again after the third number, I just ignore him and get on with the game.

After I'd brought her new box of crackers over on Saturday, Mrs. Wang had tried to get me to stay for dinner. I think. Anyway, I had picked something up at the market that wasn't buttered noodles when I was there on her errand, and I'd been kind of excited about it so I'd had to decline. She'd turned up again yesterday, too, and we walked in silence to Regent's Park where she had worked on a knitting project while I read a book. When we'd returned home, I felt strangely like I'd spent the whole day with a close friend. The way that she had patted my arm when we parted told me that she felt the same. I liked the way it felt so natural to slip into that with her. We could hardly speak to one another but spending the day with her had been the most pleasant afternoon I'd had in months. I can't remember the last time I made a friend so easily. There's always been some sort of pretense involved, drinks or coffee as a trial run... almost like dating. But with Mrs. Wang it all felt different, like I'd always known her.

"All right, Angus really does have a bingo! Five squares in a row! Good job, Angus!" I cheer as I hand him a sleeve of chocolate biscuits. It's ironic that I'd be rewarding Angus with biscuits after the soggy, slobbery way that we'd met and even more ironic that he was the day's first winner given his slow understanding of the game. The latter got its fair share of grumbles from the other residents; until Angus started distributing the chocolate biscuits, that is.

If it weren't for the accents, I almost would have thought that I was back in Cleveland, doing the thing that I've always done. It almost feels like my life is the same as it always was; that Jake and I got married and that Becca is still my best friend. It almost feels like I can call Mindy up after work and talk to Teddy about Field Day. And then I hear someone speak and I remember.

"Is everything alright, dear?" Jane's voice asks sweetly as I'm packing up the game components. I guess I'd been lost in my own thoughts a little more than I'd realized, but I offer her a reassuring smile.

"Just feeling a little homesick," I reply. I don't want to burden her with my problems, she already has enough of her own by being Linda's constant companion. I expect her to walk away then, instead she places her hand on top of mine reassuringly.

"I've had my share of those days since moving to this place," she offers. It's something I hadn't considered, but Jane probably moved here voluntarily when Linda's family told her it was time. She'd given up her life and her freedom to be a source of comfort for her best friend at the end of her life. The thought of that breaks my heart, reminding me again of Becca and the way we used to joke about going to the nursing home together.

"She was right, wasn't she? Linda?" Jane asks. She must have seen it on my face. I'd almost forgotten that Linda had so accurately guessed the situation that really brought me to England. I hadn't admitted it then and I don't admit it now to Jane either. But somehow, she knows.

I've been afraid of people finding out the truth ever since it happened. I'm so ashamed. And to have other people knowing that shame just adds to the feeling. It's embarrassing. How did I not know? What signs did I miss? Surely there were some, or something other people noticed that raised red flags? I've tried to ask Mindy this several times, she was the closest to the situation and would have noticed if there was anything amiss, but she always says that she never saw any signs at all either. As far as she was concerned, everything was going exactly as it should. So, if there had been any signs, I missed them all. That's why I feel so ashamed. I was so caught up in work and planning the wedding and trying to have a perfect life like my sister's that I completely missed all of the things that could have saved me the heartache and the shame.

"Why don't you come up and join us for a cuppa?" Jane interrupts my thoughts. "We like to sit and have a cup in the afternoon before supper."

"Oh, I don't know if I'm supposed to. I'm still on the clock," I answer quickly. It's not that I don't want to spend some time getting to know Linda and Jane, it's the thing that I've most wanted to do since I started working here. However, there are policies about what we can and can't do with residents and I don't want to cross any lines.

"It's alright," Jimmy says from over my shoulder then. I didn't even know he'd been standing there. If I think about it, Jimmy isn't that bad looking. He has a nice smile and handsome eyes, though he's got a bit of a belly, which is only accentuated by his work uniform. But I don't think about it.

"They're not going to come looking for you, and if anyone asks, I'll say you're on a break. You do have those in America, right?" he continues snarkily. I smile and assure him that I am, in fact, aware of breaks. "Well, then. Don't turn down the lady's offer."

And so, without another thought, I find myself following Jane to her room and sitting across from Linda at the small table while Jane makes tea.

It's a nice room, you can tell that Jane has taken great care in making it as homey and familiar as possible. I would guess that was for herself as much as it was for Linda. It's slightly smaller than my flat, with a bed against one wall. All of the furniture feels very much like it belongs to an old woman. It reminds me of my Grandma Betty's house, of Mrs. Wang's flat, and even of my own subleased temporary home not far away. I wonder how she did it, made it homey I mean. These rooms usually all look the same and yet, somehow, she has managed to make it her own.

Linda is muttering something to herself as she sits, it's so soft that I can't make it out but whatever it is seems to make her happy, so I don't try to intervene. I'm only just realizing that I've never spoken to Linda without Jane's assistance so I wouldn't know where to start even if I tried. That's not something that ever would have bothered me in the past, but something about these two women makes me feel nervous. Maybe it's because I know that in another lifetime, they would have been my friends.

Or maybe it's because even in this one, I desperately want them to be.

"I hope you like Earl Grey," Jane says. She sets a steaming teapot down on the table. I haven't been to any official English teas so I'm not sure if she's using a teapot to serve the tea because she assumes that's what I'm expecting or because that's actually the way it's done. In my flat, I just pour hot water from the kettle over a tea bag directly into my mug. Back in Ohio I was even lazier, putting a mug of tap water straight into the microwave for heating. Whatever Jane's reason is for using the teapot, though, I like the touch.

"Oh, I do!" Linda replies excitedly, even though the comment hadn't been directed at her. There's a glazed-over look in her eyes and I just catch Jane looking away sadly.

"Earl Grey has always been Linda's favorite, ever since we were girls," Jane adds. She regains her composure and turns back to pour.

Linda has returned to her muttering and now I can faintly make out the melody of "A Bicycle Built for Two." She smiles and sways in her seat as Jane pours her a cup of tea but Linda hardly seems to notice, she's too caught up in her song.

"Daisy, Daisy..." Linda suddenly sings at full volume. "Remember we used to sing that song with Janie during the war?"

"I remember," Jane answers. I feel like a fly on the wall, sipping my tea, unsure of where to insert myself into their regular daily life. Jane shakes her head sadly and pats Linda's hand like she had done to my own in the recreation room.

"How often does she get like this?" I ask. I'm not an expert on dementia, but I've been around enough people with the disease to understand its progression.

"More and more often these days," Jane replies. I nod in understanding, though I can't possibly imagine what Jane is feeling as she watches her friend deteriorate.

"I moved here by choice to be with her," she starts after a moment. I had already deduced this on my own, of course, but I let her continue. It's clear that the thing she needs most is to talk with someone who is aware of what she's saying. Because I'm willing to listen, I find I am soon privy to the reason she came to live here by choice.

Jane Reynolds and Linda Suthcliffe had met when they were ten years old in 1941. They'd lived blocks from each other their entire lives, but Linda went to an all-girls school while Jane received a thorough education through the Church of England, so their paths had never crossed. But the night they met, their families had been forced underground by Hitler's Blitz on London and they had ended up taking shelter side by side. Jane's mother sang softly with them to drown out the noise of the battle overhead and by the time they had reemerged above ground the next day, they'd become inseparable. Linda's older brother was killed in the war and her mother was never the same after his death. Linda practically grew up at Jane's house after that; Jane always felt a particular responsibility toward Linda. They ended up together at the University of London at the end of that decade and to hear Jane tell it, you'd never seen two more rambunctious girls. They had their run of the city, Linda always had men chasing after her, and Jane had had a few romances herself. And though she'd never married, Jane had been there to support Linda for every step of her life's journey: marriage, children, career changes, grandchildren, her husband's eventual death... it was like, Jane joked, poor Marty had gotten two wives for the price of one.

"She named her daughter Daisy, after the song we sang that night," Jane concludes. "Daisy Jane."

There are tears welled up behind my eyes, I can hardly hold them back, but I manage, swallowing down the giant knot that's formed in my throat with the last of my tea. The story of their friendship is the most beautiful love story I've ever heard in my life, and it makes me simultaneously incredibly happy and insanely jealous. This is a kind of love that it feels like I might never have.

6.

It takes a month of bingo to feel like the residents, and even some of the other workers, begin to acknowledge me in the halls. It's nice to finally feel like I have a bit of a presence here. For a while I felt like I was moving through my life like a ghost, so I'm happy when I receive another invite from Lily to join my co-workers for a drink after work.

I haven't been out to the pub with everyone since the time they grilled me about America. I don't know whether that means they haven't gone again or that I just wasn't invited, but I've tried not to spend all my time thinking about everyone doing things without me. Besides, Mrs. Wang and I have developed a routine of drinking jasmine tea and playing mahjong every night after dinner. I'd learned to play in one of the homes I'd worked at back in Cleveland, and Mrs. Wang had been so excited to make the discovery. This ritual is something that I've come to look forward to as I head home each night. Still, I tell Lily that I'd love to come even though it's trivia night and I don't want to play; mostly because I know that it's probably not healthy to spend all of my free time with an elderly woman who only speaks Chinese. I feel only a little bit guilty about it, Mrs. Wang always watches for me to come home in the evenings.

Frankly, these days I'm looking for anything that can help me pass the time so that I don't spend it thinking about Jake, Becca, Mindy, or my life back in Cleveland. Work has helped some, now that I'm fully immersed in my job, I have plenty to keep me busy until I get home. And then when I'm playing with Mrs. Wang, we can't talk about it and that helps some, too. Going out tonight will be just one more thing to distract me.

I keep trying to tell myself that I should no longer care; that I should be over it by now. After all, it's been almost eight months. But then again, Jake and I were together for four years and Becca and I had been best friends for nearly three decades. I think that's why it still stings. Truly, they did me a favor. I literally almost went through with marrying him, and I would have been none the wiser. They did me a favor, but the betrayal stings worse than anything. And even if I am ready to be over Jake… I think it's going to take me a while longer to get over Becca.

"Earth to Molly," Cat waves her hand in front of my face. I've been lost in my own thoughts again, the worst kind of company for a night out.

"Sorry," I stammer. "I was just thinking about…"

"Fuck em'," Jimmy interjects before I can finish. "You moved here for a new life, right? So, let's have that then."

He raises his pint to tap mine and the rest of the group chimes in with a hearty "hear, hear!" It fills me with the unexpected warmth of friendship, and I take a long sip of my drink to keep from getting too emotional about it. I don't have time to anyway, just then Cat announces that trivia is about to start, and Lily and Tom follow her into the back room to play the game. No one says anything when I don't follow and Jimmy stays behind with me as well, so at least I'm not a total dork who is sitting in a pub by myself.

That makes me think of Sam, who I haven't seen since the night that he was sitting here in the pub by himself. I've tried to come up with excuses to see him, but I don't know what I'd say if I did manage to make that happen. Still, I've spent a good deal of time thinking about him since then, even when the timing isn't right. Like right now, when I'm supposed to be out with my maybe new friends.

Tonight, it feels different in the bar than when we were here the last time. Maybe it's because it's familiar to me now. It's no longer some strange, foreign landscape but a place where I'm beginning to feel that I belong. It no longer feels odd to walk up to the bar and order a beer or to sit at the same table with this group of relative strangers. The only thing that's missing is that Sam isn't sitting at the bar, watching us out of the corner of his eye. I'd be lying if I said that I hadn't silently hoped, in agreeing to come tonight, that he'd be here too. That would have been the icing on the cake. Now that I've already been given the third degree by my co-workers, we're able to just hang out together and it feels like all of the other times in my life when I've gone to a bar with friends.

Even though I'm having fun, Mrs. Wang has crossed my mind more than once. I wonder what she thought when I didn't come home as usual after work or if she sat and played mahjong solitaire instead. I feel bad that I had no way of even calling her to let her know the reason for my absence. Even if I'd had her phone number, how would I have been able to make my point? So much of our communication relies on images. Tomorrow when I see her, I'll have to show her a picture of friends hanging out together to convey where I went tonight. Somehow our special way of talking to each other always seems to work out just fine, but it doesn't work if we can't see each other.

"You're really in your head tonight," Jimmy says over my shoulder as he comes up behind me. We were on our third round as a group before the others went off to play trivia, but the way his speech has slowed I can tell he sped ahead when none of us were looking.

"I guess I just have a lot on my mind," I answer. He sets his beer down hard on the table, causing mine to splash up over the side and scoots in close.

"Still hung up on what that bastard did?" he asks. I shrug, it wasn't what I'd been thinking about just then, but it was never far from my thoughts. It's a lucky guess on Jimmy's part, of course. But when a girl runs halfway around the world to escape her life, I guess it's easy to assume there was a man involved. Not that he knows any of the details, it was just a lucky guess.

"I just don't understand how I didn't even notice that anything was going on!" I erupt, unloading the entire story on

Jimmy. The way it spills out, I can tell I've had quite enough to drink. It's not that I feel particularly drunk, but I haven't been this honest with anyone about what happened in eight months and it's obvious that the only thing helping my honesty now are these two and a half beers.

"You're so much better than him," Jimmy says finally. It seems like a standard response considering I've just finished giving him all the details of the worst thing to ever happen to me. He places his hand on my knee under the table and I don't move it. I'm not sure whether that comes from my candor, the three beers, or a sense of genuine loneliness, but when Jimmy leans in to kiss me, I don't stop that either.

The kiss is a little sloppy, given the alcohol consumption involved, but I don't hate it. It has been over half a year since I'd kissed anyone, six years since I'd had a first kiss with someone new. I can't even remember the last time I kissed someone like this in a bar. I can't even remember the last time I kissed someone like this at all.

These are things I've been trying to remind myself of over the last eight months. There hadn't been passion in my relationship with Jake for at least a year. It had gotten comfortable for us to live our lives and passion was an afterthought. Maybe that's why he turned to Becca, maybe he'd found passion there. Becca was passionate about everything she did all the time, whether it was cooking dinner or decorating a float for the homecoming parade, Becca went all in with a kind of passion I'd rarely, if ever, witnessed in someone else. Of course, Jake would be drawn to that. His very life is passion - as a firefighter, so much of his job relies on passion and adrenaline. It seems only natural that he'd want a partner that exudes the same. It's easy to see why they would have ended up in each other's arms. Ugh. I hate them. I've spent eight months trying to make sense of all of this but every thought I try to use to help myself rationalize leads me back to what Jake and Becca did and makes me angry. I think that's why I'm so stuck.

I'm in my head again, while kissing Jimmy. That's not fair

to him and I pull myself back into the moment before he has a chance to notice. It feels nice. His arms are strong as they wrap around me, his tongue knows exactly what it's doing as he works around inside my mouth. It is a good kiss, and I don't want to stop myself from enjoying it, but I'd be lying if I said I wasn't imagining what it would be like to kiss Sam. I may like kissing Jimmy, but I have a feeling I would love kissing Sam.

"God, Molly, you're so sexy," Jimmy whispers when we part for air. I glance around for the others, wondering who might have witnessed this escapade, but they're still playing in the other room.

"They'll be in there for a while yet. Cat takes trivia very seriously, and Lily and Tom go right along," he says.

"You don't want to play?" I ask.

"I'd rather be here with you," he answers flirtatiously. He has a nice smile, it brightens up his whole face and makes him look cute in an adorable way.

"Yeah, I'm getting that vibe," I laugh. Honestly, I can't remember anymore who came onto who, it just happened kind of naturally and easily. I had forgotten what that could feel like.

When I'd met Jake, it hadn't been that way at all. The guys from his firehouse had come by the facility I was working in at the time to give a lecture to the residents about what to do in case of a fire. I'd set the whole thing up and after they'd finished Jake sent the rest of the guys back to the truck while he asked for my number. I gave it to him reluctantly because he said he wasn't leaving until I had and I was worried about causing a scene. He'd called me that night and asked to take me out that Friday, again he wouldn't take no for an answer. At first, he'd always schedule our next date while we were still on the current one, making it harder for me to say no. It was Becca who helped me to see what was so great about him back then, so by the time he asked me to be his girlfriend, I really did like him. But none of it was ever easy or effortless, not like this.

"So," Jimmy starts and then pauses. "Do you want to get out of here?"

As much as I hadn't been expecting to kiss him in the middle of the crowded pub, I expected this question even less. I don't think I'm the kind of girl who goes around kissing men in bars, tonight notwithstanding. I know I'm not the type of girl that goes home with men that she's been kissing in bars, but a part of me wants to say yes. Maybe what I need is a rebound, someone to have passionate, meaningless sex with to help me get over what I'd had with Jake. I had no doubt that Jimmy would treat me well, he seems like the kind of guy who'd even make me breakfast in the morning. But I don't want my first-time post break-up to be passionate and meaningless. It has been fun kissing Jimmy, but I don't know if I can take it beyond that. At least not tonight.

"Oh, I... no. I don't think that would be a good idea. I mean, we work together. It could get awkward and I'm so new there," I manage to say finally.

Jimmy's face falls a little. Had he thought our drunken make out had actually meant something? Had he planned on kissing me tonight in hopes that he could more easily sleep with me?

"But I *like* you, Molly. Haven't you noticed?" he asks. It's as if he thinks the fact that he likes me is enough to make me rush off and jump into his bed. I hadn't noticed and I tell him so.

"Please! It couldn't have been more obvious. What about how I cover for you whenever you go have tea with those two old lezzies? That's not allowed but I *covered* for you," he's getting angry. And after the way he talked about Linda and Jane, I am too. Right at that moment, the three other members of our party emerge from their trivia game, and I've never been happier to see them.

"Everything alright here?" Tom asks. Jimmy's posture indicates that it's not, but he doesn't speak.

"Um, yeah, it's fine. I think Jimmy's a little drunk," I offer, sweetly. Maybe it wouldn't be a big deal to them, but I don't want anyone to know about what's happened here tonight. Instead, I excuse myself and head quickly for the door.

I'm not sure what just happened exactly. It went from lighthearted and fun to something almost scary very quickly and I didn't like it. How am I supposed to go back to work tomorrow and think about doing my job when I might have to face Jimmy knowing things ended this way? I mean, I know, I was definitely kissing him, too, but does my word mean nothing? Like the fact that I was kissing him means that I most certainly want to sleep with him now? I know it's been a while since I've been single... but that just doesn't seem right to me. It's so confusing, and I'm not sober enough to think about this. That's a major part of the problem. All I want to do is get back to my flat (sneak in, really, so that Mrs. Wang doesn't notice) and sleep all of this off. I can't try to think about it until my head is clear anyway.

7.

Things aren't any more clear when I wake up. Had Jimmy ever wanted to be my friend? Or had he only ever been motivated by the fact that he liked me? I'd never been very good at being able to tell. In high school, Becca always used to tell me that so many boys liked me, but I only ever noticed that boys wanted to be my friend. In fact, part of the reason I'd ended up with Jake was because he made it clear that he had no interest in being my friend, though that put us at odds in our relationship for other reasons. I had always thought it would be nice to be friends with someone first, but the fact that Jimmy used the pretense of friendship to skip straight past that stage leaves me wondering what's true. Jimmy had been friends with Lily, Cat, and Tom for a while. What if they were all in on it, too? It's all too much to think about, even sober.

The good news is that Jimmy has the day off. He's the last person that I want to see today, and it means that I can focus on my work and allow that to distract me until I have more time to think. Because the other part of it that I can't wrap my head around is the part that I played in what happened. I may claim that all I want from Jimmy is friendship, but I kissed him back. I didn't pull away or say no. I even considered leaving the bar with him when he asked. What does that say about me? What does that say about the kind of person I am? Do I actually want friends, or do I just want to sabotage every chance I have for real friendship?

"Good morning!" Cat says cheerfully. She brushes past me into the employee lounge. My biggest fear had been that Jimmy had started talking as soon as I'd left the pub and gotten all of our co-workers on his side. But Cat's greeting tells me that he stayed silent. That's confirmed as she continues. "Sorry about Jimmy last night, he can be a nasty drunk. What happened between the two of you anyway?"

I don't answer, shrugging my shoulders slightly. If I decided to tell, I'd be doing the exact thing I'd been afraid of Jimmy doing last night after I'd left. If I expect that silence from him, then I should offer my silence too. I still have a lot to think about, because the fact of the matter is that I'm more confused than angry. Until Jimmy turned on me, I had enjoyed kissing him and I don't want anyone else to be in our business about it.

"Well, I'm glad you've started coming out with us," Cat continues after my silence has gone on for just a beat too long. "It's nice that we outnumber the boys now. Makes it harder for them to gang up on us." I try to make myself as cheerful as Cat, offering a small laugh and a bit of small talk. But I'm just not as cheerful as she is, I haven't been cheerful in months.

"Did you hear about the meeting today?" she asks then, her tone turning much more serious. I had heard about a meeting for all of the department supervisors but not the reason it has been called and I tell her this.

"Sam's coming," she answers matter-of-factly. It's a simple enough answer but all I can think of is his name flashing on a neon sign inside my brain. SAM! SAM! SAM! I hope this recognition isn't also flashing across my face. As thoughts of Sam push in, thoughts of Jimmy push out, and for that I'm grateful.

"Sam is Linda's grandson," Cat explains. At first, I'm confused because I know this already, but then I realize that she's trying to do me a favor by explaining it because I've never met him and while I feel like I know him from my deeply fulfilled fantasy life, I only know him by the group's reaction to seeing him that first night at the pub.

"He's in charge of her care and he likes to come in and have these meetings about her progress as if she's the only person we care for here," she goes on.

"Oh, that's kind of sweet," I say.

"It was kind of sweet the first time, but now it's just exhausting. We have to get her freshly washed and primped and make sure the whole place is spotless. He's always bringing printouts from the internet about new treatments for her condition or ways to change her diet to assist her cognition. Like we don't know what we're doing here," she goes on. So far, I haven't spotted the problem with Sam. I mean, sure, it's time consuming that he wants to come in and meet with everyone all at once, but I've sat through plenty of those meetings in my career and they are always helpful in making sure that everyone is committed to the same level of care for the patient.

"He's just such a pompous prick," she exclaims finally, getting to the real heart of the issue. My heart sinks a little, Sam's a jerk. I guess I should have expected it, no one that good looking is ever a nice guy. "Not bad to look at though," Cat throws over her shoulder as she heads off to start her day.

I hadn't been told to prepare for the meeting, though I assume I'll need to attend. As activities director, I've found through the years that family members like Sam are very interested in providing insight into the types of activities their family members should be doing. I try to never let it get to me; sometimes that's easier said than done, but in the end, I try to remind myself that we all want the same thing for the person in our care. I feel confident that Sam and I will see eye to eye. After all, I've developed a soft spot for his grandmother and her friend, more than I have for any of the other residents. If anyone is looking out for her best interests around here, it's me.

Sure enough, I receive word about my need to be in the meeting as soon as I emerge from the breakroom. Some of my colleagues act like it's the end of the world to have to present in front of Sam, but it doesn't bother me. I already feel pretty confident about what I'll say, and prepping a short presentation helps to keep my mind off Jimmy and on Sam for just a little while longer. There's so much to unpack about last night that I'm actually grateful for the respite that work offers.

"Right this way, Mr. Collins, sir," Sheila is bumbling in a way I've never heard as she leads Sam into the small conference room right off of her office. There aren't enough chairs around the table for all of us, so I've taken one in the corner away from the group. It's the perfect vantage point for me to survey the room and look attentive in the meeting while also providing me a direct view of the man of the hour.

Everyone blubbers all over themselves as soon as he steps into the room, much in the same way that Sheila had been doing on her way in. It's more than just his good looks, though, I know that he pays a lot of money for both Linda and Jane to live here and to keep Linda out of Memory Care. Everyone falls all over themselves to give Sam a glowing presentation of the facility, it's almost comical. The chef tells Sam about Linda's diet and then Sam provides some material about the benefit of a Ketogenic diet for people with dementia, and then the chef blubbers over himself as he explains how they try to offer low carb alternatives. Then the head of housekeeping talks about how her staff cares for the living space and Sam provides some documentation about the chemicals in cleaning supplies and their effects on the brain. It's not hard to see, after the first couple of presentations, why these meetings have come to be dreaded.

Soon, I'm being introduced to Sam Collins for the very first time and talking about our weekly schedule and the activities in which Linda likes to participate... which is not at all how I'd imagined or practiced our first introduction all of those times in my bathroom mirror.

"Have you read the journals about activities that keep up cognition and motor skills?" he launches immediately after I've finished my presentation. Instead of blubbering, though, I have a comeback all ready to reply.

"I have. We try to provide as many of those freestyle activities to our residents as we can. Jane usually gets Linda to sit down and color every day using the printed sheets we provide. You can usually tell how she's doing that day based on her strokes of the marker. We also work with puzzles, and she is particularly drawn to those. The more intricate ones seem to be getting more difficult for her to grasp, but she's happy to put the pieces together whether or not they fit. I have put in a request for some cognitive development puzzles. They're similar to the kind you or I might buy as a gift for a new baby, but they're specifically designed for and targeted toward senior adults with dementia. They're cardboard or wood in a distinct shape with a peg in the center. We used them in my last facility back in Ohio and our dementia patients did very well with them," I respond confidently. My colleagues look across the room at me as if they can't believe I've had the nerve to speak to Sam with so much self-assurance. It's the same thing I would have said to anyone else who had come in and wanted to know how we were helping their grandparent, but apparently around here, Sam is a god. This is also true in my fantasy life, but I am trying my best to keep that separated from my work.

"Right then. Good," he says. He stares at me quizzically for a moment before turning back to Sheila to see who goes next. Once my part of the meeting is done, I kind of tune out everything else and just watch Sam. Internally, we're already all on the same page about Linda's care so I know exactly what everyone else is presenting to Sam and I don't need to listen.

After the meeting, Cat practically accosts me on the way out of the room. "Oh my God. I can't believe you've gone and done that!"

"Done what?" I say, trying to sound innocent. I know exactly what she means.

"Gone and talked to Sam that way! I'd watch out for Sheila on that one if I were you!" Cat warns.

"Cat," I say finally. "What am I missing? I mean, I get that he's good looking, but that can't be the reason that everyone is so gaga over Sam."

"Oh darling," she says sympathetically, "I forget you're new here sometimes. Sam Collins is one of the biggest television presenters in the country!"

"Is that all?" I am genuinely surprised that it's not something bigger than that the way everyone carries on, really, they're just star struck.

"Is that all? What more could there even need to be? The fact that he keeps his Nan here is huge for our business. Everyone else wants to put their grannies here too in hopes they'll make friends with Sam's."

"So, we're extra nice to him so that he doesn't move her to a different facility?" I ask.

"Well, yes. And I mean, he is handsome, so that certainly doesn't hurt," she admits.

I had no idea Sam was anybody. I had only ever heard his first name, so I had never been able to look him up and while Mrs. Wang and I watch television almost every night, it's usually the BBC News with Chinese subtitles. Does it make a difference for me to know that Sam is famous? Not really... it's easier to have an unrequited crush on a celebrity than it is to have one on your patient's grandson. This is what I'm thinking about as I make my way from the meeting back into the recreation room.

"Molly, dear," Jane calls out to me from their usual table as soon as I enter the room. "Come meet Linda's grandson, Sam."

I put on my best smile and make my way over to my friends. I think it's safe to call them that, aside from Cat and the rest of my coworkers, Linda and Jane are the closest things to friends that I have in this place. Still, I've never made friends with any of the residents at any of the homes where I've worked in the past. Fraternization is generally frowned upon as it can show nepotism to one resident over another.

"Molly is it?" Sam asks. He extends his hand to shake mine, looking at me with the same intense stare he'd given me in the meeting.

"Nice to meet you," I smile, accepting his hand and shaking firmly.

Sam's about to open his mouth to say something else when Linda interjects. "Sammy, she's the one that I've told you about.

Jilted. Single. Looking for love," she chides him. I can tell by his body language that he is as uncomfortable with the way this conversation is going as I am. He brushes his hand through his hair and looks away sheepishly. I have to stop myself from wishing that it were me rubbing my hands through his hair. This is the first time in the history of my career where I've wanted for one of my residents to follow through with the promise to set me up with their grandson.

"Now Linda, I never said I was looking for love," I laugh, trying to break the tension. It's true. I'm not looking for love. I haven't been able to think about love or finding it in months. I wouldn't say I'm not looking for Sam, though. Even while I haven't been able to think about finding love, I've had no problem whatsoever thinking about Sam. Up until now, it's always been harmless.

"I just know these things," Linda says. She picks up the marker she'd been using and resumes coloring on the page in front of her using neat, precise strokes. She's having a good day.

"Well, I appreciate all of your help with Granny," he says politely. "These two can be quite the ornery bunch."

I look at them fondly before I respond. "Ornery women are the best kind if you ask me."

8.

An online search for Sam Collins doesn't produce anything particularly juicy or exciting, which seems strange to me if he's as famous as I've been told. I find only what I already know that he's a television host covering entertainment and that he's born and raised in London. There's no scandal, no photographs of him doing anything other than looking professional. The worst I can find are some fan pages on social media where women (and some men) express their, apparently, unquenchable thirst for him. Which, I mean… same. Either he has really good people working for him, or he really is as squeaky clean as he appears. Still, now that I know more about him, it's nice to be able to do some sleuthing on my own, and to have some actual photos of him to fuel my fantasies.

I'm just about to click onto page two of the image search in the hopes of finding something akin to my sweaty t-shirt fantasy when there's a knock on my door. I know who it is before I even open it. I'd been worried about Mrs. Wang being angry with me for not coming straight home after work last night, but I can tell by the use of her usual knock that she's already forgiven me.

"Hello, Mrs. Wang," I greet her. A smile fills her whole face when I do, and it makes me forget all of my cares for a moment.

"I'm sorry I didn't come home right after work last night," I begin, wondering if she's understanding me at all. "I went out for drinks with some of my coworkers." Even if she doesn't understand, she smiles and nods right along with every word anyway. I haven't had a chance to pull up a picture of friends to give her the illustrated version of events, so I have to hope that she understands enough English to follow along.

"OK, Moll-ee," she says, patting my hand. It's the most coherent sentence she's spoken to me, and the first time she's ever attempted my name. My heart swells at the thought of her sitting at home during the day and practicing my name as she waits for me to come over and play mahjong. My heart swells, too, knowing that she's not upset with me that I didn't tell her about my plans, all instantly feels forgiven.

Perhaps it shouldn't bother me so much that I hadn't been able to get in touch with her about my change of plans. But that's the kind of thing that friends are supposed to do. They're supposed to call and let you know that something has come up. So, the fact that I hadn't been able to do that for Mrs. Wang, the one friend I have in London whose friendship I don't have to question, bothers me. I know myself to be a better friend than that.

Mrs. Wang follows me into my flat without me having to give her an invitation, which at this point doesn't even faze me. When she first started waiting for me to come home, I found it invasive that she'd invite herself right into my apartment. Now if she didn't follow me, I'd be worried that something had happened between us or that she no longer felt that connection with me.

"Mama?" a man's voice calls from the hall. I'm almost startled until Mrs. Wang jumps up excitedly from the spot where she's been sitting at my small kitchen table. "Nǐ zài nǎ?" the voice continues.

"Sheng!" she calls out to him as she runs toward the front door, throwing it open excitedly. As soon as she's across the threshold she hurls herself into the man's arms. It's the fastest I've ever seen her move, and to be perfectly honest, the entire situation is fascinating to watch. Sheng looks up and sees me then, standing in the doorway, and he immediately breaks the embrace, his face turning apologetic.

"I'm so sorry, was my mother bothering you?" the concern in

his voice is endearing. I realize then where I've seen him before, in the pictures Mrs. Wang has shown me of her family. I had surmised that they lived in London and that's why she was here, but I'd never seen any sign of him around her flat until tonight. Foolishly, I'd imagined that she was all alone in the world, just like me.

"No, not at all! We're friends!" I exclaim. I'm definitely overcompensating for his concern but working in a convalescent home makes me acutely aware of children who feel their parents are burdensome and there's nothing that bothers me more. Mrs. Wang beams at me as if she knows exactly how I feel about her. I hope that she does.

"Wǒ de Moll-ee," she tells him, pointing at me. I have no idea what she's said, other than my name. As soon as Mrs. Wang and I had met, I'd downloaded a language app, determined to learn to speak the language to surprise my friend. So far, the only phrase I've learned to say in its entirety is "Wǒ de xuēzi li yǒu yītiáo shé" which translates to "there is a snake in my boot" and does nothing to further our friendship. It's not fair since Mrs. Wang always tries to use English when she talks to me. It would really come in handy now that she's talking to her son, although he speaks English, I'd love to hear both sides of their conversation.

"Ah, yes, Molly. Of course," he says, extending his hand. For just a second it reminds me of Sam extending his hand in the same way just hours ago, a thought I'm not expecting.

"My mother has told me so much about you, I apologize that I didn't immediately make the connection," he continues as we shake. His Chinese accent is only very slight when he speaks English and he's dressed in a perfectly tailored suit that if I had to guess I'd say was custom made on Savile Row.

It's easy to tell how much Mrs. Wang adores her son. As he speaks, she hangs on his every word in rapt attention, whether he's speaking English or Chinese. The expression of pride and love that she wears on her face can't be wiped away, it's the kind of parental love that usually makes me feel a little bit jealous. My parents had only ever seemed to love Mindy. But for some reason, I just can't bring myself to be jealous of Sheng Wang. Maybe it's because I know that on some small scale, Mrs. Wang shares some of that love with me too.

"I came to pick her up and take her to our home for dinner. Would you like to join us? I'm sure my wife wouldn't mind," he tells me before turning to his mother and explaining to her what he's asked me. I know this is what he's doing because her face lights up with that radiant smile again and she turns to me nodding emphatically.

"I wouldn't want to impose on your family time," I say. Besides, it might be kind of nice to have a night to myself to eat crappy food and watch crappy television and think about what happened with Jimmy last night while also looking at more photos of Sam on the internet. This day seems determined to keep me from collecting my thoughts.

"Come, Moll-ee," Mrs. Wang adds. It's less of a request and more of a demand, I will come whether I like it or not. It makes me laugh out loud. I'm starting to learn more and more about my friend's fiery personality, and I have to say that I like it.

The Wang's house in the Fitzrovia part of London is the type of Terraced House I'd only ever dreamed about or seen in the movies. It's perfectly inconspicuous and is made out of the same beautiful brick that is reminiscent of Dickensian London, in my mind at least. It's exactly the kind of place where I had pictured myself when I'd imagined what type of person I might be able to become after my move. I have to remind myself that I'm just a visitor here, and that I am yet to become anyone other than who I'd tried so hard to leave behind.

"It's been my goal, ever since we purchased this home five years ago, that my mother should come and live here with us. There is a separate apartment on the ground level that's currently undergoing renovations for her use. I'd hoped to have it finished before she came from China last year, but we ran into delays with the permitting. So, we've been putting her up in the flat in the meantime and feeling terrible about it. Until she met you, that is," Sheng tells me as we enter the house's main foyer. The inside of the house is even more beautiful than the outside, it looks like it could stand in for an *Architectural Digest* piece on feng shui in the modern home. I don't know what I was expecting but I feel startled by the appearance of money that surrounds me. Of course, Mrs. Wang has never been able to tell me anything about her son, so other than knowing he existed and that he lived somewhere in London, I never would have pictured him living this lavishly, especially not given Mrs. Wang's flat.

"I know what you're thinking, why wouldn't we put her up closer to us? But she wouldn't have it. We looked at several flats when she first arrived and that was the only one she was willing to accept us paying for," he says, as if reading my mind. "I had half a mind to just buy the whole building so that at least I could make sure she was being looked after. But Mama likes her space and her freedom too much, which I swear will be the death of me. That's why my wife, Jie, and I were so grateful to hear when she started talking about her new neighbor and the time you were spending together."

Jie, I find, is one of the most beautiful, and also one of the sweetest, women I've ever met. She is dressed from head to toe in designer labels but unlike some women I've met with a similar style, she never once says a word about it. I know that the decor inside the home is entirely her doing, I can tell as soon as I'm introduced to her because I can picture her sitting and having a cup of coffee in every single room of the house that I've seen so far. Their son, Jasper, runs to and fro wearing a red cape around his shoulders until he spots his grandmother and squeals "Nainai!" loudly.

Mrs. Wang lights up when she sees Jasper, more than I even saw her do with Sheng. I'm enjoying just watching her be in her element like this, with her family. They're obviously her true joy and I'm sorry that we have the language barrier to hinder her being able to tell me all about them. I'm sure that if we could talk about them, I'd know everything in the world that there is to know about Sheng, Jie, and Jasper Wang.

"I hope you like Chinese food," Sheng says politely as we make our way to the dining room. "We weren't expecting guests, so we didn't order out. My wife prepared the meal."

"I'm sure it will be delicious. I don't know that I've ever had real Chinese food, just the kind that comes in a cardboard carry out box," I reply. As soon as I've said it, I wonder if it's rude to comment on the commercialization of the cuisine. Sheng just laughs, though, and tells me he's sure I'll like this much better.

As we sit down to eat, I'm struck by the fact that not only is Jie beautiful, well-dressed, and seemingly intelligent, but she also cooks their meals and has the ability to silence a rowdy five-year-old with one simple look. She's basically a super woman and I'm in awe, though I've just met her.

Mrs. Wang munches happily on her meal, chatting away in Chinese with her family. Occasionally she turns toward me and smiles widely, as if I'm included in the conversation or have any idea what they're saying to each other at all. I don't mind not knowing every part of the conversation because the food is delicious. All I've ever been able to cook well is pasta with store bought sauce so I'm always excited when I get to enjoy a home cooked meal. I feel the familiar pangs of homesickness as I think of the many evenings I spent at Mindy's. She'd gotten all of the cooking prowess, by the time I had been old enough to learn, there wasn't anyone who wanted to teach me. When I was in Ohio, it hadn't mattered, I could always go to Mindy's for home cooking anytime I wanted to but now that I'm here on my own, it's something I've missed. Now I feel content sitting here with them, being a part of this family unit. It's something I haven't experienced since I left home and even though there is a language barrier, families are families all over the world. To be honest, with the exception of Mindy, sitting here around the table with the Wangs feels better than it ever did sitting with my own family for all those years.

They try to make small talk with me too. I learn that Sheng works for a Chinese investment firm that has several properties in both the United Kingdom and the United States. I'm most surprised to learn about the time he has spent in Cleveland, and I get to talk about my hometown with someone who isn't totally unfamiliar with it. Jie is an orthopedic surgeon, which just further cements her superhero status in my mind. Even Jasper is fully bilingual and already appears to be succeeding in life far more than I. Still, with all of their accomplishments, they don't make me feel inadequate at all.

After dinner Mrs. Wang joins Sheng to get Jasper ready for bed and I follow Jie into the kitchen where I insist that she let me help with the cleanup.

"I'm sorry we didn't have a fancier meal for you, if I'd have known you were coming, I could have prepared something else," Jie admits apologetically.

"Are you kidding? This was great! Thank you so much for allowing me to join you. Mrs. Wang didn't give me a choice," I answer as I accept the towel she has held out to me to dry a dish.

"The transition has been difficult for her, so we try to cook traditionally whenever she comes over. It's customary in our culture that we care for our aging parents and that we all live together in one home. Sheng tried for years, when his father was still alive, to get them to move to London and they refused. My husband is so much like his father was, stubborn, unwilling to budge. When he passed away, Sheng insisted that his mother come and live here. She still didn't want to come but he insisted that it was his responsibility to care for her now and he would not have it any other way. I think she chose her flat on purpose because she knows it's farther away and costs less money than Sheng would have liked. But that's Mama Ting, always tormenting him," she tells me as we wash.

"Ting," I repeat under my breath, it's the first time I've ever heard Mrs. Wang's first name.

"We're so grateful for you, though," Jie continues. "You have been like an angel sent to us to be Mama Ting's friend. Ever since she started talking about 'My Molly', that's what she calls you, Sheng has been able to breathe a little easier knowing that she's not totally alone over there. I don't know what we'll do when

Mama Ting finally comes here, I can't bring Sheng to think about it. In his mind, she belongs here and that is that. But to separate the two of you, that will be harder than my husband believes."

'My Molly.' It makes me smile. No one in my life has ever claimed me before, and it feels so special that the person who finally has would be Mrs. Wang. I've grown so attached to my neighbor and companion, I guess I should just call her what she is, my friend. I think of her as mine too. 'My Ting.'

9.

I've been planning my first big event at work since almost the moment I got here. Something about these people and this setting reminds me of this phase Becca and I had in fifth grade where we were obsessed with post-war America. Well, really Becca was obsessed with it after she found an old yearbook of her grandmother's and I just went along with it because if I wanted to see Becca, I had to be obsessed with it too. We'd go over to her house after school and listen to this AM radio station that replayed broadcasts from the era, and we'd pretend that we were older and that our boyfriends had just come home from the war. It was silly and we were just being kids, but that phase has always helped me feel a special connection to the residents in the homes where I've worked over the years. This phase lasted for several months, and we managed to log a lot of time with the AM radio, so it's always felt like I'd shared a part of my childhood with these people. As soon as I stepped off the plane in London, that whole phase came flooding back to me and I'd worked night and day to find a way to bring those radio shows to life. I'd hired a band called 'The 45s' to come in and perform a concert. They play all the old radio standards, and their online videos show that the lead singer runs the whole act like one of those old radio shows. I've never been more excited for an event at work, and I know that the residents are going to love it.

The planning has helped me to be able to actively avoid Jimmy. I can't say for sure that he's been avoiding me too, but it sure seems that way. We almost never find ourselves in the same place at the same time, and when we do I use my work to distract me. I know I can't avoid him forever, but I'm happy to try for as long as possible. It makes me wonder if I should have noticed that he liked me. Was he trying to be in the same room with me all those times when we ended up together? If he's actively avoiding me now, was he actively pursuing me before and I was just totally oblivious? It wouldn't have been the first time, I suppose. Still, I'm glad that I haven't been forced to confront the awkwardness that happened between us.

I've told all of these things to Mrs. Wang, and she smiled and nodded as she always does, but it's hard to know whether she's understanding me or if I'm talking to a brick wall. Still, even talking to a brick wall is better than having no outlet at all. I had showed her some of The 45s online videos and used Popsicle sticks representing Jimmy and me… but that's the best I could do.

I love her, she's my best friend in London. We spend every evening together playing mahjong and watching the news. Sometimes we drink tea or have dinner together. But I miss having a friend who answers me when I talk about my life with them. I miss having a friend who talks to me about her life, too. I never get to hear anything about Mrs. Wang's life, and I would kind of like to. I had loved Sheng and Jie and Jasper and I have been anxious to hear more about them, if only Mrs. Wang would try to tell me. Instead, I talk her ear off and she listens contentedly, whether she understands me or not.

I'm so lost in thought, putting battery operated candles out on the tables for a little mood decoration, that I don't even notice the commotion making its way down the main hall until it arrives. One of the female residents screams, and it's only then that I see the bleached blonde, spiked hairdo that has entered the recreation room.

"I'm looking for Molly," comes the voice that accompanies the hairdo, and it takes me almost a full minute to take him in. Leather vest with metal spikes and no shirt underneath, tight black pants, combat boots, and enough eyeliner to sell *Sephora* out of stock.

"Can I help you?" I offer, finally. Nothing about this situation makes any sense at all and I have no idea why he'd be looking for me.

"Are you Molly?" he asks. I don't get to answer, though, because I'm distracted by three more gentlemen dressed just like this one coming into the room with musical equipment.

"You're not... oh, God. Are you The 45s?" I ask as it dawns on me what is happening. I ordered a band, and a band has arrived. Only, all of this is horribly wrong.

"No, we're Pistol Whipped. We are imitators of the greatest band of all time, the Sex Pistols," he answers me confidently. *Oh, thank God.* My heart is just beginning to slow down when he speaks again.

"The 45s couldn't play today, they had another engagement, so Hugo sent us," he says. Hugo is the band promoter whom I'd spoken to by both phone and email several times as recently as yesterday. He'd assured me that everything was set and that The 45s would be here to play their show as promised. And now, here I am looking at someone I've been told is called Johnny More Rotten.

I'm speechless. Utterly and completely speechless. This was supposed to be my big moment, my chance to prove to the people who hired me that they made the right choice by seeking me out and bringing me all the way across the ocean to plan events like this one. Now all I'm succeeding at doing is proving that all of us are fools.

"Hugo here," comes the voice on the other end of the phone once I've finally regained my wits.

"Hugo, it's Molly. We spoke just yesterday confirming The 45s for my event this afternoon?" He's quiet on the other end, so I already know that he knows why I'm calling.

"You remember me, then? Great. I'm wondering if you can explain to me why I am now looking at a band that's apparently prepared to play the Sex Pistols greatest hits for a room full of people in their eighties and nineties?"

Hugo stalls for a moment, I can hear paperwork shuffling in

the background. "The 45s had something come up last minute, a paying gig..." he starts before I interrupt him.

"I'm paying!" I remind him.

"Er, right, well they aren't able to be in two places at once. But Hugo always makes sure you have a band to cover your event so Pistol Whipped is there to be at your service," he spits out.

"So, you've sent a punk rock cover band to play at a care home for the elderly?" I ask him, spelling it out in as simple language as possible. While it is entirely his fault, he's not the one who is going to get the brunt of the blame. That is going to fall solely on me and I'm just trying to bide my time before the reprimand comes down.

"Well, I've instructed them to only play the classics. Look, lady, you paid to have a band and I sent you a band. I don't know what the big deal is," Hugo says. Pistol Whipped is almost done setting up and I feel bad to tell them they have to leave now, but I don't know what else I can do.

"Alright there, Molly?" Jimmy says from behind me. Of course it would be in this moment that my luck in being able to avoid him runs out, Jimmy is the last person that I want to see while I'm dealing with what could potentially be a career ending disaster.

"Not really," I admit before I find the entire saga spilling out of me. I didn't mean to tell Jimmy the whole story, I would rather have told anyone but Jimmy. For some reason, though, I can't seem to stop myself from telling him everything whenever he asks. He seems to have that effect on me for some inexplicable reason. I expect him to laugh in my face, to tell me that it serves me right after everything else, but he doesn't. Instead, he takes it upon himself to get Pistol Whipped out of the building with sincere apologies for the time wasted and an assurance that they'll still be paid. Then he finds an online radio station that plays all of the songs that the band was supposed to play, and he tells the residents that we're having a listening party instead.

"You don't have to do all that," I tell him once he's gotten everyone settled and the music playing.

"I know, but that's what friends do," he offers me a smile. Friends. It's an unexpected statement and it opens up the floodgates for the tears I've been holding in ever since this whole disaster started. Jimmy nods and then turns back to his work, even asking one of our more agile residents to dance.

The listening party is a huge success. Even people who weren't originally in the room stop as they walk by, just to listen to a song or two. Several residents dance, others sing along. I'm especially surprised to learn that ornery old Angus has the most angelic singing voice. But none of that is thanks to me. None of this would have happened if it hadn't been for Jimmy and I don't know where that leaves me. He said we were friends, but now that I know his true feelings can it ever just be that? Now I'm always going to question his motives. Is he being nice to me because he wants to be more than friends? Or is this really just what friends do? It's all so overwhelming that the tears start flowing again.

I'm going to have to face Sheila eventually, to tell her what happened and why the plans changed. But I don't feel emotionally prepared for that just yet. I'm going to need a little bit more time to gather my thoughts and figure out exactly how to present this. Can I take credit for Jimmy's quick thinking? Should I? I don't even know. For now, I just want to sit in this corner and cry.

I've been sitting with my body hunched into a ball, my head against my knees, so I don't see what's going on. Once I know that things are going well, I can't keep watching. So, I don't see the happy men and women dancing and tapping their toes to the music, I don't see the staff getting involved in it too, and I don't see when Linda crosses the room and sits down on the floor beside me.

She was part of the reason that this place had continued to remind me so much of my post-war phase. Linda's dementia had made the war a very real part of my everyday life at work and had kept the idea of doing this event in the forefront of my mind. So, it's only fitting that she would be the one to join me now.

"It's okay to be frightened," she tells me, putting her arm around my shoulders. "The bombs can't get to us here."

Although her timing and location are totally off, the act of comfort still means just as much as it would have if I'd been down below ground with her as a child. It's the thought that counts, as they say, and today Linda's thought is providing comfort to someone who is huddled in a corner. That's the most meaningful thing in the world to me.

10.

It was a horrible disaster. That's the only way I can put it. This was the event that was supposed to be my shining moment, the thing that was supposed to show Greenfield Care that they had made the right choice by reaching out to me and bringing me on, and I failed. Sure, it all turned out fine in the end, but that was no thanks to me. Jimmy was the one who had to step in and make it right, all I did was panic and buckle under the pressure. And that means that I'm back to owing him again, which is not something that I want to have to do. Based on what happened the last time, I can't help but think that he's just storing up these favors in his back pocket to use against me at a moment when I least expect it. Sure, he says he's helping me out as a friend... but I feel like there's so much more to it than that. Not to mention that this time, what he did was so much bigger. This time he literally saved my job. How do you get on with owing somebody like that?

What's more is that no one has talked about what happened. I suppose I should be grateful that my screw up flew under the radar. I had made such a big deal about it. I'd gotten all kinds of approvals from Sheila and her team in order to bring in the band... but no one has said anything. I know that's not an accident, I know that is Jimmy too. He's continued his unspoken vow of silence and now I've made it all the way to my day off without a word.

Truthfully, I'm relieved. I've been working so hard the last few weeks that I'm looking forward to spending the day laying around in the bed that is starting to feel more and more like mine. I have two days off every week, but I spend most of them playing tourist in my new city or visiting with Mrs. Wang next door. Although I've grown to love her company, I'm happy that she's out shopping with Sheng today and that I can be home alone for a change. I haven't just laid in bed and allowed myself to wallow since my very first week in London. It's crazy how that feels like a lifetime ago. Not that I necessarily need to wallow anymore. I'm not over what happened by any means; but the longer I'm here, and the more things I have in my life to keep me occupied, the better I feel.

I haven't done much of anything related to my old life since I've arrived in London, to be perfectly honest. Beyond the necessities of paying my living expenses and trying to make it to the market at least once a week, I'm so far behind on life that it isn't even funny. After everything happened with Jake and Becca, I'd disabled all of the notifications on my cell phone so that I wouldn't have to deal with people and their stupid questions. Then when I got a new mobile in the UK, I hadn't even bothered to connect any of those accounts to it. The only person outside of London with the number is Mindy, and I'd given her very explicit instructions about how she is to never give it out to anyone, even our parents, under any circumstances. She knows how to reach me, and that's enough. Apart from Mindy, I don't want to be found. I haven't even checked my email or any of my social media accounts in months. Back in Ohio, the thought of going almost totally offline seemed like it would be impossible. But I think if I hadn't done it when I did, I would have gone crazy.

I don't know what prompts me to open up my email today, but as soon as I do, I regret it. There, in the middle of all of the coupon offers and online shopping deals is an email from Becca that's dated just three days ago and my blood runs cold. A part of me, the part that misses my lifelong best friend, wants to open it immediately but another part, the part that remembers what Becca did, wants to delete it without even opening it at all.

Instead, I sort through the other thousand or so emails that have accumulated in my inbox, get up and make a cup of tea, then change my mind and pour a glass of wine, take a shower that's so hot I feel like my skin might melt right off my body, try on everything that I have in the closet, then hang everything back up using a new system of organization that takes at least an hour to decipher, go downstairs for Indian food and then eat it in front of the TV until I'm so full I might burst. And then, when there is nothing else left to do, I pour another glass of wine and open Becca's email.

From: BecBecBecca@cmail.net
Sent: Wednesday, 10:37pm
To: MollyWalton713@cmail.net
Subject: London Trip!!!

Molly!!! I can't believe you live in London, that's so crazy and exciting! We always talked about living somewhere else, but I never thought either of us would ever really do it! I've never been anywhere outside of Ohio, as you know, so you'll have to tell me all about what it's like to live in Europe!

Speaking of never having gone anywhere, Jake and I were talking about how inspiring it is that you just took charge and moved to someplace new for no reason at all. We decided that it's time to take a trip together and we were thinking what better place than to visit London?! I can't wait to see Big Bill towering over the London skyline for real like I've always seen in pictures. Plus, we'd love to meet up with you, it's been way too long and I miss you like crazy! We'll be there for five nights starting the 15th of next month. Let's grab lunch!

Love ya!
Becca

That's it. That's the whole thing. No apology. Nothing.

She talks like she and Jake have been together forever and that I've always known about it. Not to mention the fact that they think I packed up my whole life and moved to another country for NO REASON AT ALL?! And she may as well have signed it the way we used to sign our passed notes in middle school "LYLAS!" *Love ya like a sister*. What a joke. I feel so many conflicting emotions at once. I feel angry, I feel sad, I feel betrayed... and weirdly I feel a little happy to have heard from someone back home. I know that's not how I *should* feel... but it's how I *do* feel.

There are three things that I take away from her email though. One – she's not that bright... her reference to "Big Bill" instead of "Big Ben" makes me laugh. It's the kind of spiteful laughter that feels good deep in my soul (and probably maybe makes me a terrible person). Two – she's done the exact thing I warned Lily against on that first night at the pub. Asking what London's like because a person has always wanted to visit Europe. Maybe, subconsciously, when I'd said that that night, I'd been thinking of how it was exactly the kind of thing that Becca would do. And three – it gives me comfort to know that at least they're still together now. I think I would feel worse if Jake had broken my heart the night before our wedding and then he and Becca hadn't ended up together. I guess that's weird. I suppose I shouldn't want either one of them to be happy. But I'd rather that they're happy together. It's all just such a confusing thing to even have to think about.

What do I do now? I wonder. That part of me that wanted to open the email right away wants to respond, but I don't know at all what I'd say. Of course I'm not going to see them. When I moved out of the United States, I promised myself that I would never have to see Jake or Becca ever again. It never occurred to me that they might make their way to London. I mean, these were two people who thought the idea of a "fun vacation" was making the drive down to Cincinnati. It had been a big deal that Jake and I were going to spend our honeymoon in Niagara Falls. The promise of that three-and-a-half-hour drive made it feel like we were going to get away and it had taken a lot of work to convince him that we should leave Ohio for our honeymoon at all. Now he's coming to London. In another country. On a plane. With Becca.

"I think you should try to see them," Mindy says into the

phone as soon as I've finished reading her the email. I'd called her because I didn't have anyone else with whom to share my outrage. But instead of being outraged, she says this. She'd even giggled at Becca's "Big Bill" faux pas.

"Are you crazy? No!" I retort.

"They're obviously making the effort to try to see you, and don't you think it will help you get some closure?" she asks. The only thing that would give me closure is having the recurring fantasy of Jake's genitals being twisted and mangled by a torque rod while I look on smiling come to fruition, but I don't say that out loud.

"I can't believe you're suggesting this. I thought you were on my side, Min," I tell her.

"I am on your side, but I just think you'll be better off if you see them instead of spending the rest of your life hating them. All the energy you're wasting on hating them could be going toward building your great new life!" she continues. It's the first time she's alluded to my new life being great and I can't bring myself to tell her the truth, especially not now.

"No, Mindy. Just… no," I repeat, shutting her down in the same way I do every time she's tried to discuss Jake or Becca with me.

We hang up shortly after because if she's not giving me the answer that I want to hear, then I have nothing to say to her right now. I know that's not the point of a dialogue, but I didn't exactly call her to have a dialogue. Hanging up when you don't like where the conversation is going is the way we've always handled things in my family, and right now it's working well for me. It's the middle of the morning back in Cleveland so I know she has time to talk, and I miss my sister more than I'll ever admit, but I can't talk to her about this if she's not going to agree with me. Maybe someone should tell her to go have lunch with her ex-fiancé and former best friend who are now together and see how she'd react. Maybe then she'd understand.

I sit and stare at the email again. I still don't know what to do. I keep reading it, looking for clues, but all I find is more rage.

I know that if I respond now, it will say something that includes a lot of four-letter words. And if I do respond, I want to look like the bigger (and in this case, smarter) person. Right now, I just need to put down the phone and walk away. That's easier said than done, though. I haven't heard Mrs. Wang puttering around next door yet, and there's nothing on TV. I'm bored and lonely and Becca's email has only served to remind me of the fact that I am bored and lonely.

Without even realizing what I'm doing, I'm picking up my phone and texting Jimmy to see if he's free. I owe him after all... but as soon as I hit send, I realize what I've done. I throw down my phone and run out the front door just in time to see Mrs. Wang slowly and methodically climbing up the stairs.

"Moll-ee," she says softly, as if she knows I need a friend. "Come. Tea."

11.

*N*othin' how bout you?

That had been Jimmy's reply on Saturday night. His first reply. He'd sent several in follow up after I didn't respond, culminating in the dreaded double question mark. I never sent him anything else. I couldn't, I was too embarrassed. But I'd spent all day yesterday reading over and over his messages trying to decide what to do. I had come to no conclusions, there really is nothing that I can do.

I had thought about telling the truth, but there doesn't seem to be any way to do that without making me look unstable. I thought about lying and saying that I had meant to text someone else, but that didn't seem very believable as I've made it pretty clear that I don't have a lot of friends here. I also thought about lying and saying I'd been drunk, but that just led me back to the instability problem. There was nothing I could do about it, except ignore it, and hope that Jimmy will ignore it too. The only solid conclusion I was able to come up with was calling in sick to work but avoiding Jimmy forever at the detriment of my job doesn't seem to be a very good option either.

So that's why I'm standing in the breakroom, waiting for my cup of tea to finish steeping. It's funny, I don't think I'd had more than a dozen cups of tea in my entire life before I moved here. Every time I was sick, and Grandma Betty was forced to look after me while my parents worked, she would make me a cup of generic black tea with massive amounts of lemon and honey added, rendering it almost undrinkable. Back in Ohio, I was always more of a coffee drinker. But spending my time with

Mrs. Wang, Jane, and Linda, has really turned me onto drinking tea. Now I genuinely enjoy the soothing warmth of a good cuppa (and I'm learning the lingo to go along with it.)

I'm just pulling the bag out of my cup when I spot Jimmy out of the corner of my eye. It's futile to hope he hasn't spotted me; the break room isn't large and we're the only two people in it. My plan of ignoring him and my text at all costs falls away completely when, at the last second, I decide to hold my head up tall and proud. I don't know where the idea comes from, since this is not at all what I had planned or rehearsed. I'd been fully prepared to act like I had no idea that anything at all had happened.

"Hey Molly, how were your days off?" Jimmy asks. It seems like a simple question, but his tone holds so much more weight, it's almost accusatorial. I deserve his accusation, he told me he liked me, and I used that information to my advantage, only to turn around and ghost him completely. I guess that I'm that kind of person now. I want to tell him that I'm not; that it wasn't the real me who had sent him that text, that I'd been beside myself with emotion after receiving Becca's email.

Before I have a chance to respond, though, we're both distracted by the commotion outside the door. "We've got an emergency in the tower!" someone shouts.

"That'll be Mary, I expect," I find myself saying under my breath. It brings a slight smile to my face to think of Linda's joke each time one of these emergencies is called. The smile, I'll admit, comes a little bit from having been saved from this awkward conversation with Jimmy, too. Who wouldn't want to be saved from that? My smile is short-lived though, no sooner has the wave of nurses and assistants gone down the hall than Sheila appears in the doorway, frantically signaling for us.

"Molly, Jimmy, we need you both to come. It's Jane, she's fallen, and she's hit her head," Sheila pants. It's clear she's been running for a while. The paper cup of tea no longer appeals to me, and I abandon it on the table as I rush to follow Sheila toward the resident tower.

I know the way to Jane's room by heart, I've been invited there for tea several times and it's the only resident's room number that I'm sure I know from memory. But today, going there now, it's like I have never seen these halls before in my life. I just blindly follow Sheila. My mind is numb and I'm mentally kicking myself for making Linda's joke about the emergency. *It can't be Jane. Please let it be anyone but Jane.*

I almost forget Jimmy is beside me until he speaks, "Don't worry, I'm sure she'll be alright. Sometimes they just take a tumble and then they're right back up the next day." He's trying to reassure me because he knows what Jane means to me, but when I look him in the eyes, I know that neither of us really believes what he's said. A fall is almost always bad, and one with this much response is almost always worse.

"Don't move her! Don't move her!" someone is shouting when we finally make our way into Jane's standard issue quarters. The warm, inviting feeling I'd had when I'd been invited all those times for tea is gone, replaced by doctors and nurses and assistants shouting at each other in every direction. This is bad and all I can think to do is look for Linda.

"She's there, in the corner," Jimmy tells me, somehow knowing exactly who I need to find. And sure enough, Linda stands in the corner of the kitchenette, trying to make herself as small as possible. Her eyes are wide and full of fear. She reaches for my arm as soon as I've come to her, though I know she thinks I'm somebody else. It doesn't matter to me, though, whether she thinks I'm Molly, the activities director at a nursing home, or Mrs. Smith, her Sunday School teacher from 1941. It doesn't matter as long as she knows that whoever I am today is here by her side.

"They're bombing again, Mummy," she says in a soft, child-like voice. She grips my arm more tightly, if she weren't such a slight little thing, it might have hurt. "We have to get to the shelter."

"We're in the shelter now, we'll be safe here," I tell her. She turns and looks at me.

"But someone's been hit. I heard the plane come over, and then the crash. There was blood," she tells me emphatically, mixing current events with those from her past.

"The doctors are here now. They're taking care of... the person," I say. I don't want to say her name. I don't want to tell Linda what's happened, not yet. I've been trying to use my body as a shield between Linda and the commotion surrounding Jane. Not that she's aware of what's happening, but it seems like the right thing to do. I haven't had a chance to look to see if there's blood, whether that's something from Linda's memories from the war or the thing she grabbed onto from this real-life situation. There's just so much happening in the room that all I feel equipped to do is protect Linda from seeing her friend this way. I know it's what I'd want someone to do for me if it were my friend.

"On my count – One... two... THREE!" I hear someone yell as Jane's lifeless body is lifted carefully onto a gurney that has arrived to take her to the hospital and I turn my body away from Linda to watch. The fact that people are calling out her vital signs is the only way I know that she's still hanging in there.

"Where's Janie?" Linda asks me then. It's enough to almost break me down. I do this every day in my line of work, but it's different somehow with Linda. I want so desperately to tell her the truth, but I know she wouldn't understand right now anyway. Right now, in Linda's mind, it's 1941 and London is being bombed by the Germans and for now, that's probably the safest place for her to be.

"They're taking her to another shelter," I find myself saying. "She's going to another shelter where she'll be safe. And we're going to stay here at this shelter because we're safe here."

Linda has been watching the staff work with the emergency medical responders, but I have no idea what she's seeing as they work feverishly on her friend. I've never been grateful for someone having a delusion before, but if it has to happen to protect Linda from knowing what's happening to Jane, then now is the perfect time. Eventually she'll be lucid. I've seen it happen often enough that I know it will be coming sooner or later, and then she's going to start asking questions. Jane has been by her side since they were children, I can't imagine what it will feel like for Linda once she knows.

"Alright then, Miss Linda?" asks one of the Memory Care nurses I've seen assisting with Linda's care when Jane wasn't able to in the past. Linda looks at her but doesn't release my arm and I do my best to pry myself away. It makes sense that Memory Care will be looking after her now, so in a way it's like I'm saying good-bye to the both of them. It's just in another wing of the building, but Memory Care feels like a world away, like a black hole that absorbs everyone who enters. It's all too much, too finite for me. I had prepared myself from the moment I'd learned of Linda's condition that she would eventually have to make the move. But I hadn't anticipated having to say good-bye to Jane too, and especially not on the same day.

I haven't said good-bye to Jane yet. She's still being strapped in for her ride to the hospital and I know that now's my chance – but I just can't make myself do it. It's like some subconscious hope that if I refuse to say good-bye that she'll have to keep living. I know the way these things go; I know that when a fall gets this kind of response, it's never good. People Jane's age don't bounce back from this. From a fall, maybe, but not from hitting her head. Once she's wheeled out of here today, that's it. Even though I know it's true, I just can't make myself believe it yet.

I've never been good with goodbyes, I moved thousands of miles away to avoid them. They make me think of painful things, like my parents' divorce and my dad leaving to move to his own house. There's no such thing as a good goodbye, now I'm even more certain of that than ever. And as I watch them wheel Jane away, I'm reminded again.

"Are you alright there, mate?" Jimmy asks me as I steady myself. He says it with genuine concern and for the first time since I've known him, I don't question his intentions. Even still, I don't take the time to answer. I have to get out of this room as soon as possible or I might lose it.

I don't know where I'm running. I can't tell because even though I've tried to keep the tears from falling, they've started anyway. I'm not looking up and I'm not paying attention when I run right into a body.

"I'm... I'm sorry," I stammer as I try to wipe the tears from my eyes. Instead of being chastised, I feel a pair of strong, male arms wrap around me.

"It's alright," Sam says into the top of my head. "I'd run too, if I could." I hadn't even thought of him, how they would have called him as soon as Jane fell, that he'd rush to get here for Linda as soon as he was able to. It was the first time I hadn't thought of him since I had seen him the night at the pub.

"She's having an episode," I tell him, regaining my composure and pulling away from his embrace. "She thinks she's in a shelter during an air raid. She was asking for her, so I told her that Janie was being taken to a different shelter today... not exactly a lie."

Sam nods solemnly and thanks me for my help. His eyes are piercing, I feel like he's boring a hole in my face until I have to look away. I've imagined staring into those eyes dozens of times, but now standing here like this, it feels nothing like what I imagined. He gives my shoulder a gentle squeeze before he continues down to Jane's room. In any other context, I never would have tolerated a hug, or even a touch on the shoulder, from a resident's family. But this is different, not because it comes from Sam, but because there is a mutual sadness, a mutual love for Linda and Jane. I wouldn't have been able to share my grief with anyone else.

12.

J ane died shortly after arriving at the hospital. All I can think about is how I didn't tell her good-bye. Usually they don't tell us those kinds of things, these people are our business and once they're gone we're expected to get on with our jobs. It's something that comes with the territory, and we're expected to adopt an 'out of sight, out of mind' mentality. But Sheila comes to tell me the news as soon as she gets the call. It seems strange, especially since Sheila tends to be the type of person who follows protocol exactly.

"Sam thought you'd want to know," she explains, as if reading my mind. "He asked me to tell you right away." Her tone isn't that warm or comforting, though I suppose when you've worked here for as long as she has, death becomes just about as normal as brushing your teeth. I'm surprised that Sheila doesn't question why Golden Boy, Sam, would want me to know the news first, but I guess maybe my close relationship with Linda and Jane hadn't been that much of a secret.

"So, what will happen now?" I ask. She knows I mean with Linda, and I already know her answer. She'll be moved to Memory Care, it's inevitable now.

"I wish she had other options," Sheila says, speaking candidly for the first time in our working relationship. "But without Jane, I just don't know what else we can do with her. Jane had a way of calling her back out somehow, none of the rest of us have been able to do it. Though she has taken a fancy to you."

I smile at the thought. I know I'd taken a fancy to Linda, too, but I could never be her friend the way that Jane had been.

I could never keep her present in the way that Jane had been able to do. Part of what made them so good for each other was that they'd been together for so long. Jane could draw her out because Jane had been present at almost every single memory Linda's mind chose to revisit. I wish Linda had other options, too. Unfortunately, the nature of her disease eliminates more options than it creates. Even Sam has to be able to see that now, especially without Jane here to help.

"When will she move?" I ask. I'm not expecting Sheila to give me an answer, the schedule for residents has nothing to do with my job whatsoever. I am here to plan the events and not to ask questions about who does or does not come to them. I'm surprised, actually, that Sheila is entertaining so many of my questions now.

"I'd imagine by this evening. I'll have to send some assistants to pack up her things," Sheila responds, but I cut her off before she can continue.

"Can I do it? I'd like to help," I say. Sheila shrugs and dismisses me. We both know the planned activities for the day aren't going to happen after this morning's excitement. Everyone will be more than happy to be parked in front of the television for hours without someone shouting bingo numbers over the sound of the BBC... except maybe for Angus, who has managed to win every bingo game that he has ever played.

Linda's room is identical to the one where Jane had lived but it looks so much different. Although they were always together and almost indistinguishable from one another, it's their living spaces that set them apart. While Jane's room had been cozy and inviting, filled with quilts and flowers and decorative throw pillows, Linda's looks like it could double for a museum exhibit on the mod era. Pops of color are everywhere and the art that hangs on the wall would make even the most amateur collector jealous. Linda is sitting on the couch when I arrive, the nurse in whose care I'd left her in Jane's room earlier is in the kitchenette washing the few dishes that had been left out in the room. It looks like Linda is waiting, though for who or what I may never know. She sits upright with her hands on her knees, the posture resembles that of a small child. I wonder if this is what she looked like to Jane on the night they first met inside that bomb shelter.

"Sam had to go back to work again, he works so hard," she says to no one. "He said someone would be coming to help me pack up my things."

"Here I am!" I exclaim both in answer to Linda's statement and because I don't think that either of the room's occupants has noticed me at all.

"Right, well I've already begun over here. I don't know why we need to pack up most of these things as they won't be moving with her. The Memory Care rooms are much smaller than this and there just isn't room for all of these trinkets. It's a waste of time to have to pack it up. Should be on the family to do it. If it were up to me, all of this would end up in the bin," the nurse says to the wall. It's not an uncommon attitude in this business and yet I continue to wonder why someone would bother working at a job they hate so much. Sometimes the work is inconvenient, but it's ultimately about helping people have a better experience at the end of their lives and it's a job that I do with pride.

"I can take over. I don't mind," I tell her. In fact, I'd kind of prefer it, though I don't say this. I'm excited to have some time alone with Linda and it's clear that this nurse is not the right woman for the job. She doesn't even answer, just sets down the bowl she'd been drying and steps toward the door.

"Fine by me. But don't expect any help from that one," she points at Linda. "I've told her to sit there and not to move a muscle."

It breaks my heart to think that Linda moving to Memory Care means that she's going to have to be around this nurse more often. I know that not everyone in the world has compassion for everyone else, but it's not Linda's fault that her mind has deteriorated. She certainly didn't ask for dementia; nor did she ask to have to give up her freedom and move to a care home, or for her lifelong best friend to have an accident... I know that her family must know all of this, Sam is extremely involved in her care and I'm sure he's had all of these thoughts. That's probably why Jane was here, too, why she agreed to come along. Jane knew that she was the only person who could properly look after her friend. Now that she's gone, everything that they had tried to keep from happening to Linda will come to pass. It's not fair.

"Where shall we begin?" I turn to Linda with a smile. I don't want to spend this time with her in a fog of sadness. It's easy to picture what she must have looked like as a child; her eyes grow wide as she takes in my words. It's hard to tell from the look on her face whether she's here or somewhere else.

"I always say it's best to start with the small things," she says. Her voice startles me, it sounds more confident than I've ever heard it. "Like the pictures of my family. Things we know I'm going to need when I get over there. We can sort things into categories: things I'll use, things my family can take home, and things for the bin like that awful woman suggested."

It's the first completely lucid moment I've ever spent with her. They have been so rare since I started working here, in fact, that I thought moments of total clarity had become a thing of the past. She'd always hovered halfway between two worlds, but here she is, talking like she knows exactly where she is and what's going on, where she's going and what will happen to her when she gets there. I had spent time imagining what type of person she'd been before she got sick, based on Jane's stories and my own wild imaginings. It has never occurred to me that she might have such a take-charge attitude; that had seemed like Jane's role. But then again, that could have been because by the time I met them, it had to be Jane's role.

"That's my husband, Marty," Linda explains as I pull a black and white wedding photo off the wall. "Wasn't he the most handsome man you've ever seen?"

Marty was handsome, I can see Sam's features in his face. The same eyes and the sculpted face under a crop of brown hair. Linda is positively radiant in the photo. She's wearing a tea length white gown with long lace sleeves and a pillbox hat. The smile on her face rivals the gleam off the string of pearls which had adorned her neck.

"It was May 16, 1954, a Sunday. Happiest day of my life," she continues.

My own wedding was supposed to have been on a Sunday, everything had been cheaper when booked on a Sunday and we were more than happy to cut costs where we could. I picture my own dress, which I'd tried on for Becca just before she drove me to the rehearsal, with its lace sleeves that matched Linda's almost exactly. Weddings have been one of the harder things for me to be able to accept since... the incident. I know that there are people in the world who have wonderful, happy marriages... but I just can't deal with weddings. Looking at Linda's photo now reminds me of why, it puts me right back to where I was on that night.

*   *   *

"Thank you all for coming tonight. We really appreciate your love and support," Jake said. I beamed beside him.

"I'm especially glad that Molly has the support of a loving family," he continued. Mindy and I exchanged a look, but I hadn't thought to look at either of my parents. Instead, I reached for his hand but he pulled back, turning to look at me.

"Molly, I'm sorry. I can't do this." He didn't even look that tender, he didn't look like he was sorry at all.

"What do you mean? I said you didn't have to give a speech..." I began but he put his hand up to stop me. Becca had come up behind me then, to offer support I thought.

"I can't go through with marrying Molly tomorrow. I'm in love with someone else."

It was cliché, the kind of thing that only happened in movies. Not the kind of thing that happened in real life to anyone... especially not to me. I couldn't believe it and had just turned toward Becca for comfort when she walked past me and took her place at Jake's side.

"I'm sorry, what?" I asked. It was the dumbest thing I could have said, but to be honest I'd never felt more stupid in my life. How had I not seen it coming?

*   *   *

I don't want my memory to cloud the time I have with Linda. This really may be it. And the fact that she had had a beautiful wedding and marriage had no reflection on the fact that my own engagement had ended so disastrously. As I come back to reality, I find that she's continuing with the story of Marty even though I hadn't asked her to. Of course, I'd have been happy to hear her talk for hours, I didn't care what she talked to me about.

"I'd had fun before Marty; Jane and I used to paint the town. Every dance, every movie, we were there at the front of the line, and we had our fair share of men clamoring to be right there with us. But when I met Marty, I just knew that something was different. He made me laugh, oh how he made me laugh. Not a girlish giggle the way I might have put on for other boys before, but genuine laughter deep from inside. We spent so many years laughing together, always sharing a private joke. He was older, I was only twenty-three when we married but he was already thirty and somehow that felt so much more worldly and mature, though it was only seven years. I don't know what I did to deserve Marty, he was not the type of man that a 'wild' girl like me should have ended up with and his mother made that fact known. But he was such a good man, he worked hard for our family and treated Daisy and me like we were queens. And then one day, in his sixties, Marty just dropped dead. The doctor said he had an undiagnosed heart condition. That was 1989, I'd only gotten thirty-five years with him," she concludes. I can see the glisten of a tear in her eye, and I can tell how much telling the story has affected her. I don't know what to say, but I find that I don't have to as Linda starts to speak again.

"My grandson, Sam, he's so much like his grandfather. It's amazing, really, since he was so young when Marty passed. Some days I forget that it's Sam standing in front of me, not Marty. But Sam is so good to me, just like Marty was," she says. She's holding a picture of Sam now. They're dressed up in black tie style and it looks like they're on a red carpet. Of course Sam would have taken Linda with him to that kind of event, it's obvious that he adores his grandmother just by the way he's so invested in her care.

I open my mouth to reply just as Linda exclaims something about the puppies and I realize that she's gone again, back into the regresses of her mind. Maybe it's better that way, for her to live in hallucinations and memories in a world where Jane and Marty are still alive and by her side to keep her laughing through all of the pain.

13.

I can't wait to crawl into my bed and cry. That's the only thought that sustains me through the rest of the day at work. I can keep it together knowing that as soon as I get home, I'll be able to let it all go. I'm not supposed to let residents' deaths affect me; it's part of the job, something I've come to expect from my line of work. But this one is different. Just about anyone else could have passed away today and I would have been fine, but this was Jane. I'd grown to love her as if she was my own grandmother in the short amount of time that I'd known her. More than that, I'd grown to love her as a friend. I had admired her loyalty to her friend, even when it meant sacrificing her own quality of life. She had been the type of person that I can only hope I might become someday. And though I'd known her for just a little while, her loss leaves me with a gaping hole.

My tears aren't solely for Jane, though. It's been a while since I've allowed myself to have a good cry, mainly because everything about my new life has been coming at me so quickly that I've needed to be *on* and alert at all times. I couldn't take the time to cry because I needed to move on. But, between Becca's email yesterday, my immediately regrettable text to Jimmy, and Jane's death today... I feel like I could cry for weeks, and I probably won't feel better until I do. Everything feels so overwhelming.

I can admit now that when I first moved to London I was running away from my problems. I know that I had tried to paint it as something else at first, but now that I'm a couple of months in I can look back a little more objectively than I could then. I had hoped that by moving somewhere so far away, I'd be able to start over in a new life and forget about everything that happened. I thought that it would be possible. Instead, I've been plagued by my problems even here. I'm beginning to wonder if they'll ever go away. I'm beginning to wonder if the problems are following me because I am the problem.

I've just buried my head under the covers that still don't feel totally like mine when there's a familiar knock at the door. I groan under my breath. I am not in the mood for Mahjong today, I am especially not in the mood to sit in silence with my Chinese friend. I can't do it, I've already had to deal with too much today. I don't want to deal with anything else, not even with her. But the knock persists.

"Moll-ee," I hear from the other side.

She knows I'm home. She always knows. She waits on the other side of her door when she knows it's about that time and she listens for me to climb the stairs. It would make it easier to pretend I wasn't here if I knew she hadn't been waiting for me to arrive, instead there's nothing that I can do. I am trapped.

The tears had begun to fall before I even made it to the bed, and they've only gotten worse from there. I do my best to wipe them away as I sit up and put my feet on the floor. The knocking continues.

"Moll-ee," she repeats. "Open."

It's fitting that the majority of Mrs. Wang's English words are commands. It fits her personality so well. Not that she's demanding, but she knows what she wants and will be stubborn about it until she gets her way. Exactly like what she's doing right now, because she wants me to open the door.

When I do finally get there, I don't say a word or even smile. Instead, I stare at her incredulously. I'm not mad at her, she's not behaving any differently than she does every other day. But I don't have it in me to express any other emotion right now. She notices right away, reaching a small hand up to caress my cheek.

"Oh, Moll-ee," she says softly. Neither of us moves; we stand on either side of the threshold of my flat, looking into each other's eyes as she strokes my tear-streaked cheek softly. It's such a sweet gesture on her part, so gentle and kind, that I know the tears are going to start again at any moment. I don't deserve her. And it's not that I mind if she sees me cry, I don't, but I can't help wishing that I had a way to explain to her what has me so upset.

"Mrs. Wang, I'm not in the mood to play today," I tell her, hoping that she'll understand. She nods like she does, but that's not necessarily saying anything. She pats my face softly and drops her hand.

It's been one of those days. The kind where you've had just about all you can take and you don't even want to deal with your friends. Mrs. Wang seems genuinely concerned, though, so I tell her why I'm crying, even if she can't understand a word of it. Because even if she doesn't understand all the words, she seems to have a way of understanding my heart. When I've finally finished, between the sobs and the sniffles and the heavy tears, she looks at me with so much kindness that it almost feels like everything wrong in the world has been put back right again. And then she gives me a simple hug.

I don't know how long we stand there, Mrs. Wang's little body wrapped tightly around mine. She's never hugged me before, we haven't had much physical contact at all. I've been careful about initiating anything because my work training is so ingrained, but I've thought dozens of times about giving her a hug good-bye when we've parted at the end of one of our many evenings spent together. It's a different feeling than what I might have imagined. Mrs. Wang is so tiny that I would never have thought that her grip would be so tight. I feel such security in being held by her that I silently hope the hug never ends. I honestly can't remember the last time a friend had hugged me so earnestly and securely. Becca hadn't given me a hug like this since we were kids.

"Come, Moll-ee," she says finally, after she releases me. I'm reluctant to let go of the hug but I allow myself to be led to a seat at my own table where I wait while she prepares tea for us and then takes her seat across from me. She stares at me kindly as she sips her tea with one hand and pats my hand gently with the other.

If you'd told me two years ago that I'd be sitting at a kitchen table in London, drinking tea with my best friend in the world, who happens to be a seventy-year-old Chinese woman who hardly speaks any English, I would have laughed in your face. Two years ago, I thought that I was going to spend the rest of my life in Ohio and live a happy existence that mimicked my sister's as closely as it could. I never could have imagined this life that I have now or the people who are in it. I still can't imagine it on some days, and it's all right here in front of me. There are days I think that I'm going to wake up back in my bed in Cleveland, as Jake's wife, living the life that I had always planned. Mrs. Wang squeezes my hand softly, drawing me back out of my thoughts.

"Moll-ee," she says seriously. She sets her tea mug down, giving me her full attention. "Moo-vee."

Her face wears a grave expression, and I can't figure out why she's so serious about watching a movie. A couple of weeks ago, we'd been watching television while playing like we do on most nights when Sam appeared on the screen. It was the first time I'd caught a glimpse of him even though Cat had claimed he was one of the most famous television personalities in the country. When his face had popped up, I'd been beside myself. He was covering a movie premiere at a theater in town, and it was easy to see why Mrs. Wang would have confused my excitement over seeing Sam in this way for excitement over seeing the film. Ever since then, she's been trying to get me to watch that movie with her. I guess that means she doesn't understand me when I pour my heart and soul out to her either. If she did, she wouldn't be making such a ridiculous proposition right now. None of that does anything to explain her grave face, though.

"No, I don't want to watch a movie," I reply. She shakes her head.

"No. Moo-vee," she repeats, this time pointing at herself. It doesn't make things any more clear. She wants to watch a movie? Then why is she telling me? She can go watch one in her own flat without my company. And I kind of wish that she would.

"Right. Movie. I don't want to watch one," I say again.

"No. No. I," she says, poking her finger hard into her chest, "moo-vee. Sheng. Three weeks."

Oh. I get it now. She's moving. To live with Sheng. In three weeks. The apartment must be ready. That was why he needed to take her shopping yesterday, so that she could pick out items for her new home. She's leaving me, just like everyone else has. I stand, pushing my chair back dramatically, and nearly spill my mug of tea.

"Moll-ee," she tries to call after me as I turn and head back toward the bed. I don't know why I'm mad. It's not a surprise that she's going. Jie had told me the details of Sheng's plan when I had gone to their house for dinner weeks ago. But I hadn't been prepared for how soon it would happen. I especially wasn't prepared to get the news on a day that I already want to forget. The layer that it adds to my sadness is unconscionable.

"Moll-ee," she says again.

"Mrs. Wang, go away!" I shout. I feel like a teenager again, throwing myself down on the bed. If I'd had a bedroom door to slam, I would have done it just for effect. Instead, I grab the extra pillow and use it to cover my head completely, willing her to leave. It's a few minutes before I hear her get up from the table, wash out her mug, and head out the front door. I can hear the dejection in her footsteps and feel a pang of longing for her, but instead of calling out for her, I double down and pull the pillow down more tightly over my ears.

It's not her fault that she has to move, I know that. And I know I still have three weeks left with her here before she's gone, but it still makes me sad. Mrs. Wang has been the one thing that has made renting this borrowed flat feel like home, without her I'll be back to square one. I know that I can still see her after she moves in with Sheng, but I won't have a reason to stop by and I doubt he'll be willing to bring her back around here. I'm not ready for our friendship to end yet, and I'm not ready to think about our friendship ending on the same day my friendship with Jane was forced to end without my consent. Part of me wants to chase after her, give her the same kind of hug that she gave me, so that she knows how much she means to me. But I just can't bring myself to do it. Tonight I need to wallow, and I'll have to hope that she's willing to forgive my anger tomorrow.

14.

You know when you're being talked about as soon as you enter a room by the eerie silence that begins as soon as you come through the door. That's how I find out that I'm not being invited out to drinks with the rest of the group again. I tell myself it's fine, I wouldn't have wanted to bring the awkward new Jimmy/Molly dynamic down on the rest of them anyway. I'd managed to not only get some alone time with Linda yesterday, but also successfully avoided Jimmy for the rest of the day in the process. It had been a win/win for me. Now, though, I see how all of this is going to have longer term effects. I am not the one who gets to keep the friend group. Which is fair. They were his friends first. It just makes me sad. All of the friends I've made so far in London are dropping one by one in one sense or another. It adds salt to my wounds when on her way out of the breakroom, Lily forgets about me and calls "see you tonight!"

It only takes me half a second to realize that she's leaving me alone with him. It takes me only half a second more to abandon my tea for the second day in a row and high tail it out of there. I still haven't had time to think of what I want to say to him to explain what happened. It wasn't that I particularly wanted to sleep with him, it was just that I wanted to forget about the world for a few minutes. Really, anyone would have suited fine... but Jimmy was the person I had access to. How do I explain that? Especially knowing that he genuinely likes me. There is no way to make it seem like I wasn't trying to exploit that knowledge.

"Molly, a word?" I've no sooner stepped out of the break room than Sheila calls me into her office.

"Is everything okay?" I ask, as I step in and close the door behind me.

"Have a seat," she says gravely. I can feel my heartbeat immediately quicken inside my chest as I take a seat in the chair opposite her desk. I thought that we might escape the band incident without her notice, but I can't think of anything else that this could be about. I'm about to open my mouth to defend myself when she starts talking again.

"Molly, it's come to my attention that you are in violation of our fraternization policy," she starts. So, that's it. Jimmy finally tattled on me for my afternoon tea parties with Linda and Jane. I guess I should have known that I was setting him up for this when I pretended like I never propositioned him.

"I…" I begin but she holds up her hand, clearly not finished.

"We work hard to make our facility a comfortable home for those who are entrusted to our care, and to have two employees romantically involved with one another is something that can't be tolerated, I know you're young, and you're new in town so you're on the prowl," she continues. "But we just can't have this kind of thing going on here. You understand." On the prowl? What am I, an animal?

Oh. Well, I'm glad that I didn't start talking about the two things that I thought she was calling me in here to talk about, that would have just been digging my own grave. I nod, pretending to take in the severity of the situation. I must end things with Jimmy. *Darn.*

"Oh absolutely. Yes. You're right. Of course," I say.

"You kids think you can sneak around behind my back; that I don't hear about the things you do," she smiles knowingly, "but things always get back to me. I'm always aware." I try to keep the smile from creeping from my mind onto my face. She obviously doesn't know everything or we'd be having a very different conversation right now, but of course I don't want to let on that there might be anything else of which I am guilty.

"So I assume you've already talked to Jimmy?" I ask her. I'd been in drama club in high school, because Becca told me that if I wanted to hang out with her after school I'd have to join, and the skills I had learned then, that my mother told me would never be practical in my real life, are finally coming in handy now.

Sheila shakes her head and says she got to me first. "I'm sorry to have to nip it in the bud when it's just blossoming, but it's for the best of everyone involved."

I nod again, sigh deeply, and sit back in the chair. If this is all it was then this is the least of my concerns. Keeping the band disaster a secret and sneaking off to spend time alone with some of the residents are things that could cost me my job, but what she wanted to talk about isn't even a thing that really exists. I mean, okay Jimmy and I kissed, but it's not an actual relationship; it's not anything that has to end because it was never anything that actually started in the first place. It's not that big of a deal in the scheme of things, as long as it's not something that I can lose my job over.

I don't know what I would do if this job were to fall through. I'm in the country on a work visa, and if I don't have work, then I have to leave. I'm not ready to go back to Ohio yet – the pain there is still too real. I need more time away from that place and those people and that means that I'm going to have to make sure I find a way to stay out of trouble and off of Sheila's radar. I guess it's for the best that I have no friends and that I'm uninvited from group hangouts, at least that means that I'll still have a job tomorrow.

The walk to the recreation room isn't long, but my mind is heavy with the weight of what I know now so it feels like it takes forever to get there. What I know is that Jimmy blabbed. He didn't rat me out for the things I would have thought mattered more, but he'd bragged about our kiss and maybe even about my text. Jimmy has been talking and that's precisely what I don't need.

"Almost time for Bingo, aye Molly?" Angus says as soon as I enter the room. Of course he's ready, Angus is always ready for Bingo. I smile, trying to put everything else out of my mind. I need to focus on my job, that's why I'm here.

"Sure is, Angus. I've just got to get everything set up," I answer. Angus shakes his head and when I follow his gaze, I see that Jimmy is putting the finishing touches on my usual Bingo setup.

"Ready then, Molly? I saw you were talking to Sheila and didn't want things to be delayed," Jimmy says when he sees me.

In theory it's a kind gesture. A week ago, I probably would have spent an hour analyzing why Jimmy was trying to help me and whether we could ever truly be friends. But after my talk with Sheila, I just see him and this whole thing as a problem. I call him over to a quiet corner of the room where we can talk privately.

"I was with Sheila because she found out that we hooked up and she was reprimanding me for being in violation of policy. She said she's going to talk with you later today, too. So now all of this," I say, gesturing to the Bingo set up, "looks really bad."

He nods. "I'm sorry, Molly. That was my fault. I couldn't help talking about it," he admits. I give him a look that says I obviously know it's his fault. It certainly wasn't mine.

"But you didn't…" I start.

"Mention how you propositioned me? No," he says with a bite in his voice. Ah, here it is, the conversation I've been dreading.

"Yeah… I… I'm really sorry. I've just been going through a lot; and I heard from Becca and she's coming to London, and I didn't know what to do and I panicked and then I immediately knew it was a bad idea. You know, because of the policy," I ramble. Jimmy doesn't respond, I can see the fire in his eyes, and it makes me hope he stays silent.

"Look, I don't mind being used and ignored. But let's not pretend for a second that we're friends, alright?" he responds. "I helped you today because I know how much Angus looks forward to these games and I've got a soft spot for the old bugger. Something that I know you understand. So, let's not go on as if I did any of this for you."

I can feel tears welling up behind my eyes again. I swear all I've done for days is cry and yet I somehow have more tears back there somewhere. Jimmy walks away, leaving me standing in the corner working to choke back the knot that has formed in my throat. It's not him that's making me cry, it's not the situation we're in, it's just everything compounded together. It's the fact that I have no friends, that I'm not a good person, that maybe there's a chance I'm not even very good at my job.

I hear Angus gathering the group for Bingo, he's become my sort of number two for the event, but I don't care. It suddenly feels like the walls are closing in on me and I can't breathe. Before my mind even knows what my feet are doing, I've left the Bingo game behind.

"We've got to stop meeting this way," Sam says with a laugh when I turn the corner and crash right into him. You've got to be kidding me.

"You're telling me," I reply. What are the odds of my turning a corner and colliding with Sam again? Out of all of the people who could be walking through these halls, what are the chances that I would run into him?

"I wanted to thank you," he says then, "for everything you've done for Granny, and for Jane too. The fact that they mentioned you says so much about who you are, and I know that things were better for Jane at the end because you were here."

I don't know what to say. I hadn't been expecting any kind of thanks, I'd befriended Linda and Jane entirely out of my own selfishness and the desire I had to be like them someday. If anything, they made my life far better than I ever could have made theirs. Jane's death had been devastating to me, it's still devastating to me, it will continue to be devastating to me for a while. They had given me a reason to get out of bed and come to work every day just because I'd looked forward to seeing them.

"How is Linda doing?" I ask finally. I've never been good with compliments and this one feels particularly hard to take, it seems the easiest thing to do is to change the subject.

"She's getting settled. I was just on my way to visit her, if you'd like to stop in," he replies. What I need to be doing is pulling myself together so that I can get back out there and lead a rousing game of Bingo, but I can't think of anything I'd rather do than visit Linda in the Memory Care unit.

I do my best to keep up with Sam's quick stride, but his height means that one of his steps is equal to at least two of mine. I'm so busy trying to match his pace the whole way that I don't even notice that we're walking in silence, which is fine with me. It saves me from the awkwardness of having to address his compliment.

Memory Care has a completely different feeling than the rest of the facility. Elsewhere, residents are free to roam and make their own decisions about how they want to spend their days. But in Memory Care, security is tighter since patients are prone to wandering off and forgetting where they were headed, or worse, where they've come from. It's sad to see so many who once had great, vibrant lives reduced to such a low. What might they be doing still if only they had their minds? It's one of the more difficult parts of my job, seeing people like this. Maybe I'm overly compassionate, that's what Jake always used to tell me, but it's hard to see them so dehumanized by their own minds.

The nurse whom I had relieved of packing Linda's belongings gives me the once over when she sees me enter the unit with Sam, but I decide to ignore her. Our paths cross so rarely that it doesn't matter to me whether or not she knows that Sam is doing me a favor by allowing me to pay a visit to my friend.

I've never been to this side of the home before, and these residents don't fall under my jurisdiction as activities director so I'm seeing it for the first time as the nurse waves us past her little station in the center and Sam leads me to the first of two halls. It feels so much more sterile here, like a hospital instead of a place where people live. I understand why, of course, as people descend into dementia even the most simple, everyday object can become a hazard so it's easier to keep everything out. Still, I feel bad to think that the residents of this unit have to live out their days in a place like this.

I don't know what I'm expecting to find when we get to Linda's room, but everything is in complete upheaval. She's taken all of the linens off of the bed, thrown all of the pillows onto the floor, and knocked over everything laying on top of the small bookshelf under the window. It takes me a second to realize that the soft hum we heard as we approached the room was Linda muttering softly to herself as I'd often seen her do when she was with Jane.

"They're coming, Sam said they're coming. They're going to have to pack everything up so that we can move. Janie, Janie? Are they here yet, Janie? I know they're coming, Sam said they're coming. Why won't you answer me, Janie?" she is saying under her breath as she moves frantically about the small space. It breaks my heart to see her like this, to see her left alone here without supervision or companionship. It's obvious she misses the friend who has been by her side for decades, this is a lot of change for her to have to deal with all at once. I wish I knew how to calm her the way that Jane had been able to do. Instead, I watch as Sam rushes to her side and speaks soothingly to her, convincing her to sit down on the edge of the bed before he calls for assistance. I excuse myself, because I am no help to the situation, and I can't afford to be neglecting my job duties after my talk with Sheila this morning anyway.

"Molly, wait," Sam calls from behind me when I've almost reached the double doors.

"Jane's service will be Saturday. I know that she'd want for you to be there. Like I said, the way she spoke about you, it says a lot. I know you meant a lot to her," he continues. I can feel the knot in my throat that tells me tears are coming, there's something so comforting in knowing that Jane thought of me the same way I thought of her. Sam pulls a slip of paper from his pocket and hands it to me, on it, I'll find out later, are printed all of the details for Jane's service. I'm sure that just like with Linda's care, Sam is footing the bill.

"Thank you, I would be honored to be there to remember her," I reply before he turns and walks back to Linda's room. And I know that my words are true, I can't think of a better way to honor Jane than to be there to celebrate her life.

15.

It's raining on Saturday. That's not exactly unusual for London, I've learned, but I had hoped for a sunny day for Jane. She'd brought so much sunshine to my life in the short time I'd known her that it seemed like what she deserved. The somber weather is a better match for my somber mood, though. I haven't been to a funeral in years. Being almost entirely estranged from my parents means that I don't get the latest family news, and I'm not typically in the habit of attending services of the people with whom I work. I've never been invited to the funeral of a resident ever in my career until now. But my friendship with Jane was the first of its kind in my career too, so it's fitting that her funeral would be my first.

The church where the service is being held is a beautiful Neo-Gothic building just southwest of Hyde Park and as I approach in the rain, I can't help but feel like I'm in the opening scene of a snappy, London set romantic comedy. All I had known about London before I moved here was from movies and I've tried so many times since I moved here to pretend that I was in one of them. I've tried to pretend that I am the down on her luck heroine who rebuilds her life into accidental perfection much to the chagrin of her nemesis... but life is not a movie and everything about my life truly feels stranger than fiction anyway. Nobody would want to watch this movie.

Inside the church is even more beautiful than the outside, with stained glass windows and vaulted ceilings. I've always loved the architecture of churches like this, they're something that we don't have enough of back in the states. Although a small crowd of mourners is gathered at the front of the church, I feel like an imposter, having known Jane for such a short amount of time, so I take a seat near the back. From my vantage point I can see Linda, sitting quietly in the front row with her hands folded quietly in her lap. A woman who must be her daughter, Daisy, sits beside her while making small talk with some of the other guests, a man in a wheelchair sits on Daisy's other side. Sam walks amongst the groups, thanking people for coming. He looks so at ease among the throngs of well-wishers, dressed in a polished black suit with a matching tie, I can't help but stare. Thankfully I am sitting back far enough that to follow my gaze would only lead your eye to the crowd.

I had considered before that Sam would have paid for all of Jane's arrangements, but I hadn't thought about how he also likely planned today's affair and would be cohosting with his mother. Jane had told me that she'd never married. She'd never had a family of her own, choosing to be by Linda's side throughout her life instead. When Linda had become a mother, Jane had become an aunt. When Linda had become a grandmother, Jane had practically become one too. Sam had taken care of them both even though he'd only ever had an obligation to Linda, and he was continuing to do it even after Jane's death.

"Molly!" Sam exclaims when, after a few minutes, he notices me sitting at the back. Of course, my eyes hadn't strayed from him since I'd first spotted him making the rounds. If I didn't know better, I'd say he smiled when he saw me. Alas, I do know better, our relationship is strictly professional. It is a nice fantasy for the moment, though.

"Thank you so much for coming." He leans in for a chaste hug which I am more than happy to oblige him. In any other circumstance, a hug would be entirely inappropriate, and I know this, but given the setting and that we're both here to mourn Jane's death, a quick one doesn't hurt anything. Though it's not technically our first hug, that day in the hall was less of a hug and more of me crashing into Sam while not paying attention and him offering empathetic comfort to a person who was mourning the same loss. This quick hug is voluntary and thus better than that last one.

"Of course! Thank you for inviting me, I am glad for the chance to honor her in this way."

Now that we've made small talk, I'm not sure what else to say. It doesn't feel right to comment about the church or the weather. Instead, I allow Sam to excuse himself and watch as he makes his way back to the crowd. I could move up and join them, now that I've been acknowledged, but I feel more comfortable in the back. I haven't been inside of a church in ages and sitting in the back gives me a quicker escape route if I need one.

As the service gets underway, I'm struck by how little I know about Anglican traditions. Every religious funeral I'd ever attended growing up had been at my grandma's nondenominational Christian church and those services rarely had a set structure. It was the same church where Jake and I were supposed to have had our wedding. Part of the reason I haven't spoken to my mom since then is because Jake's calling off the wedding had made her look bad at the church she's barely attended for her entire life - it's the one where she and my dad were married and where Mindy had her wedding, too. But not me, and that ruined everything, apparently.

Jane's service is lovely; I know she grew up attending church and went to the school at her parish for many years, so I feel that she would have liked the religious ceremony. I'm sure Sam was certain of that too. Even Linda stands and sits and kneels at all the right parts, I'd imagine it's something that's in her so deeply that she can never forget. I just try to remain unseen in my spot at the back so that if I'm doing anything wrong, no one notices.

Once it ends, I'm not sure if I'm supposed to leave or wait to be dismissed or how it works, so I linger in my seat for a minute or two, observing others to see the proper etiquette. This is how I catch Linda's daughter throwing me glances as she talks to Sam. After a few seconds he gives her a hug and a kiss, offers the same to Linda, and then makes a beeline right for me. I actually do the cliché glance over the shoulder to see if Kate Moss has slipped into the church behind me.

"Hi," I say stupidly when he reaches my pew. I'm feeling way more nervous with him standing in front of me than I might have thought, I've been practicing for this moment for weeks, but I can't remember any of the witty and flirtatious things that I had planned to say.

"Do you want to take a walk?" he spits out, and it sounds almost as stupid as my "hi."

"It's raining." This is even more stupid as I obviously do want to take a walk, among other things, with him.

"It's let up a bit, I think." This conversation is proof of why no one would want to watch this movie, our awkwardness is cringeworthy. I realize he's waiting for me to answer about the walk, but I can't seem to find the words.

"So?" he asks finally, tired of waiting for my response.

"Oh, yeah, um, yes. A walk sounds great!" I stammer. And that, kids, is the story of how I end up on a walk with one of London's most eligible bachelors.

I'm surprised, when we step out of the church, to see that it has indeed stopped raining, though the cloud cover indicates it could start up again at any time. The weather gives me a good distraction because I can think of absolutely nothing to say to Sam at all. I know he must feel the same way, too, because we walk the first several hundred feet without talking.

"Thanks again for coming," he says finally when we're about a block down the street. I don't know whether he means on the walk or to the funeral until he starts speaking again.

"Jane spoke about you so often; I know she would have wanted you to be here. Even Granny talks about you sometimes, always reminding me that there's a girl at her home I should meet," he says with a chuckle, sheepishly digging his hands into his pockets.

"I knew from the minute I saw them on my first day of work that these ladies would be my friends. They had something special, and I wanted in on it," I admit, looking down at my feet as I speak. "And Linda tells me every time she sees me that she has a grandson I should meet."

"You're so good with her, the way you talk to her, the way she's been able to trust you... we don't see that very often anymore," he goes on. "How'd you get to be so good at it?"

"It's probably equal parts years of experience and having basic human compassion, I guess. Plus, a little bit of watching Jane with her," I reply, adding the second part as an afterthought. Sam stops walking then and laughs, forcing me to look up from the ground and look at him.

"They were really something together, weren't they?" he asks. I can see it written on his face without him even having to say a word: they don't know what they're going to do now that Jane's gone. She was the raft that had kept Linda afloat, and now that she's gone there's nothing to do that.

"My mum tried to care for her for a while, we'd all agreed that it made the most sense for her to be in a familiar place where she had the most memories. But she couldn't do it, it was too hard on her. My dad, I'm sure you saw him there today, the man in the chair, has MND and my mum is his primary caretaker. At first, we thought maybe she could look after them both, but after a week with Granny, we knew it was too much. That's when Jane stepped up and offered to move to a care home with her," he says as he starts walking again. I'm not expecting his steps, so it takes me a few paces to catch up. I'm not familiar with what MND is but it doesn't seem like the right time to ask.

"The prince lived there for a while," he says suddenly, pointing toward Kensington Palace as if he's my official London tour guide, before continuing on his way toward the park.

"Didn't Jane's family mind?" I ask. Even though I know already that Jane hadn't had a family of her own, Sam doesn't know that I know this and it's both a question to dig a little deeper into her story and the one that seems right to ask.

"Might have if she'd had one," Sam says back quickly. "They were two peas in a pod, Granny and Jane. I've known Jane my whole life. My mum knew Jane her whole life. My granny's known Jane for practically her whole life."

"Right, they met during the war. Jane told me that," I chime in.

"They did everything together from that point on. Went to the same college and university, joined all the same organizations... I think Granny was always the one who decided what they'd do, and Jane just went along with it. I'm sure she told you that my great grandmother completely lost it after the war, Granny's brother was killed in combat and her mother never recovered from the loss. Jane was just always there to serve as Granny's protector and that lasted all the way until the end," he says.

"But your grandparents fell in love and got married, Linda told me that story herself when we were packing up her things. Why didn't Jane?" I ask.

"When my grandparents met and married, they leased a flat in Paddington and Jane leased the one next door. When they eventually moved into the house where my mother was raised, Jane got a flat around the corner. It was sort of like my grandad had married them both. Granny never seemed to notice that Jane wasn't interested in finding love. I've thought for years that Granny probably knew how Jane truly felt about her; that to Jane it was more than friendship, more than having an honorary sister, it was something much deeper..." he continues.

"Love," I say matter-of-factly under my breath.

"I think so. Though I would never have dared to say anything. I think Granny knew, and I think she accepted it though the kind of love she returned was different. And I don't think that Jane minded that either. They had some unspoken, or maybe they did speak about it once upon a time, we'll never know, agreement to accept love from the other in whatever way it came without infringing on the other's happiness," he adds.

"That's really beautiful."

"Really? You don't think it's a little sad?"

"Well, sure but in a tragically beautiful way. I knew from the first time I saw them together that theirs was the kind of friendship that I wanted, the kind I doubt I'll ever have."

"You didn't leave any lifelong friends behind back in America when you came over here?" he asks earnestly. It's sort of like ripping a band-aid off all over again when I decide it's time to tell him my story. I don't know where the desire comes from since I've been so judicious with the story ever since leaving my old life behind... but right now it feels like something that I need to tell.

"Well, that's quite... something," he says once I've finished spilling my guts. I know I've probably made things even more awkward now, but it was either tell him the story (which his granny had figured out within seconds of knowing me and has already told him, whether or not he believed it) or pretend that I had no friends back in Ohio which didn't seem like it would make me all that appealing either.

"I'm glad you're here," he adds then, which is not what I expect him to say at all. On top of that, he throws in his megawatt smile. "Can I take you out for a drink sometime?"

When I got up and got ready for Jane's funeral this morning, I did not in a million years imagine that I'd be asked out on a date by Sam Collins. I never would have even imagined I'd be taking a walk with Sam Collins or having any kind of conversation with Sam Collins that wasn't strictly related to the care of his grandmother. None of this feels real - that I'm standing in Hyde Park with one of London's most sought-after men who is asking me out for a drink. Surely I'm going to wake up any minute to the sounds of Mrs. Wang singing loudly through our thin walls.

16.

I still can't believe that Sam wants to go out with me. It was one thing when it was just an unrequited crush, but it's something else entirely to know that he likes me too. I wonder if he's spent as many hours thinking about me as I have spent thinking about him? Is that something that guys even do? I know Jake didn't, he didn't give himself the time. He just decided that he was going to have me on the first day we met and that was that – he didn't give me the time to think about him for hours either, come to think of it. I wonder how long it will be before Sam asks me out for that drink officially? It's all too much to bear, maybe it would have been better for the crush to go on unrequited and then things wouldn't have to be so complicated.

"Well, it sounds like things are going well for you, Moll. I'm happy to hear it," Mindy says. Of course, I hadn't been completely truthful as I filled her in about how happy I am and how I've made so many new friends. The only thing I haven't lied about is Sam, whom she had promptly Googled and approved, though I know from my own searching that she hasn't uncovered very much about him at all. If I tell her the truth though, about how I'm not exactly happy or how all of my friends are senior citizens, she would start insisting that I come back home and live at her house for a month or two while I figure things out. Even as hard as things have been in London these last few weeks, there's nothing about the trouble that makes me think for a second that I want to go running back home.

"I ran into Becca last weekend. Did she tell you?" she changes the subject.

"Why would she have told me that? We don't talk."

"Oh, I thought maybe you had been talking again after she reached out. She told me that she and Jake are going to see you when they go on their vacation next week. I'm really happy you decided to see them, I think you'll be happy that you did."

This is news to me. I still hadn't responded to Becca's email. I was never able to figure out what I wanted to say, and every time I sat down to try writing it, I'd get angry all over again so my response wouldn't have been what I wanted it to be. Instead, I'd deleted her email altogether so that I didn't have to keep looking at it every time I opened my email, it was only allowing my rage to fester and grow. I tell Mindy this and that I have no plans to see them.

"You should go, don't you think it would be nice to see them?" she asks so sincerely that it genuinely hurts me.

"No, it wouldn't be nice. It wouldn't be nice at all." This is the point in the conversation that we inevitably always reach, when she wants to discuss Becca and Jake and I do not.

"Look, Molly, I know they betrayed you. I'm not trying to tell you not to feel betrayed by them. I honestly can't believe what they did, and only after they let you plan a whole wedding. But don't you think you'll feel better once you can put it behind you? Maybe seeing them would help you to be able to bury the hatchet and get on with your life, even if that means they're still not in it," she says.

"The only place where I want to bury a hatchet is right in Becca's..." I start but Mindy cuts me off.

"I get it, you're still angry. Just at least tell me you'll consider it. They're going to be there whether you see them or not. Wouldn't you rather see them on your terms than run into them by chance?"

Mindy has a point, though I don't want to admit it. I would be horrified if I ran into them around London. And I know the city is huge and I could easily avoid them by just avoiding everything that's touristy, since I can guarantee that's where they'll be. But with my luck, they'd be on a walking tour right past my front door. I do have to at least think about it. Mindy's right about that too, until several months ago, they were two of the people that I loved the most in the world.

"Fine, I'll think about it."

"I just think that it will help you to be able to forgive them."

"I don't want to forgive them." It's true, what they did is unforgivable. What they did was the reason that I moved to another country. Why should I have to be the one to forgive them? After what they did to me? It's one of the most absurd requests I've ever heard in my life and I don't care what my sister thinks of me for saying so.

"You can still be angry, no one is telling you not to be. You have every right to be frickin' pissed. I can't believe what they did to you, either one of them. But wouldn't you feel better if you could be the stronger person and forgive them? They don't deserve any more of your headspace. So maybe seeing them could be the final push you need to say good-bye to the whole situation."

"I don't know, Min. But I promise you that I'll think about it, okay?" This appeases her. I do mean it when I tell her that I'll think about it, too. Thinking about it doesn't guarantee that anything else has to come of it. Thinking about it is all that I owe anyone.

"That's all I ask. I've got to go. Teddy is trying to make us lunch on the stove and it's not going well." She says her goodbyes quickly and hangs up. I feel a pang of longing at the thought of my nephew, whose current obsession is with cable cooking shows, and how if I'd been home, I would have been invited over to taste whatever he'd concocted. I'd been there for his entire life until now and the thought of missing out on the rest of his childhood occasionally makes me sad.

Mindy's right about Becca though, I have given her and Jake so much of my time over these last several months. And I should be able to forgive them, I mean, what they did to me shows exactly the kind of people that they are and they're the kind who deserve one another. But I still don't know if I can forgive them yet, in any capacity. Maybe seeing them would help, Becca was the one who extended the olive branch after all. Maybe seeing them in my own environment would help me be able to see that I truly am better off without them.

From: MollyWalton713@cmail.net
Sent: Sunday, 5:43pm
To: BecBecBecca@cmail.net
Subject: Re: London Trip!!!

Hi Becca,
It's good to hear from you. I'm glad to hear that I've inspired you to travel. You both definitely need to get out more. Haha. Sorry it's taken me so long to respond, I've just been so busy with work and my friends. I think I'm probably free for lunch on Saturday if you don't already have plans. There's a great cafe in Piccadilly Circus, if that sounds okay let me know and I'll send you the details.
Talk soon,
Molly

I hit send before I can change my mind. Of course, I know of no cafes in Piccadilly Circus. But it seems like the kind of place that would impress Becca. I know her better than I know anyone and there is nothing she loves more than being surrounded by a crowd. Piccadilly, with its large electronic screens and hordes of double decker tour busses, can serve as the perfect locale for me to pretend like my life is great and that they did me a favor by getting together.

In reality, I don't know what I've just done or why I've done it. After my conversation with Mindy, it just seemed like the right thing to do and now that I've sent it, I can't take it back. I am committed to seeing the two people who I want least in the whole entire world to see in less than a week. I wish that my life was awesome and that they didn't know me well enough to be able to tell when I was lying so that I could really show them. Instead, I know they'll be able to see right through me... unless...

Today is a day of impulsivity and I'm done dialing before I can talk myself out of it.

"Molly," Sam answers after only a couple of rings. I take a deep breath while I collect my thoughts, deciding to start with the small ask before the big one.

"Hi, sorry to bother you. I wasn't sure who else to ask." I try to make my voice steady, but what I'm about to do could ruin everything."It's no bother, I'm happy to hear from you. How can I help?" He's so polite that it almost seems fake. I mean, who talks like that in normal conversation? But, then again, Sam is polite for a living. That's literally one of the primary tenets of his job, he probably can't help it.

"So, remember how I told you about Becca and Jake? My ex-best-friend and my ex-fiancée who are together now? They're coming to London next week and somehow, I got talked into seeing them on Saturday," I pause and wait for Sam to interrupt, but he doesn't. Another tenet of his job: active listening.

"I told them that I knew of this great café in Piccadilly Circus... but I don't. I wanted to sound confident and I figured that as Americans who have never set foot outside of the state of Ohio, they'd find Piccadilly exciting and glamorous. I thought that maybe you'd know of some place where we could meet, being a Londoner and all," I realize how ridiculous I sound. When I talk to Sam it's like the words don't compute from my brain to my mouth.

"What kind of meeting place are we going for? Is it a full lunch? Just a quick cup of coffee before you send them back to the special ring of hell that they call home?" he asks. His joke makes me laugh, especially since it's one that I've thought of already many times myself.

"I agreed to lunch because I'm an idiot. But the shorter and less formal it can be, the better. I don't know why I said I'd do this. It's going to be a disaster."

"There's a little coffee shop right next to *Lillywhites*. It's the kind of place that wishes it was in Paris, they serve tea cakes and finger sandwiches and that's about it by way of food. They have an outdoor area, too. I assume your American friends will want to sit out in the busyness?"

"Calling them my friends is a gross misuse of the word," I reply shortly. His breathy laugh makes my stomach flutter, it also makes me remember the other reason, the real reason, for my call.

"Thank you, I really appreciate it. I want to show them that I'm doing well and that I'm better off without them. And I was thinking that one way to do that would be to show them that I've already moved on and that I have a hot new boyfriend and I was wondering if maybe you would want to come and pretend to be that person?" I spit out practically in one breath.

"You want me to pretend to be your boyfriend to impress people that you claim not to care about?" he asks. Putting it plainly like that makes it sound so stupid.

"Well... yes?" I can think of nothing else to say.

"I don't know, Molly... that seems like it would be a little weird. I understand where you're coming from, I really do. But I just don't think I'd be comfortable."

I don't know what answer I was expecting or why I thought that this would be a good idea. I should have known better than to try to rope Sam into this.

"No, I understand. It was silly of me to even ask. Just forget it." I'm certain that I've ruined my chances of ever getting that date until he speaks again.

"But you think I'm hot, though?" he laughs. Ugh, men. They're the same in every country.

17.

I like Sam. Up until this point it's just been a crush, but I can admit now that I truly like him. He's gorgeous, sure, but he's also funny and thoughtful and smart and kind. I'd imagined all of those things about him when he was mostly a figment of my fantasies but getting to know him in real life has far exceeded my expectations in every single one of those categories. All I want to do is to be able to tell someone about it, that's what girlfriends are for after all. Becca and I had spent so much time talking about boys over the course of our friendship that you'd think it was all we ever did. I've tried bringing it up to Mrs. Wang and she always tunes in as if it's the juiciest gossip she's ever heard, but I feel selfish talking about me all the time when we only have a few more nights to spend together.

The time for Mrs. Wang to move in with Sheng and Jie is coming up fast and I don't know what to do about it. Yes, I'll be able to go over there anytime I want to visit, but I have this crippling fear in the back of my mind that once she's gone, our friendship will be out of sight and out of mind. So instead of dwelling on what happens when she's gone, I've been trying to focus all of my time and energy into the fact that I still have her here. Every night we get together to play mahjong and drink tea, and it's almost like nothing has changed and that she won't be moving and leaving me all alone in this borrowed flat. On other nights I help her pack her belongings into cardboard boxes and I try not to let her see how much I'll miss having her right next door. One night last week, I ordered Italian take out and we ate Spaghetti Bolognese by candlelight. I never imagined that I could have such a good friend with whom I shared so little, and now she's leaving, and I don't know what that means for me or the life I've attempted to build here.

There's not much to this life with Mrs. Wang gone, really. I came here for the work, but it was work I could have done back home. It is work I have done back home. I just didn't want to be back home anymore. I didn't want to be around reminders. I wanted to run away. I only came here for the work because the work was familiar, something I could do in my sleep while I figured out the rest of my life. Only, I haven't figured out much of anything. I don't think I've really tried, honestly. I've been waiting for better things to materialize without having to work for them because I have felt like the universe owed me that. I have a job that isn't very challenging, I am crushing on a man who probably only feels moderately attracted to me because I am such a mess, and I have exactly one friend who is way too good for me. Without her, what do I have?

I've just sent Mrs. Wang back to her own flat on Wednesday night when there's a knock at the door. I know it's not her because she always uses the same soft three rap cadence and this one is different, decidedly stronger, and I'm not expecting any male guests.

"Who is it?" I ask skeptically, quickly scanning the table by the door for something I could use as a bludgeoning tool. There's nothing except a small porcelain bowl intended to collect keys, and that's not going to injure anyone.

"It's Sheng Wang," comes the unexpected reply. I glance through the peephole to confirm that it is, indeed, Sheng and that Jie is by his side. My heart flutters a little in my chest, I may have a romantic crush on Sam, but I have a massive girl-crush on Jie. True to form, she looks flawless in a pair of black pants and a brightly colored cable-knit sweater pulled over a crisp white button down. I'm so busy admiring Jie's attire that I nearly forget to respond to the knock. Jie offers me a friendly wave as soon as I open the door.

"Sorry to stop by so late, we were going to pop in on Mama,

but my work meetings went later than expected," Sheng says. I tell him that I have already sent her back to her own flat and move to close the door again but he puts up his hand to stop me.

"We wanted to see you first, if you don't mind," Jie says then and I'm suddenly incredibly embarrassed of my flat. Not only is it not my style at all, it's also a mess. Mrs. Wang had only just gone next door and our tea things are still strewn all around my small kitchen area. I have no choice but to let them in, and neither of them seems fazed in the slightest by the clutter.

No one speaks for several minutes as I offer them tea and move to put the kettle back on. I can't help but wonder if Mrs. Wang knows they're here or why. She is usually so attuned to what is happening on the other side of her door, and I doubt that a visit from her beloved son would go unnoticed. I half expect her to come walking back into my flat without knocking as soon as she hears their voices and even go so far as to get out an extra mug, just in case.

"I'm sure you're wondering why we've come," Sheng says as soon as I've set the mug of tea in front of him. I realize too late that I've served him a novelty mug with a picture of an old woman in a bikini on the front. Though I have been wondering why they've come, Sheng doesn't give me a chance to answer.

"Jie and I have been talking about what a huge blessing you've been for us, helping with Mama and all. You have no idea how much of a relief it's been to know that she hasn't been all alone here in this tiny flat that she insisted on letting." I can tell from his tone that Sheng still can't believe his mother chose to cram her belongings into the tiny, one-room flat rather than accepting his offer to put her up in a place of better comfort.

It's funny, he says that I don't understand how much of a relief it's been to know that she wasn't alone here, but I do. I understand completely because I've been so relieved to not be alone here as well. That's why I'm so heartbroken over her departure. Our friendship might not be conventional, but it's been exactly what I needed during this transition period, and I think the same is true for her. When I tell Sheng this, he smiles.

"You are very dear to my mother, too, Molly. I never stopped to consider how difficult it might be to bring her here to London. I was trying to do the right thing, trying to do what is expected of a son to take care of his mother. But I never thought about whether she'd be happy or if she'd have friends. I wanted to get her here so that I knew she was safe and being looked after, but I never gave the adjustment much thought beyond that. Then you turned up, a woman with a similar story, having left your country and your life behind to start over again here. And by some miracle, you leased the flat right next door. It is sort of remarkable the way it all worked out."

It is pretty remarkable. I hadn't looked at it from that perspective, but the way Mrs. Wang and I found each other really is nothing short of miraculous. I could have moved into a flat next door to literally anyone, but somehow, I ended up next door to this woman who was also brand new to town who has become my friend. I couldn't have predicted the outcome in a million years, and it truly is remarkable.

"I'm going to miss having her here," I admit. "I've been trying not to think about it. I know I can visit, but it's just not the same. Your mother has become my best friend."

"In all of London?" he asks with a tone of disbelief.

"In all of the world, if you can believe it," I laugh.

"I think Mama Ting feels the same way," Jie says then. She's been quiet, allowing her husband to do the talking, it's clear from his delivery that he's been practicing what to say.

"It's funny because we've been trying to think of what we can do with Mama Ting once she moves. All she talks about is 'My Molly' and the things you do together, I am just sick at the thought of having to separate you. Then I remembered, and I was just telling my husband, how you work with the elderly, as a carer," Jie continues. I don't work as a caretaker, though that's a common misconception. Normally I would speak up to clarify but Jie is sending me a look that says I would be better to keep my mouth closed so I do just that.

"And we thought, that's perfect! It would solve all of our

problems!" Jie has a lightness in her voice as if she's just let me in on a special joke.

"I'm sorry… I'm confused," I reply.

"You see," Sheng starts, "You, Molly, are one of the only things that makes London tolerable for my mother. You, and I'd imagine Jasper. We were thinking that perhaps we could have you come live and work for us, as a sort of companion for my mother. It would put my mind at ease to know that she is happy having you with her, and I think you would be a huge help in our home." He seems nervous to ask, as if he's over-stepping some kind of invisible boundary that I have in place. Is he? I'm not even sure. A question like this wasn't on my radar in the slightest.

"You want me to come and work for you?" I don't know what to make of their request.

"Yes. You've been such a good friend to my mother, and I think having you there would help all of us with the transition. The downstairs apartment is fully equipped so it has its own kitchen and bathroom plus multiple bedrooms and a sitting room, so you could move into the apartment right along with her. And obviously we'd compensate you," he adds.

I can't quite believe what I'm hearing. They're offering to pay me to live at their house and spend time with my friend. It's a strange combination of too good to be true and something that doesn't feel totally right. I choose to hang out with Mrs. Wang because I want to, it feels strange to consider getting paid for it.

"Sheng, you know your mother better than I do, but in a million years do you think she'd be okay with me essentially being paid to be her friend?"

He laughs and shakes his head as Jie starts to speak. "We thought of that, and no she probably won't like it. BUT it's better than the alternative which would be to hire a nurse who would treat her more like a charge than a friend."

"She doesn't need a nurse," I reply quickly. She's perfectly capable of taking care of herself and I've watched her do it for months now. I know that they know this too.

"You're quite right," Sheng answers. "But while a nurse isn't appropriate, we need something to do with her. We have a housekeeper who comes in to clean and we have a university student who comes in to help with Jasper after school, but we don't have anything to do with Mama. If you were there, my mother would be occupied during the day, and she'd get to keep her friend."

I don't know what to say. This is an offer outside of anything I ever considered a possibility and I'm going to need some time to think about it. Mrs. Wang is my friend, and I don't want to jeopardize our relationship by suddenly becoming someone tasked with taking care of her. She won't like that one bit. But I love the Wangs, I had known instantly upon setting foot in their home that they are a wonderful family with whom I want to spend more time. There are so many things to consider that I don't know where to start.

"I know you need to think about it, we've sprung it on you quite suddenly and I'm sure you have a lot of questions," Jie says. Sheng is tapping his fingers nervously on the table like he's afraid he's done something wrong. I've observed his mother do the same. I assure them that I will think about it and will let them know as soon as I've made a decision. I don't know why it's weighing on me so much, they're giving me the opportunity to not be separated from the only good friend I've made since I arrived in London – what more could I need? Still, I have so many questions running through my mind.

"What about my visa? It's tied to my employer, and I don't know how that would work." I don't expect them to have the answer but it's the first question I think of to ask.

"I have a great immigration solicitor, he helped with all of Mama's paperwork, and he can find a solution for you. Is that your only hesitation?" Sheng responds more quickly than I expect.

It's not, I still have so many hesitations; but I don't know how to ask everything else, and I also don't want to hear all about how Sheng has an answer to all of my questions. It's clear they've already given this a lot of thought and I need to do the same. Choosing Mrs. Wang would mean letting go of Linda. And even though I won't be seeing her anymore now that she's in Memory Care, I don't feel quite ready to say goodbye. It's a lot to think about.

I hear their voices through the wall after they've left my flat and gone next door. I wonder if they're telling her about the offer they've just extended. I hope not. If Mrs. Wang knows, it will make it harder if I decide to say no. And if I do say no and she knows that, then that will be the end of everything.

I'm not sure if I want to say no, I just don't know what I want to say. I moved here to do the same job that I've always done because it was something familiar and at least I'd have one familiar thing going for me. Could I do something else, though? Someone is giving me the opportunity to choose my friend - is that a choice I'm ready to make?

18.

There are certain things in life that a best friend is supposed to help you with, certain things that are just a part of their job description. One of those things is helping you to pick out the perfect dress to wear when you see your ex again for the first time so that they know exactly what it is that they're missing out on. When your best friend doesn't speak the same language, it's a little more complicated than just sitting on the bed and drinking wine while you gossip about how ugly the new girlfriend is. I feel confident, though, that Mrs. Wang will be able to rise to the occasion – she's just going to require a little more explanation.

"I want to tell you a story," I say on Friday night. She sits right down in her favorite armchair in my cramped seating area, her face conveying that I have her absolute attention. I've told her the story of Becca and Jake several times already, but I've never been sure if she's understood, so tonight I've come prepared.

I'm seeing them tomorrow and I still don't think I can face them alone. Though I completely understand Sam's not wanting to come along, it was a lot for me to ask of him and now that it's all said and done, I feel a little silly. If the roles had been reversed and he'd asked me to come and pretend to be his girlfriend so that he could make his ex jealous, I don't think I'd have said yes either. It's hard to imagine facing them tomorrow alone, though, and that's why I need Mrs. Wang tonight. I need the confidence boost that I can do this, the kind I can only get from my best friend.

Silently I kneel before her in the chair, my laptop on my

lap. I decided that since visual aids work so well as a way for us to communicate, the best way for me to make sure that we fully understand each other is to provide her with an electronic presentation, I haven't progressed enough in my language studies to rely on that yet. I'd spent my entire Thursday night, after we'd had our tea and said our goodbyes, working on it and it had helped to ease my mind and to keep it off of Saturday. As the presentation opens and the brightly covered opening slide illuminates the screen, Mrs. Wang's face lights up.

It was hard to figure out how to get started but I decided to start at the beginning, scouring all of my old files for pictures that showed Becca and my friendship over the years. The first slide featured animation of our childhood photos along with our names.

"Moll-ee," she says softly as she taps the screen on my photo.

"Yes, that's me, and that's Becca," I tell her, pointing to the other photo.

"Beck-uh," she repeats, sounding out the name.

"We were best friends growing up back in Ohio," I continue. They're the same words I've said a million times, but I'm hopeful that tonight they will hit Mrs. Wang's ears differently. I'm hopeful that she'll be able to understand why I need her so much tonight.

The slides continue as I include more and more of our childhood pictures. I'd deleted all traces of Becca and Jake from my social media profile after the rehearsal dinner, but I still had a big folder of scanned photos that I had used to make the slideshow which was supposed to have played during the reception. They included so many pictures of Becca and me as children that I hadn't needed to look far at all to find what I needed to tell Mrs. Wang this story.

After I've clearly established our friendship, narrating along with each slide, Jake is introduced. "This is Jake. He was my fiancée," I explain as a picture from our engagement appears.

It had been a very Jake kind of a proposal. We were at a park near his house where his firehouse played in a softball league with other law enforcement officers from around the city. I hated softball but I would go and watch every game because any time I happened to skip one, I'd get an earful about how all the other wives and girlfriends were there and why couldn't I just be supportive for a change? That day in particular, his team was playing in the championship and Jake had just hit a triple. As he rounded the bases, he ran over the bag at third (making sure to tag it because obviously the game was more important than his romantic gesture) and right toward the stands where I was sitting before getting down on one knee and pulling the ring out of his pocket.

"Molly Walton, will you make me the happiest man in the world by becoming my wife?" he had asked. I was completely caught off guard and embarrassed, I'd dressed in my sloppiest weekend clothes foolishly thinking that I'd just be fulfilling my role as a dutiful girlfriend at the day's game. The only way to get everyone to stop cheering and staring at us had been to say yes. I probably would have said yes anyway, but that was the specific reason that I said it in that moment, just to make it stop. Then my mom and Mindy and Becca all appeared from their hiding spot at another part of the park, and we'd all hugged and laughed. I'd wondered ever since then what would have happened if Jake hadn't gotten that triple…

Mrs. Wang draws me out of my memory by lifting up my left hand and examining it for a ring. She sets it down softly, looks back at the screen, and then picks up my hand again. I can tell she's starting to connect some dots, but I know she has no idea what's coming.

"Yes, we were engaged. And there's Becca right there, at the proposal," I say, pointing to a picture of the group after I'd accepted.

"Beck-uh. Best Friend," she says with a smile, happy to convey that she's grasping the story.

"Yes! That's right!" I hate how easy it is, sometimes, to slip into talking to Mrs. Wang like she's a child. I don't think of her as one, but with the language barrier I find that sometimes it just happens. It can tend to happen sometimes at work too, with residents like Linda who require a bit of extra patience, though I always try to avoid it if I can.

The next slide is the one to which I've most been anticipating Mrs. Wang's reaction. It's a short, animated clip that I found online of a bride and bridesmaid approaching a chapel before there is a record scratch noise and the chapel rips down the middle like a piece of paper. Then you see the bridesmaid walk off with the groom.

Mrs. Wang gasps. "Beck-uh! Best Friend!" she repeats with a completely different tone.

Since I've explained the story and the situation so many times, it no longer fazes me when people first react to what happened. I've experienced the gambit. People apologizing, people cursing Jake, people cursing Becca, I've even had people cursing me... none of it triggers an emotional response in me anymore. That is until Mrs. Wang leans over in the chair and gives me a big hug around the neck.

"Oh, Moll-ee," she says gently, caressing my hair with her hand as she holds me.

"And that's not all!" I say in a fake game show announcer voice. We've watched a lot of TV together and she quickly gets the reference.

"Becca and Jake are coming to London. Tomorrow," I add.

"London?!" she asks, looking around in a panic like they might be in my flat right now. "Oh no!"

"I promised my sister that I would see them... so I need your help."

"Anything, Moll-ee." I'm constantly astounded by the way that her vocabulary grows, especially since, as far as I know, her contact with the English language comes primarily from me and from the television. Sheng and Jie talk to her in Chinese, so she doesn't get a lot of practice.

"I need your help to pick out something to wear. I need to make them jealous," I say, getting up and walking to the wardrobe where my clothes are hung.

"A-ha!" she exclaims, knowing exactly what it is that I'm asking of her. And now comes the part where I get to sit on the bed and drink wine while my best friend goes through my closet to find the perfect revenge outfit to wear to see Becca and Jake.

I haven't given much thought to Sheng and Jie's job offer yet. I've been so preoccupied with this meeting tomorrow that I haven't been able to sit down and give this offer the kind of thought that it deserves. I know that's not fair to Mrs. Wang, because I really do love her, and I've been given the chance to keep our friendship going. It's also not fair to them because the longer I wait to figure it out, the more time they lose in trying to find someone else who might want to take the job. They've pretty much removed all of the hurdles I can think of already, so there's not any reason for me to decline. But making the choice feels scary. I've only ever done the job that I moved here to do.

"Yes?" Mrs. Wang asks, holding up a little black dress that I'd bought just days after what should have been my wedding day when I was trying all different kinds of therapy to make myself feel better. It's short and form fitting with long sleeves and a plunging round neckline. I immediately calculate that I'll have to throw on a pair of tights to combat the cool autumn weather, but other than that, it's perfect. It's totally inappropriate for lunch at a cafe in Piccadilly Circus and it is exactly the kind of thing that a best friend would encourage you to wear to such a meeting. My best friend just happens to be this seventy-year-old woman.

19.

It's been the longest week of my life as I've waited for Saturday to finally arrive so that I can just go ahead and put it behind me. When it finally does come, I wake up with the feeling of dread that I've been trying to squelch ever since I responded to Becca's email. Of course, I wasn't able to sleep in. I'd set an alarm so that I didn't accidentally oversleep, but I find that I don't need it. Better than any melody at waking me is the sense of impending doom that lingers everywhere. Apart from knowing that I'm going to look like a knock-out, today I am going to show up to lunch with my ex-fiancé and former best friend and I'm just going to wing it. That's all I can do. I've spent the better part of the week playing potential scenarios out in my head; planning exactly what to say and how I'll leave Jake in tears. But honestly, it's not Jake I'm worried about seeing. I've had breakups before, and while what he did to me was reprehensible beyond belief, I'm more angry with Becca. She's the one I'm most dreading having to see again. What am I supposed to say to her? She's the one who truly broke my heart.

When we were kids, Becca and I would spend our summers creating these elaborate, imaginative stories about our future selves. We'd be nine years old, sitting at her patio table sipping "coffee" (soda poured into mugs) while we "gossiped" about our lives: our husbands' golf games, getting our kids into private school... In every version of the lives Becca and I had imagined for ourselves, we were doing adulthood together. It never crossed my mind at any point of our friendship that anything could happen that would ever change that truth. Becca had been my person, she'd always been my person. Seeing her today is going to hurt me deeply, I know this without even having seen her yet.

After she helped me pick out my dress last night, Mrs. Wang agreed that I should set my hair in hot rollers so that it falls perfectly around the plunging neckline of my dress and forces the eyes there. I wish I could say I didn't secretly hope Jake would spend all of our meeting staring at my breasts, but I'd be lying. One thing I always had on Becca was a bigger bra size. She used to cry about it in high school when she was still wearing an A cup and I'd already grown into a C. Jake even used to comment about it when he'd first met her, and it's the only weapon I feel like I have in my arsenal today at all. I'm single, facing them alone, and still totally sad… but at least I have boobs.

It's an easy tube ride to Piccadilly and as soon as I come up above ground I feel out of place among the tourists in their blue jeans and sneakers. I don't want to be the first to arrive so I linger at a souvenir stand where I can see the cafe while I wait for them to appear. There are a million reasons for me to want to turn right back around, go back down the steps of the station, and get right back on a train heading home but I've come this far, and I promised Mindy…

That's the thing that I've been telling myself all week to keep me committed. That I'm not doing this for me, I'm doing this for Mindy. It had been her prodding, after all, that had made me respond to Becca's email in a moment of weakness. Mindy was so convinced that it would benefit me somehow to see them, and I didn't want to let her down by backing out. But the instant I see them approach the cafe, I regret it.

Becca looks relaxed in a pink maxi dress and white cardigan, it's a dress I remember well. I'd helped her pick it out at Tower City Center ages ago because she wanted to look nice at her company picnic. As soon as I see it, I know she's dressed carefully today, just like I have. Jake is still Jake, muscular, tattooed, and wearing a black polo shirt that looks like it's going to rip if he takes a deep breath. His calves, which look even bigger than they did when we were together, stick out from the bottom of his khaki cargo shorts. I should have known he'd be wearing this exact outfit regardless of the November weather, it is the Jake Caruso uniform. As he looks around for me, he takes off his sunglasses and affixes them to the back of his head. They look like everyone I knew in Ohio, but the thought of seeing them here sends a shiver down my spine. I'm just about to step out of my hiding place when someone grabs my wrist.

"Oh good, I've caught you," Sam says. I'm so surprised to see him that I can't think of anything to say.

"I got to thinking about why you would have even needed to ask me to come be with you today and it made me feel like a real wanker for saying no. I mean, if it were me, I'd definitely want someone by my side for moral support," he continues.

"So, that's what you're here for then? Moral support?" I ask. It wasn't quite my request, but I'm so grateful that he's here that I don't care. He can be mean to me the entire time for all I care, what matters is that he's here.

"Is that them?" he asks, eyeing the American couple turning wildly in circles in front of a tiny cafe.

"It is," I respond. I can't help but wonder what he thinks; can't help but wonder if he's comparing himself to Jake and wondering what I could possibly have seen in him. Maybe I wonder if Sam's thinking that because I'm thinking that. The trick with the sunglasses on the back of his head was one of his favorites, watching him do it now makes me question everything.

"Let's give them a good show then, aye?" he winks. Just as Becca spots me and waves, Sam wraps his arms around me and pulls me into a long, deep kiss.

I've spent a good amount of time imagining this moment. I always imagined Sam as a lip balm user, his lips plump and supple with just the right amount of moisture. I also always imagined that when we had our first kiss it would be in some romantic setting, like a candle lit dinner at his flat or while on a moonlit stroll along the river. I certainly never placed it next to a souvenir stand in Piccadilly Circus as a way to make my former friends jealous. That's the biggest thing that makes our real kiss different from my fantasies: I never imagined that our first kiss would be totally and completely fake.

When the kiss ends, I'm dazed, and Sam has to pull me in the direction of the cafe to get me started again. He's wearing a suit and tie and I can feel Jake staring, mouth agape, before I see him. Somewhere inside me, jilted Molly is doing a happy dance at just that part alone. Becca runs up and gives me an earnest, full bodied hug... one that is awkward, given that I don't reciprocate.

"Good to see you, Bec," I lie.

"Oh my God, it is SO good to see you!" she squeals in response. It's just like her email implied, that she thinks that nothing has happened.

"Champ," Jake says in acknowledgment before giving me a side hug that makes the awkward hug I shared with Becca look completely normal and full of warmth. I'd always hated that nickname. "Champ" made me sound like I was his prized Pitbull rather than his fiancée. He'd picked it way back when we'd first started dating after he'd taken me to a barbecue with some of his firehouse buddies and I'd dominated at beer pong. It hadn't been one of my prouder accomplishments, but the name stuck. I'm surprised to hear him use it now, though.

"Hullo," Sam says, falsely accentuating his accent. "I'm the boyfriend." Sam claps Jake's hand between both of his own and shakes with gusto. It's a comical scene and I'd laugh at the look of utter bewilderment on Jake's face if I didn't know the whole thing was an act.

"Darling!" I chime in instead, really relying on my high school acting chops. Doing so reminds me of the time that Becca stopped speaking to me for a month when I was cast to play Blanche when she only got Stella. "Go easy on them!"

Sam plays right along, dropping Jake's hand and putting an arm around my waist before turning to look at me lovingly. I feel so many different things at once when he looks at me this way. I know we're just pretending, that after this lunch we'll go our separate ways and maybe run into each other around corners at work again. But something in his look is so real, so unrehearsed... like he's looking at the woman he loves and not some crazy lady who forced him to come here and teach her former friends a lesson.

"I'm sorry, dear. I'm just so excited to finally meet some of your friends from America!" He shifts his attention from me to them and I can see Becca practically bouncing with excitement. She was always a bouncer, like the excitement of the world was too much to be contained in her petite blonde frame. I'd spent so many years ignoring this trait that I'd almost forgotten about it.

"Eh, I'd say 'friends' is a strong word," I respond, unable to hide my contempt. I feel like I can only commit to one acting role today and if that role is going to be Sam's girlfriend, then it can't also be "girl who is totally fine with seeing these people again."

"We could tell you some GREAT Molly stories!" Becca ignores my comment. I guess there was a lot that we'd come to ignore about each other over time.

"Babe, he doesn't want to hear those, let's just eat and go," Jake says then. I knew from his body language the second I saw him that he didn't want to be here - not at lunch with me, maybe not even in London at all. That made two of us who were only here to survive Hurricane Becca, the name my family had given her back in middle school because she had a habit of making everything about herself and destroying anything in her path that didn't see it that way.

I wish I had recognized sooner that Becca wasn't a good person. I wish I had seen it back then when my parents would whisper "HB" to themselves in advance of a sleepover in our basement or when she'd allowed me to take the detention she'd cried her way out of when we were caught reading *Cosmo* instead of Shakespeare in our tenth-grade English class. I always thought that my loyalty was a strength: that no matter what, I was there for my friends. But maybe my loyalty is just another way to frame my stupidity. The signs had been there for years, but I'd allowed myself to be blindsided by Hurricane Becca instead.

"I'd actually love to hear the stories," Sam says, and for the first time since this whole charade began, I can tell he's not pretending.

"Well…" Becca begins.

"How about we head inside? I'm sure you must be hungry," I interrupt before she has a chance to continue. Really, I don't care what story she might have been about to tell. But I'm with Jake and I just want to get this thing over with so that they can be gone from my life forever.

The line in the cafe is short, thankfully, which helps to move the process along. I'm just about to reach into my purse to pay for my tea and muffin when Sam gently nudges me as a reminder that today he's my boyfriend and my drink is on him. He takes it one step further and offers to pay for Becca and Jake, too. I smile at him affectionately, which doesn't require any of my acting chops, while Jake scoffs.

"You drink tea now?" he asks with disgust. That simple question tells me a lot: Jake had gotten bored in our relationship because everything was the same every day. That's why he had turned to Becca, for some variety. Now I'm a girl who drinks tea and wears sexy dresses to coffee shops and looks at her new boyfriend like he's an Adonis (because I mean…) and he is with Becca. It gives me great pleasure as I loop my arm through Sam's and we make our way to an outdoor table.

"So, what have you thought of London so far?" I ask once we're seated. It's painful to make small talk, but it would be more painful to sit in silence. I'm grateful when Sam places a hand gently on my knee, I know it's for show, but it's the reassurance I need that I'm not here alone.

"It's very big, so much bigger than I expected," Becca answers cheerfully.

"Eh, Cleveland's bigger," Jake mutters under his breath. I'm sure he must know that's not true, but to bring it up would open a whole other can of worms that I just don't want to get into. Jake is somewhat of a Cleveland loyalist. When we were together everything was always "Go Tribe!" and "Defend the Land!" - his proudest accomplishment in life was that his friends had, at some point, started to call him "The Jake", like the nickname for Jacobs Field, the former name of the professional baseball ballpark. So, of course, to Jake Caruso, Cleveland would have to be bigger than London.

"I was shocked by the size when I first got here too," I answer her, ignoring Jake's stupid aside. "I knew it was a major city, but Columbus was the biggest city I'd ever seen before I got here, so I had no idea just how major London was. I've hardly had time to see all of it. Between work and everything else in my life, I stay within a pretty small radius."

The small talk is hard, but I know keeping things superficial is the safest route. Ever since I had agreed to this meeting, I'd been rehearsing conversations in my head so that I wouldn't just immediately launch into a tirade about how horrible these two people are. Topics that I've prepared for are: the weather, the size of the city (thank you, Becca, for allowing me to rely on my rehearsed script), and food. If the conversation moves from any of these points, I don't know what I might end up saying.

"So what do you do, Jake?" Sam asks then, saving me from trying to keep it all going. It's the perfect question too because Jake loves talking about his career as a firefighter. The only thing he likes to talk about more than firefighting is Cleveland. So, I settle in with my tea and wait for the long response that I've heard a million times about the thrill of the job, racing against time to save lives... I'm surprised when Jake's answer is short and to the point before he turns the question back on Sam. I can see him sizing Sam up, trying to figure out how I, of all people, could have moved on with someone like this. I know he's hoping for a boring answer like how Sam is an accountant or a shoe salesman, just so that he can feel a little better about dumping me.

"I'm a television host," Sam says without missing a beat. "I mainly cover entertainment news, red carpet premieres, things like that." I watch Jake try to hide his expression of disappointment as I casually sip my tea.

"You're on TV? That's amazing! Do you, like, know any famous people?" Becca asks. Beside her, Jake's face has become so red that it looks like he's about to burst a vein. I have to admit that I'm kind of loving how uncomfortable he is with this meeting. It serves him right. He should be uncomfortable!

I only half listen as Sam regales Becca with stories of the people he's met. Most, like the king, I think he made up. But Becca doesn't care, she eats it right up and she can hardly wait to tell Sam about the time she met Drew Carey at a diner, which to her, is basically the same thing as having met royalty. Instead, I'm wondering how I could possibly have spent six years of my life with Jake. I guess maybe the months of objectivity help, but watching him now I can't recall a single thing that I ever found to be attractive about him. He's rude, he's impatient, he's wearing cargo shorts… for some reason these things never bothered me in all the time we were together. I guess I was just so happy to have found someone who was willing to build a future with me that I ignored everything else. I never even considered all of the reasons that I shouldn't marry him until he decided that he didn't want to marry me. In a way I should be thanking him for what he did, he saved me from making the biggest mistake of my life in marrying him.

"This has been so great, I'm really glad we got to see you, Moll. I've missed you," Becca says after a lull in the conversation. Sam tightens his grip on my knee in warning, he must know what's on my mind and it does force me to take a deep breath and think before I respond.

"Well, it was the least I could do. I mean, it was important that I get the chance to thank you," I say carefully. Becca cocks her head to one side like a puppy, trying to figure out what it is that I'm saying. Jake just stares past all of us into the distance.

"Yeah! I mean, without the two of you completely destroying my life back in Ohio I wouldn't even be here today. I wouldn't have these awesome friends or this great job and I wouldn't have met Sam. I owe you guys. You saved me from making literally the worst decision of my life and you set me free. So, thank you!"

And that's what happens when we don't stick to my prepared topics for discussion. I don't know where this is coming from exactly. I'd certainly thought of worse ways to say it to them, and the fact that I've found a way to turn it into a thank you surprises even me. I think just sitting here with both of them and realizing, maybe for the first time, all of their flaws has given me the right words to say. It's probably petty, but I don't care. They can have each other. They can have Ohio and my old life - I don't need any of those things anymore. Mindy was right that seeing them gave me closure. I doubt it was in the way she intended, she'd secretly hoped we'd all become friends again and I'd come back home, but seeing them has opened my eyes in an unexpected way and for that I am grateful.

"Well, you're welcome?" Becca says finally, she never could stand silence or letting anyone else have the last word.

Jake places a forceful hand on her arm to silence her. He's been ready to leave since they got here and now, I've finally given him the chance to make his escape. With his hand still on her arm he stands, practically yanking her up out of her seat to come with him. Had he done that to me? I honestly can't remember anymore, if he had, I'd never thought anything of it. Becca doesn't seem to think anything of it either, she just follows him dutifully. Sam stands to say goodbye, but I remain in my seat. I've said my piece and now I just want them gone. Out of this cafe, out of London, out of my life. I pretend not to notice Becca's intentions when she leans down for a hug, and it makes it even more awkward than the one she'd given me at the start of our meeting. I don't even watch them leave. I can't. As far as I'm concerned, they left me a while ago. I'm just glad that I see that now.

"I'm impressed," Sam says when he sits back down.

"With what? How great I am at picking people? You should be very concerned if I'm hanging out with the likes of you," I say with a laugh, leaning in and nudging him with my arm.

"I do have several questions. But, no, I'm impressed with how you handled yourself. You held yourself together and you got through it. Well done."

"I don't know about 'well done' but thank you. And thank you for being here, I don't think I could have gotten through it without you. Seriously, you saved me."

I expect Sam to answer but instead he leans over and kisses me. This time it's soft and gentle and everything that I had imagined in all of those hours spent dreaming about this moment right down to the butterflies that I just knew I'd feel as soon as his lips touched mine.

"What was that for? They're gone now," I say when we've parted.

"I know, I just wanted to do it for real," he says with a coy smile.

"Speaking of real, what was with that accent at the start? And that stuff about knowing the king? I mean… you don't know the king, right?" I ask. This isn't a question I had ever considered asking Sam before now, to me it would be like someone asking me if I know the president.

"I read up on things Americans like and expect from Brits - thick accents and a royal connection were the top two items on the list. I figured she wasn't going to take the time to fact check my connections. And I do have to say, I think she ate it up. How's it working for you, by the way?" I respond by initiating our second real kiss. The accent, everything - it's all definitely working for me.

It's nice to be able to kiss him when I want to, especially since I've spent so much time thinking about it. I knew that I wanted to kiss Sam from pretty much the moment I first saw him, but I didn't think it would ever happen. It was just something that I could use as a distraction, I never thought that he'd want to kiss me back. The butterflies don't go away just because it's our second kiss, either. I wonder how many more kisses it will take before I lose that feeling? I hadn't ever had butterflies when I kissed Jake, I rationalized that it was because I was too old for butterflies. But I know now that that wasn't the reason - the reason I never felt butterflies when I kissed Jake was because it was Jake.

"Okay, but really. That guy?" he laughs. I sigh and sit back in my chair.

"I don't know, I was never much of a dater. So, when we met, he just kind of decided that I was going to be his girlfriend and that was that. I think I was willing to settle because I never thought that I'd find anything better. I wasn't exactly playing the field. And I'd watched my sister get married right out of coll... university, and I couldn't help comparing my life to hers and feeling like I'd made a wrong turn somewhere along the way since I wasn't already married like she had been at my age. So, when Jake offered, I accepted and the rest is history."

"Well, I hope that you'll open yourself up to more options this time around. I think you'll find there are better things out there. Though I would like to try that trick with the sunglasses, do you think I could pull that off?"

"Don't you dare," I warn with a laugh. "Ugh, I never realized how much that bugged me until now."

"I think the fear of being alone will do that to people. We're willing to overlook a lot of things if it means we can settle. One of the things I remember admiring about Jane from the time I was a lad was that she wasn't willing to do that. She saw people's flaws for what they were, and she wasn't willing to settle. In the end, though, it meant that she ended up alone."

My ears perk up at the mention of my friend. "She wasn't alone, though."

"No, I guess she wasn't," he pauses. "God, I miss her."

"I miss her, too. I know I didn't know her like you did, but she was someone special."

20.

So, that's how it's going to be then, Molly? Aye?" Jimmy asks as he throws a newspaper down on the table beside me.

It's Monday morning in the breakroom and while I haven't had my first dose of caffeine yet, that's not the reason that I have utterly no idea what he's talking about. Until I look down. There on the cover of one of the major British tabloids is a picture of me. Kissing Sam Collins at a cafe. The headline **Sam + Mystery Girl = Love?** is printed across the image in bold white lettering.

"I guess I should have known, the way all you ladies throw yourselves all over him as soon as he walks in here. But I thought you were different. I guess I was wrong," he seethes.

I can't blame Jimmy for being mad. He made his feelings known and I did not return them. Worse, I propositioned him and then disappeared. For all he knows I'd also texted Sam that night and just went with the better offer. And why wouldn't he think that? The evidence that I've had something going on with Sam is right here in print. I can't deny it or suggest it's all in his head.

Some of the other employees, who I don't know well, are in the breakroom too and they pretend to look away when I catch them straining to see the front of the paper. It doesn't bother me if they want to see, really. All of the country knows now, what difference does it make if a few of my random co-workers know too. I just wish that one of them would say something instead of standing around acting like they know nothing and that I'm not here. Jimmy's the only person brave enough to speak up and he's the person I want to talk to the least.

Of all of my co-workers, Jimmy's the only one who knows the truth about why I moved to London. I could tell him the truth and he'd probably be the most likely to understand why I'd need backup for a meeting with Becca and Jake. Of course, he'd also probably expect that I could have asked him the same way that I'd asked Sam, that it could have been the two of us sitting at the cafe kissing and no one at all would have wanted to take our picture. There's no use trying to explain it, it won't help anything.

Like clockwork my phone begins to ring, it's Sam. I'm not surprised at all, and just like he had done by showing up on Saturday, he's saved me from having to answer to Jimmy.

"You saw the paper?" he asks as soon as I've answered.

"I just did."

"I am so, so sorry, Molly. I've only ever been photographed a couple of times. It never even crossed my mind to warn you that this could happen. But don't worry, I have a team of people for just this kind of thing. It'll be gone before you know it," he says and then pauses. I guess that explains why I hadn't been able to find any dirt on him during my countless internet searches.

"Are you in a lot of trouble at work?" he continues. "I know they're always kissing my ass over there but I'm not sure this is what they had in mind." Normally this joke would have made me laugh, but today I'm too distracted to find the humor in it.

I hadn't even had a chance to consider work or how they might react to seeing this picture. I'd been too caught up in Jimmy being the one to bring it to my attention to even think any farther than that. It was one thing to have been busted by Sheila for kissing Jimmy, but it seems like it will be an even bigger deal to be caught kissing Sam.

"Molly?" he calls me back to attention.

"Oh, sorry. I... I don't know. But I imagine I'll be due for a talk with Sheila, and I'm already not on her best side."

"Would it help if I came with you to talk to her? She seems to like me, maybe if I went in too, she'd go easier on you..." he trails off. I can tell he feels bad about this even though he has nothing to apologize for.

"What she likes is your money. If anything, she's worried about you pulling Linda out of here and moving her somewhere else. No, I should talk to her on my own. I'll let you know what happens, okay?"

"Was that your boyfriend?" Jimmy snaps as soon as I've hung up the phone. "Is he going to come in and bail you out? Probably hasn't had enough kissing yet, has he. Probably needs to come in and get some more from the whole lot of them over here, too." I do probably deserve his anger. I don't answer, though. Instead, I take my tea and head off to find Sheila, I might as well get it over with before things have a chance to get worse. He's still ranting when I leave.

By the time I get to Sheila's office I've come up with a plan wherein I don't have to lie, at least not completely. I can tell Sheila about Becca and Jake and how I had asked Sam to go with me so that I didn't have to face them alone; that we kissed so that they would believe he was my boyfriend and that I was fine. Of course, that won't account for how I came to be in a position to ask him in the first place, for that, I can only hope that she doesn't have questions. After all, she knows we've had contact about Linda before and that he invited me to attend Jane's memorial so there's a chance that that part of the story will just make sense to her. A slim chance... but that's all I've got.

The thing is that I don't think I've broken any rules. I'm not an expert on the handbook but I'd read through it after the Jimmy incident and while there are specific policies discouraging fraternization between co-workers and between staff and residents, there isn't anything expressly written about resident's families. Maybe they figured that wasn't something that was going to come up, but I'd already broken the two stated fraternization rules so why not break one that doesn't even exist too?

"Molly?" she calls from the other side of the door. I step into full view and wave awkwardly.

"I thought you might want to see me this morning," I say. If I didn't know better, I'd say she actually smiled.

"Why don't you tell me your side of things; what I maybe didn't read in the papers," she says as I close her office door behind me. And so, I do. I tell her about Becca and Jake and why I had been so excited when Greenfield Care had reached out to me about this job, I tell her about Becca's email and how my sister convinced me to see them, I tell her how I panicked and in a moment of weakness asked Sam if he'd consider going with me. Then I tell her how he initially declined, how he showed up on the day of and introduced himself as my boyfriend and how we'd only kissed to force the point on my former friends. I had no idea anyone would be taking photos of us; I didn't even know Sam was that famous. I sigh when I finish, willing her to believe it.

"Well. While I certainly understand your plight, there's just one little problem with your story," she says

"What's that?"

"There's no one else sitting at the table." She produces a copy of the paper and lays it out in front of me. Sure enough, the other side of the table is empty except for a discarded coffee mug. For all intents and purposes, Sam and I appear to be totally alone and quite enjoying each other's company. I mean, we were, and we were. But my story is true, at least it was at first.

"Molly, this wasn't exactly what I meant when I said that it would be wise for you to move on from Jimmy," she says, making a tent with her hands on the desk.

"Sam was just there to help me out, as a friend. I know what the picture makes it look like, but I assure you there was nothing more to it than that. I've looked through the policies and there isn't anything written that says we can't be friends."

"It's frowned upon," she says smugly.

"Molly, I wanted this to work…" she starts but I put up my hand. Suddenly everything makes sense, I took this job because it was a way out of my life back in Cleveland. I moved here and hoped that this job would make everything feel like it always had. But it hasn't, it never could. I think I needed to see Becca and Jake again to see that, and now I know that my life has been utterly changed, and it's time that I start living that way. If I'm honest with myself I know exactly what I need to do, it's what I should have done as soon as it became an option.

"Sheila, thank you for this opportunity. I've enjoyed my time here and I've met some amazing people. But I think it's in my best interests to resign." I stand and extend my hand. It's obvious that I'm shaking but I try to wear confidence on my face.

I'm already dialing before I even step out of her office.

"Sheng? It's Molly. I'd like to accept your offer," I say as soon as he answers.

21.

Sheng's immigration lawyer really is something special. It feels like no sooner have I accepted the job than the details of my work visa have been negotiated and arranged and all I have to do is go over to the Wangs and sign a couple of documents. It feels too good to be true. Mrs. Wang and I are going to get to stay together, I won't have to pay for my room and board, and I can finally focus on making the new start I'd set out to London for in the first place.

I don't know why it took me so long to make the decision. I think that I knew what I should do as soon as Sheng and Jie had asked me to consider the job. I was just scared of trying something different and failing at it. I shouldn't have been, this whole move to London has been a lesson in trying something different, although I guess the jury's still out on whether or not I'm failing at it. Still, I knew immediately that working for the Wangs was the right move. I should have just accepted it right from the start.

What matters is that I accepted it at all, and now I'm on my way over to the Wangs' to finalize my visa paperwork and to tell Mrs. Wang the good news. I'm honestly still a little nervous thinking of how she'll feel about having a caretaker, she doesn't need one and I've certainly never attempted to fill that role for her. We've always been good friends and I don't want her to get the wrong idea; that I'm somehow trying to leverage that friendship into a paying job. What if she doesn't want to be my friend anymore after she finds out that I'm now her employee?

"Molly! Welcome home!" Jie greets me when she opens the

door. Home. The word conjures up all kinds of mixed emotions in me. Until recently, Cleveland had been my home and I'd never even thought about living anywhere else. It's where I was born and raised and where I had planned to get married and raise my own children. Until a few months ago I never imagined having a home anywhere else, and since I arrived here, it's not something I've had, nor was it something I'd been willing to consider. When I'd called Sheng to accept the job, I'd been so preoccupied with the idea of staying with Mrs. Wang that I hadn't thought about how it meant that I'd also get to live in their gorgeous home; that I'd get to call it my home too. It had especially not crossed my mind that I would want to apply that precious word to it.

"Thank you! I'm looking forward to being here!" I respond as I cross the threshold. Inside it smells of vanilla, I can hear Jasper playing in another room.

"Sheng and Mama Ting are in the dining room," Jie says, closing the door behind me. Jie is perfectly pressed as usual: she's wearing straight legged, navy trousers hemmed just above the ankle and a navy and white gingham print button down shirt with a tangerine-colored sweater tied around her shoulders. Her black hair is pulled into a sleek ponytail. It's what I always imagined women would wear to lunch at the country club, and here Jie is just wearing it in her own home on a casual Saturday. It puts my black skinny jeans and pink cardigan set to shame (I'd chosen it carefully, too, trying to dress like I belonged in the Wangs' house.) I want to be Jie when I grow up.

"Does she have any idea I'm coming?" I ask. I've been doing my best to keep the secret, which has been easier than I would have imagined considering there's only a fifty percent chance that she would understand me if I did say it out loud.

"I don't think she has a clue. She'll be so thrilled," Jie replies. She takes my jacket and hangs it on the rack next to the door. "Can I offer you some tea?"

"That would be great, thank you." I slip my shoes off and slide my socked feet into a pair of slippers that Jie has left sitting out for me, of course they're just my size. I'd expect nothing less from Jie Wang. I can hear Sheng and his mother talking in the other room and I can't help but think how all that separates me from my future is a pair of white doors. I have nothing to be afraid of by stepping through them, but I still need a moment to collect my thoughts because as soon as I do, everything is going to be different.

"Moll-ee?" Mrs. Wang asks when I've finally made my way through the doors to the dining room. She and Sheng are sitting at the table, piles of papers are strewn across its surface, and it appears they've been deep in conversation prior to my arrival.

"Here why?" she presses after I didn't answer her first question. I'm not sure how to respond exactly, to say that I live here wouldn't be quite true yet and to say that I'm here to sign some papers wouldn't be an entire representation of the truth either. So, I stay silent and wait for Sheng to fill in the gaps.

Jie joins us in the room and hands me a cup of tea. It's not a cheap souvenir mug like what I drink from at my own flat, but rather a beautiful porcelain teacup with its own matching saucer. She's removed it from a tray of tea things, and it instantly sends me back to the first time I'd been invited to share tea with Linda and Jane, how I'd wondered if this was how everyone did tea or if it was just for my benefit. I flash back to the regrettable mug choice I'd offered Sheng the night they offered me this job and cringe.

Sheng is explaining something to his mother in Chinese, I don't know at all what he's saying except that I hear my name come up. I wonder if this is how Mrs. Wang feels when she's with me back at my flat, like the whole world is gibberish except for her name. They always say the sound of your own name is the most beautiful sound to you in the whole world. I'm feeling that right now since it's the only word I know in their entire conversation.

"He is telling her that you are here to sign some paperwork from his solicitor. She asked if you are in some kind of trouble and so he said that it's nothing like that, that you need to sign some paperwork for your visa. It's something she knows all too much about," Jie translates. I didn't even notice that she'd come to sit beside me at the table, she'd been so quiet.

On cue, Sheng brandishes the paperwork and turns to me with a pen. "Molly, good to see you. If you can just sign here and here. And then I'll sign there and there, I'll get this back to the solicitor, and we should be all set," he says, pointing to the document as he talks. Mrs. Wang says something, and Jie laughs under her breath.

"Mama Ting is onto you," she laughs. "She wants to know why Sheng would need to sign the document."

I smile as I sign and slide the paper back to Sheng. The anticipation of telling her reminds me of being a kid on Christmas, getting up early with excitement and then having to wait to open your presents. I can hardly contain myself in my seat and though I try to drink my tea to hide the excitement, the shakiness of my hand gives me away instantly.

"Well, that's done," Sheng says as he stacks the papers together neatly and sets them aside. "Shall we tell her then?"

I nod emphatically. The longer I sit here without her knowing the more anxious I'm going to get. I'd spent all night imagining the worst, imagining that she'll get mad and that our friendship will be over. It's better to rip the Band-Aid off now so that I can know for sure where I stand.

Sheng begins talking in Chinese and I'm grateful that Jie is still there to translate. "He said 'Mama, I know that you and Molly have become dear friends in the time you've been neighbors.' And then she said 'Yes, I love My Molly.'" I feel my heart burst with love and pride at hearing these words.

"Now he's telling her how we didn't want to have to separate the two of you because you've grown so close and then we remembered that you are a carer and asked if you might be interested in coming to live here with us to help at home and to keep Mama Ting company," Jie goes on. It's a polite way of explaining the job description that Sheng and I had discussed but I appreciate his discretion because it's what has most fed my fears about her anger.

Sheng speaks again but this time I don't need to wait for Jie to translate because Mrs. Wang leaps up from her chair and runs around the side of the table to me. I'm caught off guard by the way she moves, in my previous experience she'd always been so frail and slow, and now she moves like she could step out the door and run the London marathon. She throws her arms around my neck with the same level of energy, and she holds on so tightly that I think she might never let go. It's a little symbolic, in a way. After all, we'd found a way to stay together and now there was nothing that could break us apart. As she hugs me, she keeps saying "wǒ de Moll-ee" over and over again into my hair.

"What is she saying?" I ask into the air, not sure whether Jie or Sheng can even hear her.

"That means 'My Molly.' It's what she always calls you," Jie says. I can see the look of pure jubilation on both her face and Sheng's, this is exactly what they had hoped would happen for their Mama Ting. I have known, since I first met Sheng and Jie, that 'My Molly' was Mrs. Wang's particular nickname for me but getting to hear her use it strikes me in a way that I didn't expect.

It's what I had hoped would happen too. No one has ever made me feel so wanted or loved in my entire life, not even my own family, and now I get to be a part of this one. It's exactly everything I've ever wanted, and I didn't even know that I wanted it.

After Mrs. Wang finally releases me from her surprisingly strong grip, we're taken to the downstairs apartment, and I get to see where I'll be living for the first time. The too good to be true feelings just keep coming because the place is just as gorgeous as the house upstairs. White walls, marble counters, beautiful crown molding, dark wood floors, not to mention that my entire subleased flat could fit into the space at least three times. Mrs. Wang's room is the larger of the bedrooms which is fine by me since the shared living space adds plenty of room for me to be able to spread out.

"So, what do you think?" Sheng asks anxiously. He's only asking me, Mrs. Wang has already been living in the space for a week and is more than happy with the accommodations.

"Wow, this is incredible! I can't wait to move in!" I exclaim, feeling truly happy for the first time since I landed in London.

22.

Because I quit before Sheila had the chance to fire me, I'm allowed a couple of days to get my affairs in order. Really all this means to me is that I get a chance to say goodbye to Linda, none of the rest of it matters. I don't anticipate ever seeing anyone else here again, not after the way things ended with Jimmy. I know I could have handled that whole situation better, starting with not making out with him in the pub in the first place, but I can't go back and change the past so it's better to just make a clean break from all of them.

That's why I'm surprised when Cat stops me in the hall on that last day. "I can't believe you're already going so soon! We're going to miss you around here!"

"Well, I doubt that. But thank you. I'm glad that I got the chance to know all of you."

"Oh, you mean Jimmy? Don't worry about him, he's just a regular ass. Lily and I are sad to see you go! Especially now. Sam Collins! How'd you manage that?"

"Well, we're just friends," I tell her.

"If you don't want to talk about it, that's okay. I'm just a little jealous, kind of wish I'd had the gall to go for him myself."

I smile. The truth is, though, that Sam and I are just friends. At least for now. I've certainly spent a lot of my free time thinking about our friendship developing into something more. I don't regularly go around kissing my friends, recent life events notwithstanding, so that's definitely something, but I haven't seen Sam since Saturday so it's hard to pretend that there's more even though we have been talking pretty much every day in some form or another. In the meantime, we truly are just friends and I'd be completely fine if that's all we remained. Sam came through for me in a way that other friends wouldn't have, especially considering that he barely knew me, and I'm grateful. You don't find that in a lot of people nowadays. I do think that Mrs. Wang probably would have come through for me in the same way if I'd asked her to… but it wouldn't have done me a lot of good to show up to coffee with my ex with an elderly Chinese woman in tow.

"Take care of yourself, alright? And don't be a stranger! Lily and I would love to meet up for a drink," Cat says before she disappears down the hallway. It's a nice offer, though I don't for a second believe it. Cat and Lily had months to try to meet up for a drink alone with me and they never asked, why should I suddenly expect that to happen? Even if it did, I don't know if I'd ever take them up on it. Their friendship with Jimmy would make things a bit too complicated for my taste. Still, the words make me feel a little better knowing that I'm not leaving this place being hated by everyone I've had the chance to meet.

Though I hadn't prepared for it, I can now check Cat's goodbye off my imaginary to-do list and refocus on where I'd been headed when she'd stopped me: the Memory Care ward to visit Linda. I haven't seen her since the funeral, and while she was right there in the front row with Sam and his mother, I hadn't spoken to her at all. I've been so caught up in the drama of my own life that I haven't taken the time to come by and pay her a visit to see how she's adjusting to her new home. Sam and I have been talking on the phone and exchanging text messages, and he's kept me updated on what's going on with her. But I know that there is nothing but my own excuses stopping me from going to visit her myself.

There is such a striking difference as soon as you cross through the doors of the Memory Care unit. On one side of the door there is a feeling of vitality and on the other it's immediately somber. Memory Care is often where people go to die. It's where they go when they're too far gone to be able to take care of themselves, and that feeling of death, of people giving up the fight, lingers in the air. It's a sad feeling, one that I hate to have to see Linda live with every day. The way I see her in my mind, she so clearly belongs on the other side of the door, but I know that's not the way it works. I can't just will her self-sufficiency back, no matter how hard I might try.

"Oh, I know you!" exclaims the nurse I'd encountered for the first time in Jane's room on the day of her accident and then in Linda's on the day I came to help her pack. I think this is what she's referring to when I respond.

"Yes, we've worked together before."

"No! You're the one from the papers!" That is, unfortunately, not something I've been able to escape. As soon as the photo was printed, I'd become somewhat of a celebrity at work, even though I'd tried to avoid it. It's been easy enough to go unnoticed in the world since I mostly go straight from my flat to work, but around here it's a different story. I guess it has to do with the way Sam is so revered here, it's like I got some coveted prize that they've all been chasing. Honestly, it makes me all the happier to leave this place.

"Yes, that was me," I respond. I've found it best to just own up to it rather than to try to deny it. No one wants to hear the explanation about how Sam and I are just friends. They already have some version of the story in their heads whether by their own invention or the gossip they've heard that is spreading someone else's tale. My favorite fake story that has made its way back to me is that Sam brought me here from America on his own dime to spy on the care Linda is receiving and report back to him each night while we have sex. All I can do is laugh it off.

"I just came by to see Mrs. Suthcliffe. Today's my last day and I wanted to be able to say goodbye," I say, trying to change the subject.

"Well, I don't know what you need to say goodbye for. You're going to be seeing her plenty at Sunday roast and the like." If the gossip is to be believed, then this isn't such a far-fetched suggestion. Although I don't know how I'm going to have time for Sunday roast in between all of the spying and sex.

"Okay, thank you!" I say as I bypass the desk and head toward the hall where Linda's room is located.

It's not exactly the legacy I had imagined myself leaving behind here. I'd had such high hopes when I'd arrived about how I was going to transform the activities schedule here and establish a new system that would last in perpetuity long after I'd departed. Instead, I'm leaving behind the reputation as the kissing girl – the girl who will kiss just about anyone with lips if she's given the chance. It's not the greatest feeling in the world to know that's what your coworkers are saying behind your back, to know that they're formulating their own thoughts and opinions about the type of person you are based entirely on a picture in a newspaper.

"Hello, Molly," Linda says, completely coherently, when I step into her room. It surprises me, you never know when you're going to have a moment like that with her and I've come not to expect them.

"I hear you've met my grandson," she continues, with a laugh. "Isn't he a catch?" Of course Linda would have heard. I doubt she'd seen the paper herself, but the way these nurses are talking about it nonstop, it makes sense that she would have overheard a little something. Since you never know whether she's mentally in the room with you or not, you never know when she's listening.

I'm just about to laugh when Sam rounds the corner into the room, he's carrying a bouquet of daisies and I smile remembering the significance of the flower from Linda's childhood. I consider wiping the smile from my face, that if anyone were to see they'd assume I was smiling at Sam and not at the gesture, but it doesn't matter anymore. This place is as good as in my rearview mirror.

"Did I hear you talking about me? Oh, hello, Molly," he says when he sees me. He crosses the room and hands the bouquet to his grandmother before he greets her with a hug and a kiss.

"And now Molly," she instructs. Sam laughs nervously and

runs his fingers through his hair. I can feel my face turning red, but I try to play it off as best as I can.

"Oh, that's okay!" I manage finally. "I just stopped by to say goodbye to you, Linda. It's my last day here."

"Molly, I'm so sorry..." Sam starts but I stop him. He's apologized to me at least a dozen times since I told him I'd resigned and at least a dozen times I've assured him that it's not his fault and that it was a choice I should have made sooner. Still, he looks more sad than he should.

"Leaving? Where are you off to?" she asks. I tell her about the opportunity to work for the Wangs and how it's one that I don't think I should pass up. She listens intently and I almost think she's comprehending the whole thing until I finish, and she speaks again.

"Well, people need more help these days, with the war on. My brother, Arthur, had a job before he left, but he had to be replaced. We're expecting him home soon," she says then. It's amazing how quickly she can come and go from the room without ever taking a step. Sam hangs his head. I can tell he was as encouraged as I was by the state of Linda's mind when we'd arrived.

"Granny, the war's ended," he tells her. He's trying to be gentle, but I can hear the defeat in his voice. It's hard not to wonder how this might have gone differently if Jane was here, though it does no good. Maybe she could have pulled Linda back out or maybe this would have happened anyway.

Linda looks at Sam with confusion and then goes to sit down on the edge of the bed. She places her hands on her knees and her eyes are wide, like she's taking in more information than she can process. It's a look I've seen her wear more than once: on the morning of Jane's accident and later that day as I arrived at her room to pack for Memory Care. It's a look of defeat, like all of the wind has been taken out of her sails. I hate to think that this would be the way I see her last. My whole purpose in coming to work today was to say goodbye to Linda, but now that Sam's here, it doesn't feel right to share this moment.

"I should go, I have a few other things I need to wrap up," I lie.

"Goodbye, Linda. I'm glad that you've been my friend," I step forward and give her a small kiss on the cheek.

"Have we been friends? Oh, I'm so glad. I do love having friends," she answers. Her doe-like expression makes her seem younger and more vibrant, as if the disease doesn't have a complete hold over her mind.

"You have been a very dear friend to me," I say. I'm not lying anymore, and I can feel a knot rising in my throat, making it hard to continue.

I don't know if I had realized how much Linda has come to mean to me. It's funny because I've worked with the elderly for my entire professional career, but they've never had such a personal impact on me until now. They'd just been the people I worked with, never my true friends. But saying goodbye to Linda is a reminder that I'm saying goodbye to this part of my career and this part of my London journey. While nothing about my time at Greenfield Care has been conventional, it has been the link between my life here and the life I had back home. Without it, I am stepping out completely into the unknown.

"Don't cry dear, I think that you were very special to me, too," Linda pats my hand softly. It's the same thing that Jane had done to me at our very first meeting, and though I know Linda's reacting from instinct and not making the connection, it makes me feel instantly soothed. Still, I make a run for the door because I know that I can't hold these tears back for much longer.

I'm halfway down the hallway, tears streaming down my face, when Sam calls after me. I know that my face is splotchy from crying and I'm afraid to turn around and let him see me like this, but I also know I can't ignore him; we have history now.

I realize it's the opposite of the way I treated Jimmy for all those weeks. I wish I'd been able to think that way about him, like our history mattered. Not because I liked him necessarily, but because he probably did deserve better. After we kissed, I panicked. That sounds like a terrible excuse, but it's true. I'd been so caught up in my healing and my forward motion that

I'd gotten scared, and I'd hidden from him and from what had happened between us. That was what we'd always done in my family, hidden from our problems. That's why my dad ended up with a second family, because he'd hidden from the first one when things got tough. I don't know why I want to take my history with Sam into consideration when I wasn't willing to do the same for Jimmy - I guess maybe I'm just as shallow as everyone else who crosses paths with Sam. There's honestly no way I can blame Jimmy for being mad, he noticed what I was doing well before I did.

"Can I walk with you?" Sam asks as he approaches. I must have forgotten about his long strides from our walk in the park because he reaches me a lot sooner than I had anticipated and I have had absolutely no time to fix my face. I don't answer and he doesn't wait for me to, instead we just start walking and as soon as we've exited the Memory Care wing, he slips his hand into mine. I don't turn around because I don't want to see my favorite nurse through the glass doors as she cranes her neck to see and then shakes her head at me disapprovingly as if to say, "I told you so."

"Is this okay?" he asks then, as if suddenly realizing that maybe he shouldn't hold my hand in public.

"Sure," I smile. "I mean, I don't technically work here anymore."

"So, this is probably alright then, too, I suppose," he says as he brings his hand to the back of my head and lowers his lips to meet mine. It's our first kiss since that day at the cafe, and I've been dying a little bit inside each day that I have been forced to go without one of his kisses. I know I've been telling everyone that we're just friends, I've been trying hard to believe that myself, but it hasn't stopped me from wanting just a few more kisses.

I'm aware that we're still in the hallway of the home that up until today had been my place of work. And yet, now that Sam's kissing me here, I can't possibly care any less. I'd be lying if I said it wasn't something I'd fantasized about in all of those weeks and months of pining for Sam. The reality of kissing him here is so much better than anything I imagined. It's nobody at Greenfield Care's fault that I'm leaving, really, but they made the choice to leave easier. I am almost willing Jimmy to walk around the corner, but he doesn't. Instead, when we finish our kiss, Sam offers a chaste peck before he promises to finally take me out for that drink and disappears back into the Memory Care ward leaving me standing there alone.

23.

It's been a while since I've felt truly homesick. When I'd first arrived in London, there wasn't anything I could think about at all except home, but the longer I live here the more I grow to like it and understand it and not feel like an outsider. Lately, I've been so busy with trying to figure out my life that I've hardly thought of home at all. On Thursday, though, that feels different. It's Thanksgiving back in the States and while life just goes on like normal here in London, I know that the day will be anything but ordinary back in Ohio.

Mindy hosts Thanksgiving every year. She gets up with the sun to start preparing the meal and then around lunchtime my mom and Grandma Betty will show up with the pies. Mindy's in-laws are always there too, and her husband and father-in-law will sit in front of the TV watching football until they're called to the table. Now that Teddy's latest interest is cooking, I'm sure that he'll be popping in and out of the kitchen throughout the day to try to help where he is able. Even though I haven't spoken to most of them in months, my heart aches at the thought of everyone gathered around Mindy's dining room table together.

I haven't talked to Mindy in weeks, since before my lunch with Becca and Jake. Even though I had found that she'd been right, that seeing them did give me a sense of closure that I hadn't gotten on my own, I hadn't wanted to discuss it with her after the fact. I had needed some time to process seeing them and my feelings and what it meant now. Then things had started to snowball with the photo and quitting my job and taking the job with the Wangs that I got too busy to call... or I just hadn't wanted to. I've been wracking my brain for days, trying to figure out which.

If I'm being honest with myself, I'm nervous to call Mindy and tell her about the new job. I don't know why exactly except that it feels a little bit like I'm calling to admit my defeat. Like I am saying that I couldn't make it at the job I'd moved all the way to London to do and now I've already moved onto something else. In general, I wouldn't say that I'm embarrassed about it by any means. But it feels different to call Mindy and to say it out loud. I guess it's because when I'd announced my move, everyone expected me to fail. I lost count of the number of people who told me that they'd see me when I got back to Ohio. Although Mindy was the only person who didn't vocalize that to me, I know that deep down she was hoping that it might be the case, so that I'd have to come home, and things could go back to the way that they were. Knowing that my mom and grandmother would be there today, presumably asking for updates about my life, though they wouldn't be caught dead calling me for them, didn't exactly make me want to rush to the phone either. But it's Thanksgiving. And even if I'm not celebrating this year, it's still a day for family.

"HAPPY THANKSGIVING!" Mindy answers excitedly after the phone has only rung a couple of times. It's just after eight in the morning back home and I know that she's already been up cooking for an hour.

"Happy Thanksgiving! How's it going over there?" I ask, as soon as I hear her voice, I find that I'm ravenous for details of home.

"Oh, you know. Busy, busy, busy! We're eating at four!" she says. I can picture her standing in her kitchen with the phone wedged between her cheek and shoulder while she peels potatoes into the small plastic wastebasket that she's moved to the sink, so she doesn't have to slouch. Mindy's Thanksgiving routine has been exactly the same ever since she'd taken over hosting from my mom during her first year of marriage so it's pretty easy to predict.

"My mouth is watering just thinking about your turkey," I admit. "I can't believe I'm not going to get to eat it this year!"

"Well, there's always Christmas!" she says happily and I cringe. There *is* always Christmas, but I don't have any plans to try to make it home. I could, I suppose, but I don't think I will. I still don't think I'm ready to see Cleveland again, and I don't think that I'm going to be any more ready in a month than I am today.

"Yeah, maybe so!" I lie.

"What are you doing for the holiday?" she asks.

"Oh, well it's not a holiday here, so... nothing."

"Isn't it the middle of the day there, though? How come you were able to call? Aren't you at work?"

This is the part that I was afraid of having to mention. I know, deep down, that my sister will support me no matter what, but that doesn't make it any easier. Even as I say the words that I'd spent all of last night preparing: "it didn't end up being a very good fit for me, so I decided to leave," I am completely filled with doubt that she's even capable of understanding.

Mindy and I were different in many ways, but one of the biggest was that Mindy is a go-getter and I am not. Part of the reason I'd always looked up to my sister was because she always seemed to take charge of her own life. That was the reason she'd been able to have the successes that she'd had in her life, because she had made them happen. It was something that I had never done, instead I tended to wait around for things to happen to me. The only way I had ever attempted to take charge of my own life was by picking up and moving over here, even when everyone was telling me that it wasn't a rational decision. Mindy never told me that, though, and because she'd always gone after what she wanted, I had felt like she understood why I needed to make the choice. But now I'm second guessing that entirely. I know how much she wants me to come home, how much she wants to set a place for me at her Thanksgiving table this year, and my worries are that those feelings will overwhelm her understanding of why I need to do these things for me.

"So, you quit? Just like that? What happens now? Do you have to come home?" she asks hopefully. I didn't tell her the whole story, not about Sam or the photo or how I'd already been put on watch for my kiss with Jimmy.

"It's a little bit more complicated than that. And no, I'm not coming home," I respond.

"Okay, then tell me." It's what Mindy always said, what she was known for in a way. When we were growing up and our parents were too busy fighting to pay attention to me the way they'd paid attention to Mindy, I'd go into her room and lay down on her bed and tell her all about my day. Whenever I'd get to the climax of the story or if I seemed shy about sharing some details, she'd always say the same thing: "tell me." Back then that was all it took. She'd say those words, and everything would come spilling out of me. She was the only person in my family I felt listened to me, and it made me feel valued to be asked to share these intimate details with her. Now when she says these words, they tug at my heart strings and immediately beg for me to open up my entire heart to her. So, I do, just like that.

I launch into the story of Sam and the kiss and the photograph in the paper and how the Wangs had already offered me the job, so the timing worked out perfectly and how excited I am to live with them in their gorgeous home. It sounds funny to hear myself tell the story out loud, while I'd lived it, I'd just thought about it relative to the individual parts and never as a whole cohesive chain of events.

"Wow, I don't know what to say," she says when I've finished. I know that's a lie, Mindy always knows what she's going to say next.

"So, you're just going to go live with this family that you barely know? You don't even speak Chinese."

"I've been studying. And besides, with Mrs. Wang, that has never mattered," I answer.

"Mrs. Wang... this is your best friend?" I can hear the concern in her voice.

"Yes, she's such an incredible woman. I think you'd really like her."

"Molly," Mindy says seriously, after a brief pause in the conversation, "are you sure you're doing okay over there?"

Oh boy, here we go. This is exactly why I didn't want to call. I didn't want to get a lecture about my life and the way I'm living it. Mindy had always been careful not to overstep in her role as sister, I had parents and she knew that. But now that she's the only family I still talk to, I guess it is too much to ask that that kind of treatment would continue.

"It's just... being friends with old ladies, kissing men in bars, getting your picture in the newspaper for kissing a local celebrity, quitting your job – none of this really seems like you."

She's right to an extent. None of these things ever would have happened in the life of Cleveland's Molly Walton and she's the only version of me that my sister has ever known. The thing about that girl, though, is that she's the version of me who let life happen to her, and look how well that turned out. I couldn't continue to be who I used to be, that girl had died as soon as I stepped onto the plane.

"It's not like I've been proud of every single one of those things, but they feel a little like growing pains. I'm getting my feet wet and figuring out who I can be when I'm totally on my own,"

"But why do you have to be totally on your own?" she asks. I know that Mindy wants to be there for me, she's made it clear again and again ever since this whole thing first blew up. But Mindy's version of being there for me is my being in Cleveland and moving into her spare bedroom until I get back on my feet. That's where I'd lived in the months before I'd moved to London and there was not much "getting back on my feet" happening at all. About the only thing I'd been able to figure out before I left town was that I was never going to be able to go on living there. Everything was too painful: every place a memory, every person a reminder.

"I mean that I'm over here on my own," I tell her. "I know I'm not alone in the world. I know you're always just a phone call away. And I promise I'm doing well here, even if it may not seem that way to you."

"It just seems like you've changed so much."

"Well, I have. But does that have to be bad?" To be honest, I hadn't noticed how much I had changed until Mindy brought it up. For me it's just been about getting through each day, putting time and distance between myself and what happened one day at a time. Of course that experience had changed me, how could it not have?

"I don't know, I hardly recognize you anymore. What happened to my baby sister who wanted a quiet life in the suburbs?"

I know what she means, that's what I had always said. It wasn't until I'd gotten to London that I realized that that wasn't the life I wanted. That was the life other people wanted for me. That was Mindy's life.

"She was tired of being a disappointment to everyone all the time. She wanted a chance to live her own life," I say.

"Who said you were a disappointment?" Mindy sounds genuinely hurt by the accusation that anyone in our world may have made me feel this way. I consider backing away from the can of worms I know I've opened, but if I don't say this now, I might never say it.

"Mom. Dad. Grandma Betty. Maybe even you sometimes. And I don't know… it just feels like I've been living in the shadow of your perfect life, and everyone has expected me to do the things you did at the same time that you did them. I used to say I wanted a quiet life in the suburbs because that's what you had."

"What's wrong with my life?" Mindy asks defensively. That's where I knew that this was going to end up, but I hadn't been able to keep my mouth shut.

"Absolutely nothing," I say. "Seriously, Mindy. I love your life so much. But it's yours. I feel like I've never been allowed to want anything else and now I'm figuring out that I do."

She's silent for a moment and I can picture her setting down the potatoes and taking the phone into her hand so that she can talk to me more thoughtfully. "So, what is it that you want?" she asks.

"I don't know yet. But I finally think I'm on my way to figuring it out."

"Well, I miss you," she says finally.

"I miss you too, Mindy. And even though I may not have everything figured out yet, I know that I'm in the right place for now." It's one of those statements that I don't know is true until I say it. When I chose London, I'd taken a shot in the dark. I had absolutely no idea what I was doing or how it was going to turn out. And things haven't been perfect here, as my sister has just reminded me, but each of those failures has taught me so much. I never would have had any of those experiences if I hadn't taken the leap to come here.

It's been hard, ever since I moved here. Missing Mindy, missing getting to see my nephew grow up, missing the familiar streets and shopping centers that I've known my whole life, missing the familiarity of America; I didn't realize I even had that many things in my life to miss until I left them all behind. But going through each day with that pang inside of me has helped me to grow. I'm learning a new city, I'm meeting new people, I'm testing my limits... It's like I told Mindy, change doesn't have to be bad. I just needed to start believing that myself.

"I love you, Moll," she says then.

"I love you, too. Happy Thanksgiving!"

24.

I don't miss it. That was the one fear I had about quitting the familiarity of my old job to take the job with the Wangs, but it never happened. Not for one second have I missed working at that home. Well, I don't miss the job at least. I do miss Linda and, on occasion, even Angus. I wonder if anyone has kept up his daily bingo games or if he's had to take matters into his own hands? No one has called me to check in, not even Cat or Lily who insisted that they wanted to get together and keep up a friendship. Not that I'm surprised, and it's probably better for it to be a clean break.

Only, it's not entirely clean. I did get one big souvenir from my time working there: Sam. Not that I can call him mine. I don't know what I can call him exactly. We've been taking things super slow, and at this point I only feel comfortable to call him my friend. We talk on the phone almost every night, like it's high school all over again, but I haven't seen him again since we kissed in the hallway of the home. Not that that was by choice. I've been busy getting everything in order for my move to the Wangs' and he's been busy with work. But tomorrow's finally my moving day and he asked if he could come by tonight, so that's where things stand now.

It's funny, I've spent my months in London complaining about my flat: how having it come furnished meant that nothing here belongs to me and how it doesn't feel like home. And now that I'm leaving it, I've found that I've accumulated quite an array of belongings. I had arrived here with just two suitcases, everything I owned packed as tightly inside as possible. Now I've had to make multiple trips to the store to get packing materials. I didn't even realize I'd begun to collect things. Somehow the thought that I've been making purchases feels synonymous with the way I've begun making a life here; slowly and without noticing. I'd never done anything without noticing before.

I'm just taping up the last box when there's a knock at the door and I feel the butterflies flutter in my stomach immediately. They're the same butterflies that I'd felt when he'd kissed me that first time. The same ones that made me question everything I've ever done in my life up until now. The same ones I never had with Jake. The same ones that I thought might go away once the novelty wore off. Now I get them just knowing he's on the other side of the door. I don't even need to have seen him yet, don't even need to have touched him. For just a moment, I'm so lost in the feeling that I almost forget what you're supposed to do when someone knocks on your door.

"Hey!" I say, when I finally remember what the next step is and open the door wide. It's the most casual I've ever seen Sam, in a sweater and blue jeans, and while he always looks dashing in his tailored suits, the relaxed look gives him a different layer of attractiveness.

It's the first time I've had a visitor whose last name isn't Wang, and even though I'm about to move out, I can't help feeling a little self-conscious. I considered hiding all of the spoons until after he'd gone, but I'm not embarrassed of them, they're just a little weird. I can easily explain them away as a fixture of the furnished apartment. With all of my own things now packed away, the spoons are about all there is to look at, though, and I position my body in front of their case as soon as Sam steps inside.

No sooner have I closed the door behind him than his arms are around me, hands in my hair, his lips search for mine with desperation. It's intense and I'm surprised by the urgency, after a minute I need a break to catch my breath.

"Um, hi," I say, breathless.

"Hi, sorry, was that too forward?"

I laugh. As if his question needs an answer. I didn't hate it, if I'm honest. But it doesn't help me answer any of the questions I've been asking myself ever since I'd gone to say goodbye to Linda. I don't want Sam to be just some guy I kiss whenever he's around. It's fine if we stay just friends, and it's fine if it becomes something more. It's just this feeling of being stuck in the middle that I don't like.

"It's just… come all the way in. Have a seat. You know, normal things," I say, gesturing with my hands as I talk.

"Right, sorry. I've just been dreaming about kissing you again and I couldn't wait." Is this guy for real? Is that a thing that people really say? Although it could seem like it, depending on who you ask, I haven't kissed a ton of guys in the last several years. The last one had turned into my enemy and the one before him had whispered "yessss!" after we'd kissed for the first time. So having someone say they've been dreaming about kissing me is totally out of the ordinary and totally bizarre.

"How is work?" I ask, trying to make awkward small talk as we both sit on the tiny couch. It's strange that it feels awkward when I talk to him in person, but we've just spent several days where we've talked on the phone for hours at a time about whatever we could think of. I guess that's why I shouldn't care if the first thing he wants to do when he sees me is go in for the kiss. I can't even think of anything else to ask because we've already talked about everything. I already know that work is so busy that he's hardly been able to see straight and that that's the reason he hasn't been able to see me. But he answers my question politely, about how he is finally able to come up for air and that it shouldn't get that intense again for a while.

"I have a gift for you. For your new place," he says then, pulling something out of his pocket. It's so small that at first, I can't tell what it is until he opens his palm to reveal a gold locket pendant. There's no chain attached, it's just the locket itself, which I suppose is why he's told me it's for my new place and not a gift for me to wear.

"Oh, wow, it's beautiful," I say as he places it into my hand.

There's a design carved into the heart shaped amulet that resembles lace, and it's easy to tell that the piece had been well cared for and polished often.

"I found it when I was going through Aunt Jane's things. Granny has one just like it. I remember that she used to keep it propped open on her dressing table, on a little stand. I asked her about it once when I was a boy and she told me that it made it easier to see the photos and remember that way. To wear it, she said, would have been to hide those memories away," he tells me. Inside the locket are pictures of Linda and Jane as teenagers. They appear to only be fifteen or sixteen in the black and white photographs but it's easy to tell it's them. They have the exact same faces as children that they carried with them into adulthood. As I finger the locket, I find that the photo of Linda swings forward to reveal an engraving.

"My dear Janie, may we always be friends until we're old and grey. With love, your Linda," I read aloud. "That's beautiful."

"I didn't know about the engraving in Granny's until I was much older. I found it when we moved her to the home. It said 'To my darling Linda, the only friend I'll ever need. Love always, Janie.' I never thought much about it until after she died. She was true to her word all those years, Granny was the only friend she ever needed," he tells me.

"I wonder if they ever imagined what it would be like to be old women together," I ask then. "What would they have thought of the way things turned out?"

It's mostly a rhetorical question, but Sam answers it anyway. "I'm sure they did imagine it, but I'd imagine that everything turned out very differently than the way they'd planned it."

"Isn't that always the way things work?" I answer with a laugh, thinking of my own life and all of the events that led me to London in the first place. I had plans once, but life had other ideas.

"Well," he says, picking up on what I'm thinking. He leans in and tucks a piece of hair behind my ear. "I, for one, am not the least bit sorry that your plans fell through."

When his lips touch mine this time, I know that I am a goner. Now it's not just butterflies in my stomach but in every inch of my body, I feel like I'm alive with electricity as his hands make their way to my back. He holds me with such tender care that it's almost easy to forget the ferocity of his kisses, like he's starving and the only thing that will pacify his hunger is me. It takes me a few seconds to realize that I'm still clutching the locket tightly in my fist.

"Hold that thought," I say, putting a finger up to his lips. I set the locket down carefully on the end table and turn my attention back to him.

"Now, where were we?"

"I think," he says, peppering my neck with kisses. "We were right... about... here."

With the electricity coursing through my veins, being with Sam is easy. It's been obvious for a while that we have an intense physical attraction to one another, and our chemistry does not disappoint. It's been so long, and I would think that I'd be incredibly rusty, but with Sam it doesn't feel that way. Everything just clicks, and just like with the butterflies, that was something I'd never had with Jake.

Not that it's without problems. This small sofa is hardly able to seat two people comfortably, I've never even attempted to take a nap on it, so trying to do anything else presents a challenge. Still, it's so much better than I remembered and so much easier than it's ever been in the past.

"People tell me all the time that they have a grandson I should meet," I say after. Our bodies are pushed together on the small couch, so I'm forced to look at him as we both lay there, panting. "But they were always short or fat or bald... or fifteen."

Sam chuckles under his breath and I can feel the warm air on my forehead.

"You are very different than that," I continue.

"Is it too late now to tell you that this is a hair piece?" he laughs.

"Not as long as you keep wearing it forever," I answer.

"Forever, huh?"

Crap. That sounded so committal. What if he has commitment issues and now, I've scared him away? Why else would someone like Sam Collins be single? "Well, for however long forever lasts."

"Forever is sounding pretty good right now in this moment," he leans down and places a kiss on my nose.

25.

The first thing I would do the morning after my first time with a guy was call Becca. We'd made a pact when we started college that we'd share all of the nitty, gritty details with one another even if they were embarrassing or if we regretted it. It was our way of processing what had happened so far and what we wanted to happen in the future. I can still remember so vividly when I'd called her at work as soon as I'd left Jake's apartment all those years ago.

*　　*　　*

"Aha! I've been waiting for this moment!" she'd said as soon as she'd answered the phone. "How was it? Tell me everything!"

"It was… fine. I don't know what I am supposed to say," I replied.

"Oh come on, Moll! You have to give me something better than that! You called me, so there must be something that you want to share!"

"I called you because we have a deal, and you call me every single time."

"Okay, but there must be something noteworthy about it. You've been dating for weeks! How big was it?"

"Oh my god! Becca!" I'd said, appalled.

"So, pretty small then?" she'd laughed hysterically, and I'd blushed even though she couldn't see me through the phone.

"No! It was… adequate."

"C'mon Molly, you know that I always give you all the juicy details! It's half the fun!"

*　　*　　*

While I could count the number of times I'd called Becca

under the conditions of our pact on one hand, I'd been on the receiving end of at least a dozen of these phone calls. Except for one. Becca had had one first time about which she had not been eager to call me and give me the scoop. I had no idea when she and Jake had first started sleeping together because she hadn't called. And because she hadn't called, I'd had no reason to suspect anything. Maybe that's why I still remember my call to her so well.

After that phone call, she and I had never discussed my sex life with Jake ever again. I never thought much of it at the time, since talking about it with her had made me so uncomfortable in the first place. Naively I thought that maybe she was just respecting my wishes. But knowing what I know now, I've spent my fair share of time wondering about the real reasons it never came back up.

I can't help thinking about it now, even though Becca is the last person in the world that I want to think about today, because it's once again the morning after and I'm dying for someone to tell. My night with Sam was everything I had hoped it would be and more and I feel so anxious to be able to share it with my best friend. It's something that's ingrained in me and isn't so easy to undo. Fortunately, I'll be moving into my best friend's house in just a couple of hours.

Before today, I've moved exactly four times in my life. I'd lived my whole life in the house that my parents brought me home to after I was born and had only moved out when I'd gone to college. I had never counted the back and forth to my dad's condo as a real move since it was only for, at the longest, two weeks at a time. And I couldn't really count the time I'd spent at Mindy's when I'd had no place else to go after the rehearsal dinner, even though I'd lived there for several months. That wasn't really a move. So, I'd only lived in my childhood home, my college apartment, the apartment Becca and I shared, and my flat in London. That was it, in all this time, so to say that I'm a nervous wreck this morning is an understatement. I couldn't sleep all night.

Of course, being anxious about the move wasn't the only reason I hadn't slept. Sam hadn't left until this morning and our night had been spent kissing, talking, learning each other, and eventually dozing only to wake up and do it all over again. It had been amazing but coupled with the anxiety I feel about moving out of my flat, it had made for a restless night.

One thing I didn't expect was that I'd be a little bit sad to leave this place behind. It never felt like mine and I'd always called it "just temporary", but it has become all I've known about living in London. The woman I had subleased it from was incredibly understanding of my changing circumstances and said that if I ever needed a place again in the future to let her know. But as I lock up the door and make my way down the stairs to the street below, I feel just a twinge of sadness. This is the place where I had started over, the place where I'd begun to build a new life for myself. It's a bittersweet ending but one that I know is right for me right now.

I'm reminded of just how right it is for me when I knock on the Wangs' front door and am practically bum rushed by Mrs. Wang. She's been watching for me out the front window, not unlike she used to do at her flat, waiting on the other side of her door to hear my footsteps on the stairs. Something about her doing it here, now, puts me at ease. Sheng has assured me that his mother understands that I'm coming to live here as an employee. But whether or not that's true, I have no idea. She's the same Mrs. Wang that she's always been whenever I'm around and she doesn't seem at all burdened by knowing that I am here to help care for her in the way that I'd been worried she'd be. I am serious about doing my job, but I'm just as serious about maintaining my friendship with Mrs. Wang. This relationship is one of the most important in my life right now and I don't want anything to get in the way of that.

Jasper is running in and out of the room, his red cape tied around his shoulders and his arms extended out in front of him. As soon as I see Mrs. Wang, I want to spill all of the details about my night with Sam, but they're not exactly kid friendly. Never mind that, though, we have all the time in the world. I live here now.

"Moll-ee," she says over and over again as she wraps her arms tightly around my waist. Thankfully I'm traveling light since Sheng had insisted on hiring movers for my few belongings even though I had assured him it was unnecessary. Now it means that I can freely hug her back and we stand there for a while just holding each other.

"Oh, Molly, you've arrived. Just on time. Wonderful!" Sheng interrupts. I've found it's his habit to create a very detailed and specific schedule that he expects everyone else to follow whether it works for them or not. Today, for example, he's provided me with the following schedule by which I am obligated to abide: the movers I assured him that I didn't need arrived at nine, they brought my things over at ten, I was told to arrive at eleven, then we'll be having lunch and going over my duties at twelve. It's not my favorite quality in a boss, but I've certainly dealt with worse. The battle over Sheng's schedules just isn't one that's worth having right now.

He's just about to open his mouth again when Mrs. Wang cuts him off. "Sheng, shut up," she chides. Her delivery of the line is so precise that it's almost comical, but I do a better job of stifling my laughter than Jasper, who has just flown back into the room, does.

"Haha! Nainai said shut up!" he roars as he zooms past his father.

"Mama, I'm not paying for an English tutor so you can learn to talk back!" he says playfully. I think he's too stunned to respond in any other way. Not only has his mother chastised him in front of his son and new employee, but she's done so in perfect English, and she's mastered the meaning of the phrase perfectly. I, meanwhile, am equally stunned to learn that Mrs. Wang has been getting English lessons. I'd noticed that she had a few more words in her vocabulary lately, but I'd assume she'd picked them up from the hours she spent watching English television while I was working. It makes me wonder what else about her life I might not know about.

"Moll-ee, come," she says to me, choosing not to respond to Sheng or give him the chance to say anything further. I guess that's the best way to fight back against his obsessive scheduling habit, though it's not one that feels safe for me to try, seeing as he's my new boss.

Downstairs in my bedroom, my few boxes have been stacked neatly against one wall. Mrs. Wang sits herself down on the bed and watches me attentively. It's clear that in her mind, I should be unpacking and getting settled in as soon as possible. It's almost as if she knows there's something that I've been dying to tell her ever since I arrived.

"Sam," she repeats matter-of-factly after I say his name.

"Yes, you remember Sam. He's the man from the television," I remind her. She'd been on a quest to find one of his segments again after we'd caught him on air the one time. She nods unconvincingly and wanders into her room. A moment later she returns holding a copy of *that* issue of the paper.

"Yes, see. You do remember Sam," I laugh. She sits back down on the bed and sets the paper beside her, waiting for me to continue.

"It was amazing; everything that you think is supposed to happen, fireworks and rainbows and all of that. And then he stayed all night, and it all just felt so right, you know?"

"Yes," she answers, but I don't know if she does know what I mean or not.

"I've wanted this from basically the moment I first saw him, but now that it's happened, I don't know where we go from here."

"Love," she replies. Even with her one-word answers, it feels like we're having an entire in depth conversation.

"Maybe. But I think it's too early for that. I just don't know where we stand after last night. We'd been taking things so slowly and now... well, sex changes everything."

She nods emphatically, but again, I wonder if she can understand what I mean. Because of our communication limits

I've never been able to ask her what her life was like when she was younger, before she'd married Sheng's father. I don't even know what China would have been like in those years, what her life might have been like when she was a single woman. There is a very high chance that we're speaking two different languages and they have nothing to do with the words that are coming out of our mouths.

"Happy, Moll-ee," she says. I can't tell if she's saying she's happy for me until she reaches up her hand and traces my mouth with her finger. She's telling me I look happy. It's probably the first time she's ever seen me that way. It's probably the first time since I've been in London that I've ever felt that way.

"I am," I reply. "For now, at least."

I couldn't remember the last time I had felt truly happy. It was well before the wedding, which should have been yet another sign. I have a feeling that my happiness had to do with my nephew, but I can hardly remember the circumstances now. I'd felt brief moments of happiness since then, sure, like when I first saw this apartment and found out that I would be able to call it my home. But all of those moments had been fleeting. This moment feels different, and while it feels exhilarating, it also feels terrifying.

"I don't want to get ahead of myself. I don't even know if I'm ready for a relationship yet," I tell her as I fold the last of my shirts into the drawer. When I stand, Mrs. Wang reaches for me, placing her small hand over my chest.

"Careful," she says matter-of-factly. Yes, being careful with my heart is something I'm going to have to do.

26.

So, it's the red pill in the morning with food, the white pill mid-morning along with the vitamin tablet, the yellow pill after lunch, and the insulin injection each morning after breakfast," Sheng rattles off. I nod and my pen works to furiously scribble down the note, but inside I am bewildered. In all of my conversations with Sheng and Jie prior to taking this job, there had been no mention of my needing to provide Mrs. Wang with any level of medical care.

"The insulin injection?" I ask, more to myself than to him.

Diabetes? I had no idea that Mrs. Wang had diabetes. She'd always seemed perfectly healthy to me. Between her English lessons and the news of her illness, I can't help but wonder what else I might not know about my friend.

"Can she give it to herself?"

"Oh, no. She says it scares her too much."

"But she's been living alone, how has she..." I start.

"I came over every morning on my way to the office. I'm surprised we never bumped into each other," he responds before I even finish asking the question.

"Oh. Wow, I had no idea. What do I need to do? Is it just the one shot a day?" I have so many questions. The biggest is why I wasn't told any of this when I was offered the job, if I'd known I might have had second thoughts about accepting it. I'm not a medical professional. I don't know the first thing about giving someone an injection.

"It's simple, she'll help you," he says as he leads me into her room. She's sitting in a plush armchair knitting; I can faintly hear her singing to herself under her breath. Sheng says something to her in Chinese and she sets the knitting down. He must tell her how I'm going to learn to give her the shot because she nods and smiles at me before she stands.

Giving the injection itself is quite simple. I watch Sheng extract the correct amount of insulin from the vial and then Mrs. Wang holds a spot on her abdomen as Sheng sticks the needle into her flesh and depresses the syringe. As she fixes herself, he has me do the same thing and then inject the liquid into an orange.

"It can be overwhelming at first," he tells me. "I was terrified the first couple of times that I had to do it. But it does get easier. You'll fall into a bit of a routine, and you won't even have to think about it. Besides, I'm sure you've done this a hundred times."

It makes sense that Sheng would think that, over the years many people have mistaken me for a nurse or someone who has even a basic level of understanding of a patient's medical care. But the truth is, the only shots I've ever witnessed are the ones I've received myself. My job had been to keep residents entertained and active, their medical care was not part of my job description and not something that was typically done in my presence. I had told Sheng and Jie that when they offered me this job and I had thought I'd been understood.

I had wanted something different. I had wanted to step outside of my comfort zone and try living my life differently. That's what I remind myself as I follow Sheng through the rest of Mrs. Wang's basic care routine. He has it all inputted into a precise schedule, down to the minute. She starts her day at seven with breakfast followed by her insulin injection before personal grooming and going back to her knitting, all to be completed before nine o'clock. As I stare at the paper in my hand, which I'm told has been painstakingly typed by his PA, I can't help but wonder what exactly it is that he wants me to do here if the answer is not to help Mrs. Wang occupy her time.

"Too much!" Mrs. Wang says as soon as Sheng has wished her good-bye and headed out to the office. I rush to her side, afraid that Sheng has given her too much insulin, but she seems completely fine. She sighs heavily and repeats herself.

"Sheng do too much!" she exclaims angrily. "Always too much."

I can't help but laugh. When I'd observed them from afar, I'd thought that Sheng's treatment of his mother had been sweet. I had certainly never had a family member dote over me the way he does for her, it seemed endearing. But now that I'm here in the house with them, I can see how annoying it can be to everyone. Still, as an employee I have to do my best to defuse the situation instead of making it worse.

"He means well, he wants you to be happy here," I tell her. I'm annoyed with Sheng too, probably more than she is if I'm honest, but I do know that my words are true.

"I happy here. Sheng, Jie, Jas-par, Moll-ee. I very happy," she tells me. I smile at being included in her list. That she thinks of me like family and includes me right next to the people she loves most in the world is the best reminder I could ever have about why I took this job in the first place. I would give her a hundred injections a day if that's what it took to stay here.

Sheng Wang is quite possibly the most well-meaning man on the planet. Seriously, I can't think of anyone with better intentions. But he seems to be constantly acting without considering his mother or anyone else. I know he wants what's best for her, he's told me as much himself. I also know that he feels an obligation to take care of her as is the custom, and he may be going about that the wrong way.

"Molly? Are you down here?" Jie calls from the top of the stairs. "You have a delivery!"

I'm a little surprised, I'm not expecting anything. I had been careful not to provide Mindy with the new address because I still don't know sometimes if I can completely trust her not to share it with anyone else and all of my belongings had been safely delivered by the movers on Saturday. So, when I ascend the stairs and find a massive bouquet of red roses on the table, I'm taken aback.

"These are gorgeous! Who are they from?" Jie asks. I can tell she's straining to peer over my shoulder as I read the card but I'm just a little too tall and am able to shield the private note from her view with my body.

Can't stop thinking about you. Best wishes on this new adventure. With love, Sam

Can't stop thinking about me? With love? It's almost too much to bear. I can't stop thinking about him either, but I hadn't thought about sending flowers. Before Jie can read it, I slide the card into the pocket of my jeans.

I hadn't been sure how to dress for a job like this, where home and work are the same place. No one had given me any instruction, and the Wangs hadn't required a uniform. I look at Jie for inspiration but she's on her way into work and is wearing medical scrubs (which she still manages to make look chic) so I don't get any clues. I'd chosen a nice pair of jeans and a long-sleeved button down, the kind of thing I'd always worn to work. I'm grateful now for the choice since the pockets mean keeping my private business private.

"Sam?" Mrs. Wang asks when she finally reaches the top of the stairs and sees my gift.

"Yes! Aren't they beautiful?" I ask her excitedly. If a blind person heard us together, they'd probably have no idea of all of the blaring differences between us.

"Ooo, who's Sam?" Jie asks.

"Love," Mrs. Wang says, fingering the red petals. There's that word again.

"No, no, no," I wave her off. "He's just wishing me luck on the new job."

She doesn't look convinced and neither does Jie. "Two dozen red roses to wish you luck? You must really need it," Jie chimes in, laughing at her own joke.

"Who's Sam?" she asks again, now that she knows she has my attention.

"Sam Collins? The television presenter?" I offer. I'm praying that she's too busy being a rockstar surgeon, attentive mother, and fabulous fashionista to have time to watch TV, but Sam's lucky roses apparently don't reach that far.

"Oh, he's so handsome! Well done, you!" she says with a laugh. Now that I think about it, everything that Jie says sounds like it's said with a laugh.

My cheeks are hot and I have nowhere to go, Jie and Mrs. Wang both look at me expectantly as if they want me to go on about Sam. It's not that I don't want to tell them about Sam exactly, Lord knows I've already told Mrs. Wang plenty, it's just that I've been caught so off guard by his gesture that I don't know what to say. Instead, I reach for Sheng's schedule, which I've been holding in my free hand, in an attempt to change the subject.

"Looks like you're supposed to be having one cup of tea with half a teaspoon of sugar," I tell Mrs. Wang. The schedule is that detailed. I'm almost surprised that it doesn't say she should blow on each sip exactly three and three quarters times before drinking.

I think I catch Mrs. Wang rolling her eyes, but she doesn't acknowledge me. Instead, she walks dutifully to the table and sits down at what I've learned is her designated place, waiting for her tea.

"Let me see that," Jie says then, reaching for the printed page in my hand as I go to start on Mrs. Wang's tea.

"Oh dear," Jie says after a moment, placing the paper down onto the countertop. She looks at me sympathetically. "My husband means well, I assure you."

"I know that, for sure," I say. I try to laugh, but I don't have Jie's light way of speaking, and I don't know if I find it that funny. Overbearing, sure. But, funny? Not really.

"He's been worried, ever since Mama Ting arrived in the country, that she would get bored and want to go home. So, he thinks that if he can keep her busy all day, that she'll be too busy to be homesick. That's why I suggested that we bring you on," Jie continues.

I can understand Sheng's motivation. I know that he feels he has a responsibility to care for his mother, he's her only child after all. Although his detailed schedule comes from a good place, something is going to have to be done about it if any of us are going to survive this arrangement. I know it's something that Mrs. Wang agrees with me on, too. The rest of our entire day is planned out. Half past eight: help bathe and dress Mrs. Wang for the day (black trousers and a white jumper are noted on the schedule and, I'd imagine, laid out somewhere downstairs). I make a mental note that she is not an invalid and has been bathing herself on her own, without help, in her flat for all of these months. Ten o'clock: walk around the block. Eleven o'clock: Mrs. Wang's morning rest time (soothing music should be played). Twelve o'clock: lunch of steamed rice and chicken with vegetables... it's all too much, just like Mrs. Wang had said.

"He just wants to know that she's happy here," Jie says.

"But she is, she told me that just this morning. I know Sheng means well, but this makes my job harder. I mean, why even hire me if he can't trust me to fill her time wisely?"

"I happy here," Mrs. Wang chimes in. Jie smiles softly and places her hands over her heart gently. She says something to Mrs. Wang in Chinese and they both laugh.

Watching Jie and Mrs. Wang interact with one another makes me wonder what that must be like, to have a family like this. A family that cares so much about your happiness that they go way overboard to ensure you're too busy to be sad. A family who would do anything for the love of the family unit. I hadn't known that in my own family, even from Mindy. When I consider that Jie isn't even Mrs. Wang's own daughter but her daughter-in-law, it makes me wonder even more. I don't think I'd ever spent more than a few hours alone with Jake's mother during our entire six-year relationship. She was always nice to me, but what Jie and Mrs. Wang seem to share looks a lot more like genuine friendship. My heart aches for a family like that.

"I think that my husband will back off soon," Jie says and then pauses, rephrasing. "I *hope* that my husband will back off soon."

"It just feels like he doesn't trust me," I reply. It's appalling to me that anyone would think I could ever do something to hurt Mrs. Wang or that as we spend our days together, I would ever act without her best interests in mind. That hurts me more than the tedium of following Sheng's schedule does.

"He trusts you. We trust you. *I* trust you," Jie says. She places her hand on my shoulder as she poises herself to leave the house for the day. Soon I will be alone with my charge for the first time, though it still feels strange to think of her that way, and we will find out how the two of us do with time management.

27.

*T*hank you for the flowers, they're stunning. I shoot off the quick text when I finally have a moment. After our morning of dressing and walking and resting to soft music, I don't have a free moment scheduled until after lunch when Mrs. Wang's English tutor arrives. I have to admit, I'm intrigued to find out more about this tutor I had no idea she'd been seeing. Her seemingly sudden grasp of English tells me she's been receiving these lessons for longer than the week she's been living with Sheng.

"So, you're the famous Molly!" the tutor, a man in his late thirties named Tim, says as soon as we've been introduced. He's not what I was expecting. He's tall and thin with a buzz cut and he's dressed like every other man I pass on the street. For some reason I'd been picturing someone whose looks screamed academia: in my mind he was for sure going to be wearing a sweater vest and tortoise shell glasses.

"I don't know about famous, but yes. I'm Molly," I say, extending my hand.

"You may not think of yourself as famous, but you're the reason we're here!" he replies. I must give him a confused look because he immediately speaks again.

"Mrs. Wang is learning English because of you. She tells me all the time that she needs to be able to talk to her Molly."

I feel that catch in my chest again, the one I feel so often when it comes to Mrs. Wang. The one that reminds me that I am loved and that she is possibly the best friend that I've ever had in my life. If I had thought about it long enough, I might have deduced that she wanted to learn English for me. But the news had only just been sprung on me and I hadn't had time to give it much thought at all.

"Well, I'll leave you to it, then," I say when I finally find my words again and I slink back downstairs for some quiet time alone. But it doesn't last. No sooner have I reached the bottom of the stairs than my phone rings.

Sam lights up the display and my heart leaps. It's a different type of heart palpitation than the one I felt for Mrs. Wang. This one is full of lust and desire as flashes of our night together dance through my mind's eye.

"Hey," I answer. I desperately hope that it sounds as effortless as I want it to. I'm sure it doesn't since my heart is still beating way too fast.

"Hey," he says back. Unlike my greeting, his does sound effortless; almost like it's just a simple breath of air.

"Thank you for the flowers, they're lovely."

"Stunning. Lovely. You're saying all of the right words to describe what I think of you."

Seriously? I feel like I constantly have to remind myself that Sam is a professional smooth talker. That's literally a part of his job description. Sometimes the cheese gets laid on just a little too thick. I don't hate it, it's been a long time since anyone talked to me this way. But I have to take it with a grain of salt.

"Oh, wow," I say, going full Ohioan and drawing out my "o"s in an exaggerated manner.

"Too much?" he laughs.

"Just a little, but I like when you say it," I flirt.

We sit in silence for a few seconds, each listening to the other breathe; somehow it doesn't feel awkward. I like knowing that he is there.

"I was calling to see if you're free for dinner? I know it's last minute, but I really want to see you," he says, finally breaking the silence. I feel the rush of butterflies in my gut again as soon as he asks. He's been promising a real date ever since Jane's funeral, but we've just never gotten around to it.

"Dinner sounds great. I will be done at precisely five fifty-nine and fifty-nine seconds," I say. It probably sounds like a joke, and I wish it was, but Sheng has made sure that I am very serious.

Even though the day has been scheduled out down to the minute, my job is not twenty-four hours. While I live here, I am not expected to spend every waking moment caring for Mrs. Wang and it was part of my arrangement with Sheng that I should have my evenings free to do what I'd like. That could mean that I join the family upstairs for whatever they're doing, but that also means that if I want to have dinner alone or spend hours binge watching Netflix in my pajamas, I am free to do so. Poor Mrs. Wang, though, has a schedule up until bedtime (which is promptly at 10:45pm, after a period of reading and mindful relaxation).

"That's very specific," Sam says.

"You have no idea. Mrs. Wang's son has made an incredibly detailed daily schedule for us. It's like he expects us to function as a machine."

"Well, my little cogwheel, let's say I pick you up at seven?"

"I can't wait," I say, because I can't. It's been years since I could say those words, and when I moved to London, I thought that there was a very good chance that I'd never say them again. Sam has caught me completely off-guard. I'm full of energy now, so my original plans to spend some time alone while Mrs. Wang has her lesson will never work. Instead, I bypass the schedule entirely and head out in search of something to wear on my first real date with Sam.

I had never known the wonder that is *Zara* until I arrived in the UK. We'd had a store in the Beachwood Mall, but I'd have to drive all the way out there to go so it wasn't a place where I'd shopped regularly. It took me approximately one month of my London life to realize that that would have to change if I was ever going to have anything cute to wear. There are four locations within walking distance of the Wang's house alone. The early December weather is starting to get cooler in London, and while it's still warmer than it is back in Ohio at this time of year, my usual winter wardrobe of jeans and a chunky sweater doesn't fly for a date with Sam Collins the way it would have for a night with Jake. Conversely, the black cigarette trousers, tie neck blouse, and ankle boots that I select for tonight would have looked completely outrageous at any of the places Jake might have taken me, even if I didn't plan to hide the whole ensemble under a gorgeous cream-colored pea coat that was practically screaming my name from the time I entered the store. Using the word "trousers" alone would have been out of place in Jake's world. I'd had to beg to get him to take me anywhere that allowed me to dress in something other than jeans. His traipsing around London in a pair of khaki cargo shorts even during the autumn should have been proof enough of that.

I'm sneaking back in with my shopping bags just as Mrs. Wang makes her way down the stairs from her lesson.

"How now brown cow?" she asks me. It's a phrase I haven't heard in years, one we used to use as a warmup in high school drama club while staring into a mirror to watch the shape of our lips. But I understand that Mrs. Wang means it as an actual question: what have I been up to while she was gone? I hold up my shopping bag.

"New! See, see!" she claps. It reminds me very much of our first meeting when she'd invited me over in order to ask me to buy her more crackers. I happily oblige, trying on the new clothes for her and completely ignoring "14.00 tai chi in the garden." Mrs. Wang oos and ahs over everything.

I want desperately to tell her that I finally have a date with Sam, but I also want to keep that information to myself for a minute. I know that if I tell her, she's going to want to meet him and if I take the time to introduce him to her then I'm going to have to introduce him to the whole family and we might never make it to dinner. I love the Wangs and I'm so happy to be a part of their lives, but to introduce them to Sam on our first official date would be a little bit too much like bringing someone home to meet the parents and that's not something I'm ready for yet.

"For what?" she asks. Man, she's a lot more intuitive than I give her credit for.

"I just wanted to get something new. I'm meeting a friend for dinner," I reply, hoping that she won't ask questions. She doesn't need to know that I don't have any other friends, though I'm sure she is probably already aware of the fact. I know how much she wants to meet Sam and if things go well, she will get the chance. Just not tonight.

"Okay Moll-ee," she says, and I swear she sounds dejected. Like she knows it's not the truth. "Let go outside."

28.

I feel bad about lying to Mrs. Wang. Though, it's not so much lying as it is omission, I guess. I know that she knows something is going on, I can picture her waiting by the window to catch sight of whoever or whatever might be coming, just like she used to do every night in our neighboring flats. I would love for her to meet him, but tonight is our first real date and even though our relationship so far has been far from conventional, I don't think I'm quite ready to bring Mrs. Wang into it.

"You look great!" Sam says promptly at seven. He's come to the lower door just as I had instructed. I stand and stare at him, smiling like a dope until he leans in and greets me with a kiss. Okay, so my dating game is a little rusty.

"So, this is the new place, hmm?" he looks over my shoulder and into the apartment.

"I had developed such a fondness for the old one," he winks. I laugh and hit him playfully, though it's more of a push out the door. The longer we stand here, the more likely it is that Mrs. Wang will come bounding down the front steps and demand to know every detail of his life story.

There's a car waiting, a black sedan like I thought people only took in movies or at the very least in cities like Hollywood or New York. But I guess Sam is the kind of person who would be in those cities, taking black cars to fancy places and not thinking twice about it. That's something I can't even fathom. In my old life I'd had only two limousine rides, the first to my high school prom and the second as a member of Mindy's wedding party.

Both were white stretch limos with interior lighting that would change neon colors approximately every thirty seconds. I had thought that that was pretty dang fancy, but this is just a normal car in Sam's normal life, and I can't help but wonder if the girl who was excited by those rides in the white limos can be the same girl who is comfortable riding in a shiny black town car on a random weeknight?

"Does it make me sound like absolute trash to say that I've never ridden in a car like this before?" I ask. He laughs and sheepishly rubs the back of his neck. I've seen him do it before, usually when Linda has been giving him a hard time.

"Sorry, I'm sure it must seem pretentious. I was coming from work, and it was easier to pick you up this way."

"You have a driver for work?"

"The news agency pays for it if that makes it any better. It's easier to prepare for interviews and things when I can just sit here and be driven around."

He rubs the back of his neck again. "Plus, I've lived in London my entire life, so driving has never really been necessary."

I know this part is true. I'd sold my car before I'd moved over here but that was out of financial necessity as it didn't make sense to keep it and keep it insured when I wasn't even in the country to drive it. Since I'd arrived, I'd been able to get to anywhere that I needed to go by public transportation, and I think the thought of driving in this city would be frightening. I place a hand on his and give it a gentle squeeze.

"It's not pretentious. It's nice to be able to sit here with you and not have to think about how we're getting there," I say reassuringly. "Where are we going anyway?"

"Right there," he says. He points out the window as the car comes to a stop in front of a quaint Italian restaurant. "I grew up around the corner and this has always been one of my favorite spots."

"Good evening Mr. Collins," the host greets him as soon as we step inside. When he'd said it had always been one of his favorite spots, I didn't realize that meant he was currently a regular. The host doesn't even ask questions and leads us to a corner table at the back of the restaurant before taking my coat, pulling out my chair, placing the linen napkin across my lap, and propping the menu open in front of me. I like the special treatment. The only place Jake had been a regular was at a bar called Stinky's.

Dinner is delicious. We laugh and talk and sip wine through three delectable courses. I don't even notice how much time has passed until I look around and realize that almost no one is left in the restaurant. It's so easy to sit and talk with Sam like this, I feel like I could do it for hours more when he asks me if I've ever been to Oxford Street.

"They do a brilliant lights display every year. I used to love going with my parents each December. I haven't been yet this year, what do you say?" he asks.

"I say it sounds wonderful!" I exclaim, partly because I could use some holiday spirit in my life and partly because I just want to be able to spend more time with Sam.

I still haven't decided what I want to do about Christmas. I know it's only a couple of weeks away and if I'm going to fly back home, I am going to need to get something booked sooner than later. It's just that the very thought of ever going back there feels so unappealing. Instead of coming to any kind of decision, I've been blocking Christmas out of my mind altogether. That also means that I've had no real Christmas spirit.

Even with my desire for a little holiday cheer, I'm not prepared for what I see when we arrive at Oxford Street. I'd seen public light displays before, but none of them could even compare to the spectacle I see before me. Lights are suspended overhead and cascade down the front of the buildings as people move up and down the street below. I know my mouth is hanging open, but I don't make any moves to close it.

"Pretty spectacular, isn't it?" Sam asks. He takes my hand in his and pulls me onward down the street.

"We used to come every Christmas, my parents and me. I never got tired of it, even when I got to be an obnoxious teenager who hated everything."

"Were you? An obnoxious teenager I mean?" I ask.

"Weren't we all?" he laughs. "I don't know, I just always think back on myself at that age and think I must have been the worst person in the world to live with."

It's hard to picture Sam as a teenager. When I think of boys that age, I think of acne and awkward features and wiry moustaches. Sam is such a striking man that it's hard for me to visualize him ever having had any sort of awkward phase. I, on the other hand, am expecting to come out of my awkward phase any day now.

"Why'd your family stop coming?" I ask.

"When my dad got sick, about eight years ago, it got to be too hard. It would take Mum and me both to maneuver his chair. I think he felt like he was being a burden. And then Granny got sick, and we got so busy with our lives..." he trails off. I give his hand a reassuring squeeze.

"She misses you, you know," he tells me then, changing the subject. "Granny? She's asked after you more than once since you came to say goodbye."

"Aw, that's sweet," is what I say. But what I feel in my heart is *Linda has asked about me. ME! Linda Suthcliffe misses me! She loves me! Just like I'd hoped she would!*

"You could go pay her a visit. You know, if you wanted to."

Before I get a chance to respond, a woman and her teenaged daughter come charging toward us. "OHMAGOD, are you Sam Collins?" the daughter asks. She and her mother are both giddy with excitement.

Sam is nice to them, of course; smiling for selfies and signing autographs. I just stand by and take it all in. Is this what I'd be signing up for if things progress for our relationship? Would I always have to share Sam with the world? I know his job means he's in the public eye, I just didn't realize that that meant that his life was too.

"Well, you're quite pretty," the mother says to me, seeming to notice me for the first time. "Of course Sam Collins would have a pretty girlfriend."

"Thank you?" I reply. I don't mean for it to sound like a question, but I also am not certain that what she's said was a compliment.

"American? Interesting. I never would have guessed," she says before collecting her daughter and disappearing into the crowd.

"And that is another reason that we stopped coming."

"Does that happen a lot?"

"No. But when there are more people around the chances of being recognized increase. It happened the first year that we came with my dad's chair. We were walking along, pushing Dad, and someone came up and asked for an autograph. Dad was mortified. He didn't want people to see him that way, he'd always been so virile, and he wanted to be remembered for his strength. Once he knew that people knew me, he stopped wanting to be seen in public." I can hear the sadness in Sam's voice. He never talks much about his family, so I feel like I'm getting new, insider information and the more I get, the more of it I crave.

I had learned, after he'd mentioned it at Jane's service, that his father has what we would call ALS in America. I had had no idea that they referred to it by a different acronym over here until I'd looked it up out of my own ignorance. I know it must have been hard for Sam, to see his dad go through such a life altering transformation. I can't imagine what it would be like to watch one of my own parents go from being the strong, independent person I'd always known to being someone entirely dependent on the care of others.

We walk in silence for a while. Even though I'm dying to know more about Sam's life, any question that I think to ask just feels wrong in my mouth. He's not someone who shares openly, and I know that when he's ready to share more, he will. I'm lucky to be someone with whom he has chosen to share at all. For now, I'm just happy to be here with him, under these lights that make it feel like I'm living in some kind of fantasy world.

This is everything I'd imagined my first date with Sam to be. I'd spent all of those early months in London dreaming about it, wondering where he'd take me, imagining what it would feel like to walk down the street hand in hand. Actually, this is better than what I had imagined, because before it was all only in my head, but now I have Sam here with me.

"Speaking of my dad," he says, out of the blue. We hadn't been speaking of his dad for several minutes. "There is a gala on Saturday night, a holiday banquet and fundraiser for the MND Association. I'm presenting and I get to bring a guest..." he says. I know what he's hinting at, but I want him to ask me.

"Usually I take Granny but, I don't think she's quite up for it this year. So... I was wondering... erm, I guess what I'm trying to say is... Would you want to maybe come? I mean, it's a black tie affair so if you're not comfortable or you can't get off work or..." he rambles.

"I'd love to," I squeeze his hand again. Maybe I should find his awkwardness to be a turn off, but what it says to me is that he still feels the same butterflies I do whenever we're together. I hope he stays this awkward for as long as we're together so that I'll always know how he feels.

"Really?" his face lights up.

"Did you really think I'd say no?"

"No. Maybe. It's just a lot to ask you to take on. Me, my career..."

"Well, I'll be sure to let you know the second I feel overwhelmed," I tell him, reaching up to give him a soft kiss on the cheek. "In the meantime, you've given me an excuse to go find a pretty dress. What more could a girl ask for?"

I don't know if I entirely believe these words, but I believe in the idea of them. I'd moved to London with the hope to fade into total and complete obscurity as I escaped my life back home. I hadn't thought about romance at all, and I certainly hadn't thought about finding it with someone with any level of celebrity. Sam was not what I had expected, but then, not much about my life here is what I thought it would be. Still, I'm not sure what to make of Sam's fame. It is the opposite of obscurity. Can I even handle that life?

I don't know the answer to the question yet. But as Sam walks me home, I find that I don't need to know. It's a short, fifteen-minute walk, but I can't help wishing it was longer. His hand provides the perfect amount of warmth for my own and I want him to keep holding it forever.

"Thank you for dinner, I had a wonderful time tonight," I whisper when we've come to a stop in front of my gate. The lights in the house are off, even though it's only half past ten and still too early for "22.45 lights out," so I don't want to draw attention to myself by being too loud. Seeming to understand, Sam answers by way of leaning in and placing a kiss passionately on my lips. I wish I could invite him in; the kiss reminds me of his lips, his hands, his body, and the way I haven't touched any of them in several days, something that suddenly seems completely ludicrous.

"I'll see you on Saturday?" I ask instead. It's my first day on the job and I don't want to get in trouble for bringing a boy home on the very first day.

"See you on Saturday," he echoes, giving me one last chaste kiss before seeing me down the stairs and into the door of the apartment. Just like that, my first real date with Sam is over and it's been better than I ever could have imagined.

29.

Oh! That one!" Mrs. Wang cheers from her spot on a plush cushion in the dress shop. She's said it about every dress I've tried on so far, but she might be right about this one. It's a simple sleeveless dress, black on top with a slight turtleneck and a colorful full skirt on the bottom that flows out into a small train behind me. It's the perfect dress to wear on Sam's arm without making myself stand out too much. And, it has pockets.

My main goal in life had always been to have a normal life, which is to say that my main goal in life had always been to have a life like Mindy's. Her life had always seemed perfect to me, she had a happy marriage and a wonderful child, and best of all, nobody in the world knew who she was or cared. I, too, had wanted to fly under the radar in my regular job and go home to my perfectly regular husband and be happy without anyone else knowing about it. Becca used to tell me all the time that I was boring, that I should dream of bigger things, but I had never wanted to. Until now, that is. I don't yet know how to feel about the fact that I'm buying a dress to go to a gala with one of London's most eligible bachelors. So far, my relationship with Sam has done nothing but welcome unwanted attention into my life. I know I should dream bigger. This is my chance after all, and I've already failed at having a life like Mindy's. I just haven't yet decided if I'm willing to give that dream a try for Sam; because on paper, he's perfect. He's handsome, kind, smart, funny… and famous. And this dress says, "I came with him, now look at him." At least I hope that's what it says.

"That one is lovely, it's very tasteful for the kind of event you've described," the shop girl tells me. She's been incredibly patient considering I came in the middle of the afternoon without an appointment and had Mrs. Wang in tow. The only explanation is that she must work on commission.

We're defying the schedule. Today Mrs. Wang was supposed to do Tai Chi in the garden for an hour before her nap and then spend the rest of the afternoon writing letters to her friends back in China. But when I'd mentioned needing to go shopping, she'd practically beat me out the door. She was quick to forget that I'd kept my date with Sam a secret from her, and even quicker once I explained why I needed the dress. Jie had given me her blessing to take the afternoon off of my scheduled duties and I was sorry that she couldn't join us for our outing.

"Do you think I'll be too cold?" I ask, turning from side to side in the mirror. I'd spent every free minute yesterday looking at pictures from past years' events so that I could get a better sense of what to wear, or at least that's what I told myself I was doing. I'd also been scouring the photos looking for pictures of Sam and another woman. Even though he'd told me that he'd always taken Linda as his plus one to this event over the years, I wanted to see for myself. All I find though, is that Sam is a man of his word, and an ever-doting grandson. I even stumbled upon the same red-carpet photo that she has framed in her room. That did nothing to calm my nerves, of course. I feel like it means something that Sam would ask me to be his date to this event that obviously means a lot to him, especially considering the person he normally takes is his grandmother. He'd always been without a date before now. So why this year? Why me? I know I probably shouldn't read anything into it, just go with the flow and see what happens. But I've never been that kind of a person so why should I start now?

"It's an indoor event, but we could always throw a shawl over the top. It wouldn't distract from the bold skirt," the shop girl says as she quickly moves to find said shawl. Mrs. Wang leans forward and fingers the skirt delicately from her perch.

It's hard not to have flashbacks to the last time I stood in a dress shop with people mooning over me. My mom and sister and Grandma Betty were all there, sitting right beside Becca on the velour couch in the waiting area. I'd put on one bridal gown after another and paraded out in front of them as they told me that this one made me look fat (courtesy of my mother) and that one made me look slutty (Grandma Betty said that). Mindy had reminded me that it was the most important dress that I'd ever buy. Thinking back on that moment now, though, buying this dress today feels a lot more important.

"Now, what are we thinking for shoes?" the shop girl asks without asking first if I've decided on this dress. I think it's pretty clear to all of us that this is the one.

"I guess I need a heel, but I don't know how comfortable I'll be in them. I'm a carer so I don't have much occasion to wear them," I answer, going up on my tiptoes to see what some height might look like with the dress. I find it easy to use the word to describe my work, though I've always shied away from it until now.

"Well, how tall is your date?" she asks.

"My... what?" I ask. I had purposely not mentioned Sam to her because I didn't want her to ask questions. It had taken me no time at all to notice how much clout Sam's name carries around town and I didn't want to make it a habit of using it, especially not when I can't even decide if the name and the clout is something that I want for myself.

"Your date. I presume that for an event like this you'll have a date. Is he tall?" she asks as if I've misunderstood her question.

"Sam," Mrs. Wang offers. How is it that her English lessons have been so tailored toward my dating life? She can't understand a simple command, but words like "date" are right at the top of her mind.

"Right then, how tall is Sam?" the girl asks.

"Ladies, I'm right here," I interrupt. "He's tall enough that I could stand to gain a few inches," I relent, bringing myself back down onto my flat feet. The skirt cascades around me so that I can't see where I end and the floor begins.

The clerk smiles and spins on her toes, off to find me a pair of shoes. Mrs. Wang stands on the stool, something I remind myself not to mention to Sheng, who I'm sure would have an aneurysm if he saw her, and pulls my hair back, twisting it into a perfect French Twist. She catches my eye in the mirror and beams. I kind of like the feeling of her fussing over me like this, for a minute it feels like we're the only two people in the world and it feels so much more special than my last dress buying experience.

"Here we are," the girl returns carrying a box clearly labeled with the name of a designer I cannot afford, and I wonder if I look like I'm made of money. Then again, I'm in a dress shop on a Wednesday afternoon instead of holed up in an office somewhere. I think of Jie and her designer wardrobe and wonder if I could ever manage to look as chic. As soon as my foot hits the shoe, though, I feel chic, whether I look it or not.

Really, I have probably never looked more chic than I do right now. In this gown and these shoes with Mrs. Wang holding my hair up, I look like someone else entirely. I look, I think, like the person I'm becoming not the person that I used to be. Like a princess, transformed for the ball. I don't know that I would have recognized her except for these newer, fancier clothes.

"So pretty, Moll-ee," Mrs. Wang smiles at me in the mirror. I smile back, happy to have this moment with her.

"Right so that will be fifteen twenty-four and thirty-two," the clerk says, punching some numbers into a calculator. I remind myself that my credit card is meant to be for emergencies, but this certainly feels like an emergency. I've never been the type of woman to make extravagant purchases. But then again, the type of woman I'm becoming is apparently a woman who wears designer footwear to black tie galas.

As I stand in the dressing room, changing back out of my new gown, I can't help but wonder what the Molly from a year ago would think about this new woman. A year ago, I was finalizing all of the wedding details, dropping the invitations in the mail, starting to think about a seating chart... If you had asked me what I thought I'd be doing in a year my answer probably would have been: "the same thing I always do." I mean, I was about to marry Jake, so it's not likely that anything about my life was going to change at all. If you had told me that I'd be living in London, buying designer shoes on a Wednesday, I would have laughed in your face.

Frankly, I don't even know what the Molly of today thinks of this new lifestyle. I had moved to London to disappear into oblivion. It fit perfectly into the plans I'd made for my life. I wanted to fade into the background of a story that wasn't my own. So far it seems like all I've done since I got here has been to draw attention to myself. How did I even do that? All I had done were the things that I'd set out to do: go to work, try to build a social life... somehow things had turned out very differently than I'd planned.

"Oooh, Moll-ee!" Mrs. Wang calls from the waiting area just as I've slid back into my black ballet flats (normal, unassuming footwear). I know she's spotted something else that she thinks I should have to complete my look and I consider, for a moment, pretending that I haven't heard her.

"Moll-ee, look!" she says as I emerge from the dressing room, the clerk rushes in behind me to bundle up the dress for my purchase so I have no choice but to go toward Mrs. Wang. She's standing in front of a rack of evening clutches, reaching out her hand and stroking each one tenderly. They're made in all shapes and sizes, and she seems particularly drawn to a small rectangular bag covered in black and white crystals.

"So pretty," she says. I don't think she's talking to me. She sort of says it under her breath like a child and I think she might just be talking to herself as she admires them.

"You want?" she asks, holding her favorite black and white bag out to me. I shake my head and attempt to push it back toward the display, but she stops me.

"You take. So pretty."

"I don't need it. I'm already spending so much money." I push the clutch back toward the display again. It's not something that

I want to fight with Mrs. Wang over, but the price tag clearly says it's £500 and I can't think of adding a single penny to my purchase.

"I get," she says then, reaching into her canvas shopping bag for her small coin purse, which I find also contains several credit cards.

"No…" I start to protest but she stops me again.

"I always want girl but only Sheng," she says emphatically. "I want to buy pretty things. But Sheng just boy."

Mrs. Wang is defiant. I know that there is no way that I will get out of this store today unless she buys me this clutch. Even if she puts the purchase on a credit card, I worry that she can afford it. Or worse, I worry what Sheng will say when he undoubtedly reviews her credit card statements at the end of the month. How will I ever explain letting her buy me this frivolous item just because it's pretty and she wants to?

But that is the kind of thing that a best friend does, isn't it? I couldn't even begin to count the number of things that Becca and I had bought for each other over the years just because we wanted the other person to have it. That's what friends do and that's what Mrs. Wang wants to do for me. So, I let her.

She happily marches to the checkstand to purchase the clutch, tucking it into the shopping bag with the most expensive pair of shoes I've ever owned. My ensemble for the evening is shaping up to be a lot flashier than I'd hoped.

30.

Dress shopping isn't our only errand today, Linda has been on my mind ever since Sam mentioned she'd been asking about me and I figure that since Mrs. Wang and I are already out, we might as well take advantage of our freedom. So, I quickly gather up my purchases and head toward Greenfield Care. Mrs. Wang bops along happily behind me, she doesn't seem to mind defying Sheng's schedule one bit.

"Oh, hello," my least favorite nurse greets me when I enter the Memory Care unit from the street. She doesn't give me a chance to answer her back. "I'm surprised you'd show your face around here again. But your boyfriend did add you to the list of her visitors."

What is it with this girl? I wonder. Instead, I just smile. "Thank you so much! I brought a friend along with me today if that's alright," I say. I phrase it like a question, but I don't really ask it like one. She's already as much as told me that Sam has given me the power to do whatever I want around here and there's nothing she can do about it. That may be a power that I turn down in most situations, but when it comes to Linda, I relish it.

"Sure, you know where to find her. Can't say she will know you though," the nurse bites.

"Okay, well thanks again!" I smile. Mrs. Wang looks over her shoulder until she's sure the nurse is out of ear shot.

"Rude lady," she says. I stifle a laugh.

It's weird being back here even though I've only been gone for a week. When I left this place, I'd thought I was done. It already feels like I haven't worked here in years. The halls are all the same and yet they feel different somehow, it's hard to describe. It's as if all of the years of residents and their stories are trapped inside them, as if everything they've left behind hasn't yet left this place.

"Linda?" I call out as I turn the corner to her room. She's sitting in a chair under the window, a book is open in her lap, but it doesn't appear that she's reading it. Every once in a while, she runs a finger over the page and then lets the book fall loosely against her thigh. I wonder what book it is, what significance it might have had to her once.

"Yes, dear? Oh, I know you!" she says, her face lights up. I desperately want her to say my name, but she doesn't. Her declared recognition of my face is as far as it goes.

"Linda, there's somebody that I want you to meet. This is my friend Mrs. Wang," I say. Mrs. Wang has, so far, been completely silent. It's almost like she's holding her breath, afraid of inhaling any of the demons that lurk here. When I say her name, she nods and musters a weak smile, but she doesn't speak.

"Hello," Linda says. "I'd introduce you to my friend Jane, but she's not here right now." My heart catches at the mention of her name. I wonder how much longer that will continue to happen?

I take a seat at the small table in Linda's room and motion for Mrs. Wang to do the same, but she shakes her head and stays glued to the wall. I wonder what she must be thinking, I had tried to tell her dozens of times that this was what I did for work, but I was never sure if she understood.

"Mrs. Wang, Linda is Sam's grandmother," I say, trying to break the ice a little. It seems to work some. Mrs. Wang lets out all the air she's been holding in and steps gingerly toward me at the table. "I haven't had a chance to see her in a while, so I wanted to come by and pay her a visit."

"It's nice to have visitors," Linda says. "I don't get many. Only my daughter, Daisy, and my grandson, Sam. Oh, how they are good to me. Did you say that you know Sam, dear?"

"I do. He happens to be a friend of mine," I say. It seems like the simplest answer. "You're the one who introduced us."

"Did I?" she claps gleefully, just like Mrs. Wang has been known to do. "Oh, that's splendid. I do love having friends!"

I always hate seeing her like this, when she's not remembering. Today she seems more present than on other days; she may not remember my name but she's not in a bomb shelter during the war so that feels like a small improvement.

"You and I are friends," I tell her, hoping to jog her memory. She pauses and thinks for a minute, the book on her lap tumbling to the floor. The cover falls open and I see the name Jane Reynolds scrawled in perfect script on the inside flap though the title remains hidden.

"Are we?" she asks, lost. Mrs. Wang reaches out and takes my hand softly as if she suddenly understands all of it. It's comforting even though her tiny hands are cold, no one has held my hand like this since Jane died.

"You're Molly," Linda says finally. "I remember now. You're my friend Molly."

When she says my name, it feels like my heart is doing somersaults inside my chest. I never thought I could receive so much pleasure from the sound of hearing my own name spoken, but something about hearing it come from Linda changes everything. With her condition, one could never predict when they would hear her say their name again, so to hear her say it now is magical. I feel Mrs. Wang give my hand a squeeze, she's noticed it too.

"Yes! I'm Molly!" I can feel the tears welling up behind my eyes. *She remembers me!* It's the best gift I have ever been given in my life.

Before we have a chance to keep talking about our friendship or keeping Linda in the present, my same favorite nurse comes barging into the room pushing a cart. Styrofoam cups of steaming water rattle on the top and she sets three of them down on the table as if the cups have done something to personally offend her.

"It is time for her tea, I figured you'll be joining her," she says as she throws down three tea bags as an afterthought.

Mrs. Wang's eyes grow wide as she scrutinizes the nurse's every move.

"Mrs. Suthcliffe prefers Earl Grey," I tell her, thinking back to those hours spent in Jane's room sharing tea with the two of them.

"Well, good for her," the nurse retorts. She turns around and pushes the cart right back out of the room. Mrs. Wang dutifully opens each individually wrapped tea bag and places one inside each of the steaming cups. On the other side of the home, people were allowed to drink their tea from real mugs, but I guess over here they're too worried about them breaking.

I hand a cup to Linda before taking my own. "At least I don't have to have my tea with that awful woman watching me today," she says. "She's a miserable one."

Sam must know how Linda feels about how she's treated here, he comes by sometimes three times a week. Not that Linda would ever tell him the truth, she wants so badly to please him that she's likely not to say a word.

"Do you hear that?" Linda asks then. She looks around to every corner of the ceiling, Mrs. Wang follows her eyes.

"Air raid," she continues matter-of-factly. "We've got to get to safety."

Mrs. Wang looks around the room in a panic, trying to find the sound Linda has referred to. Until this moment I hadn't considered that she might have her own history with war or that witnessing one of Linda's episodes might take her back to some of her own trauma. The thought instantly puts a pit in my stomach, how could I have been so stupid? Her hand has wrapped more tightly around my own in fear and I have to use my free hand to rub the back of hers reassuringly.

"There's no air raid, Linda," I say. While addressing the one woman by name, I'm really speaking to both of them. "The war is over. We're safe here."

Mrs. Wang releases my hand immediately; my words have always been enough for her. But Linda remains unconvinced.

"No! I hear the sirens!" she exclaims.

"They're not air raid sirens. The war's over. We won!" I tell her, hoping that my enthusiasm over the allies' victory will encourage her. I try to think of the things that Jane might have done, the words she might have said to make Linda feel okay, but my mind draws a blank. The only thing I can think of is "A Bicycle Built for Two", the song I'd heard her singing on the first day Jane invited me for tea. Before I know it, I'm singing.

"Daisy, Daisy, give me your answer do! I'm half crazy, all for the love of you!" I start and then pause, waiting for Linda. I'm just about to start singing again when she speaks.

"I named my daughter Daisy after that song, my friend Jane and I used to sing it in the air raid shelters," she tells me matter-of-factly. "Tell me, how do you come to know it?"

I stop short of crying when I hear Linda speak and sound like her normal self. Maybe it's silly of me to feel so emotional, but I can't help it. It makes me think of Jane and how many years she invested in building these memories with Linda, and how much effort she put into preserving them. It makes me think of Sam and how much money he spends to make sure Linda is looked after, and it makes me sad that she has to deal with the world's worst nurse on the few good days she has left.

I hear the sound my phone makes as it vibrates in my purse. "Shit... Mrs. Wang, we've got to get you home," I say. I must not have heard the rattle of the vibration before and I'd forgotten to turn the ringer back on after we'd left the dress shop, but now I can see that I have thirteen missed calls and at least as many text messages from Sheng. I had told Jie where we were headed, but I hadn't mentioned it to Sheng for fear that he'd say no. The truth is that I'd kind of enjoyed the act of rebellion that came with disobeying his orders... I hadn't stopped to think about what that would mean for my future though.

We're on the way home. Everyone is safe. I text back to his most recent message which says: *MOLLY PLEASE. I need to know that my mother is alright.* I've really messed this up.

"Linda, we've got to go," I say to her gently, not knowing whether she'll understand or not. I'm surprised when she comes to me and wraps her arms tightly around me.

"Don't you worry about me, Sammy. I'm just fine here," she says into my ear. I'm not sure if she means for me to pass the message on to Sam or if she's mixing up names in her brain as she's been known to do (except for the name Jane which she has never forgotten or used incorrectly). Whatever the reason, I tell her that I'm happy to hear that. When I pull away, the look on her face tells me that she might not believe the words that she's saying.

It's hard to stay calm in front of Mrs. Wang as I gather our belongings and try not to rush her as I push her out the door. I don't want her to know about the trouble I'll be in when we get back to the house. If this is the last memory she has of me, I want it to be a positive one, not muddled by the fact that I am completely inept at my job. Thankfully, she doesn't seem to notice anything amiss and that helps make keeping up the charade a little easier.

As we walk to catch the tube, I do my best to fill Mrs. Wang in on Linda's condition. She nods and smiles at all the right parts, but even with her improving grasp of English, I can't be sure what she's getting. Still, I explain about her diagnosis and how that's the only reason she has to be there, and that Mrs. Wang doesn't need to be worried or frightened; how the air raids are all in her mind.

"You are good friend, Moll-ee," she says finally, just as the subway car's doors close behind us.

I smile, hearing those words from Mrs. Wang is especially meaningful. She's been a good friend to me too, the best friend I've had in a long time. Maybe the best friend I've ever had, so to hear her call me a good friend makes me happy.

Becca had never called me a good friend. Not once in our entire friendship. Becca wasn't a very good friend, I can see now, but she was always projecting her shortcomings onto me. I wasn't available for her when she needed me, I was too busy working to hang out with her, why did I need to go to another one of Teddy's birthday parties anyway? I was lucky we'd been friends for so long, she'd always tell me. Anyone else might not put up with me so I was fortunate to have Becca, she had said. I don't know how I'd been so blind for so long but now, thanks to Mrs. Wang, I can see completely clearly. It's funny how that works.

I've enjoyed my day with her today. It was nice to be able to get out and do normal things with my friend. I hate knowing that this may be the last time we get to be together. I hate knowing, especially when she doesn't know anything about that at all. As if she knows what I'm thinking, Mrs. Wang throws her arm around my waist as we make our way up the street toward the house. It's enough to make me almost forget what is awaiting me when we get home. As we get closer, though, I stop cold. I can see him standing there in front of the gate waiting for us and he does not look happy.

"Where have you been?!" he says as soon as he spots us.

I am so screwed.

31.

I remember the first time that Becca and I got caught sneaking out of the house. We were thirteen and she had managed to score us an invite to a high school party. My parents were staunchly against my attendance at what Becca called "the party of the year" because they knew the person hosting the party, a current classmate of my sister's. I never thought to question how Becca had managed to get us into the party as we got ready in her room that night. Looking back now, I wonder how my parents could have thought anything else was going to happen after they had said no to the party and then I had immediately asked to spend the night at Becca's instead. At the time, though, I whole-heartedly believed we had pulled the wool over their eyes. I can still vividly picture the black spaghetti strap tank top, flared jeans, and chunky platform sandals that I had bought at the mall hoping that they looked like I'd ordered them from the Delia's catalog. We had Becca's dad drop us off at the movies and then when we were sure his car was out of sight, we walked to the party.

Honestly, I don't even remember if I had fun. I remember there being a lot of people there and being afraid that someone would recognize me as Mindy's little sister and call her, or worse, that she might be there herself. By the end of her senior year, parties were not Mindy's thing but that hadn't stopped me from being afraid of running into her at this one when I wasn't supposed to be there in the first place. I don't remember much about the party besides that. What I do remember is what happened when we got back to Becca's house.

Her dad had arrived back at the theater to pick us up, discovered that we had not gone to see *The Mummy* like we had told him we were going to do and called my parents. They quickly figured out that we'd gone to the party even though they'd said "no" and they waited at Becca's house for us to come home. When we did finally make it back to Becca's, we tiptoed in and closed the door softly behind us before sharing a round of silent high fives and celebratory dances that we'd pulled it off... and that's when the lights turned on. I had never seen my parents so disappointed in me.

"What if something had happened?" they had asked. "What if you'd been hurt?"

I was grounded for a month, which was especially terrible because it was just as summer was about to start. And while Becca and I snuck out at least a dozen more times before we graduated high school, I never forgot how angry and disappointed my parents were that night. That is all I can think of as Mrs. Wang and I approach Sheng, even though we're grown women, capable of making our own choices, he's wearing the same expression.

"We've been worried sick! Get inside both of you!" he scolds. For a second, I do still feel like that thirteen-year-old who's just had the lights switched on. My feelings quickly change from shame to anger when I observe Sheng examining his mother as if I might have taken her out to get a nose piercing or shoot heroin between her toes. Once he has deemed her ink and track mark free, he gives her a hug and says something in Chinese which I can only assume is the equivalent of "thank goodness you're alright."

Following Sheng into the dining room, we find Jie who gives me a look that seems to say she is sorry that her husband is so crazy. Looks aside, she takes a seat beside him, opposite Mrs. Wang and me at the table. She may be sympathetic, but she's still on his side.

"Imagine how we felt, coming home and finding Mama gone with no warning!" Sheng exclaims once we are seated. I do my best not to roll my eyes, he is acting like his mother is a small child in need of round the clock supervision. I watch Jie clasp and then unclasp her hands in front of her, waiting for her to speak up and come to my defense. I might have intentionally kept Sheng in the dark, but I hadn't been so foolish as to not let anyone know where we were headed.

"What if something had happened? What if she'd been hurt?" he continues. The echo of my parents' words from that night all those years ago sets me off. It is obvious where we've been, at least partly, I've been lugging this dress bag all over London for the better part of the afternoon.

"With all due respect, sir," I start, "but why would you hire me if you didn't think I was capable of taking your mother out of the house and keeping her safe in the process?"

Sheng stays silent. His face is a shade of red I've never seen on a person before and part of me wonders if I should be playing with fire. After all, he's the one who has signed my visa and if I lose this job, then I'm out of options.

"I've given you plenty to do here, where I know it's safe! What more could you need?" he asks after a moment. Mrs. Wang has remained silent through the whole ordeal so far, just like her daughter-in-law, and I desperately wish that one of them would speak up to help me out here.

"I knew where they were," Jie says then. Her voice is soft, almost as if she's unsure she should be speaking to her husband in this way. Although I admire and respect their relationship, it's suddenly clear to me that I don't know the dynamics of how things work between them and I worry that I've asked Jie to take on more than is fair.

"You – you knew?" Sheng asks. I'm not sure if he's angrier with Jie or with me. How is it that I seem to find trouble at every job I have tried to hold in London? I never had these kinds of issues in Ohio. Maybe I'd be better off going back.

"Molly told me their plans this morning. Seeing as in the past she's been an activities director at multiple care homes, I felt confident in her ability to plan a day for Mama Ting without interference," she replies. It's not outright saying that Sheng's schedules are stupid, but it's saying a lot. Sheng sighs deeply, I can see the red draining from his face as he says something to her in Chinese.

"Molly, go to your room. This has become a private family matter and I will deal with you later," Sheng snaps suddenly, through clenched teeth. I feel myself flinch. I don't appreciate being admonished as if I am a child, being sent to my room to think about what I've done. But if I want to keep my job, now is not the time to speak up for myself. Instead, I stand, collect my purchases from the foyer, and make my way downstairs to the apartment I share with Mrs. Wang. I can hear the anger in Sheng's tone as I walk away even though I don't understand the words he's saying.

I don't know how to save this. When I texted Jie to let her know about my plans, I had intentionally not sent Sheng the same message. Was it because I knew that he wouldn't approve? I had completed the morning exactly as he'd written it and had only blown off the busy work items from Mrs. Wang's afternoon schedule. But I had done it with pleasure, as if defying Sheng's written schedule was sticking it to every man who had ever wronged me. I messed up, plain and simple. Whether Mrs. Wang is my friend or not, Sheng is still my employer. Sitting on the end of my bed, I sigh and put my head into my hands. I can't imagine going back to Ohio, but at this point what other choice do I have?

I am just finishing packing my first suitcase when Mrs. Wang barges into the room without knocking. The rest of the Wangs trail behind her, even Jasper. I don't stop what I'm doing though, I imagine they'll want me out of here tonight.

"Moll-ee, no!" Mrs. Wang exclaims, placing her hands on my wrists and stopping me mid-movement. I can't bring myself to look at her, it's heart-breaking to think of having to leave her now.

"I'm sorry Sheng, Jie," I say, still looking down at my hands which Mrs. Wang still has a hold of. "I shouldn't have defied the written list. But if you'll just give me a little time, I'll have all of my things and be out of your hair."

Someone else approaches me then, I can tell from the lightness of foot that it's Jie. She lifts my chin gently to face her. "It's okay, Molly. You're not being fired," she tells me. I finally allow her face to come into view and in doing so, I can see Sheng behind her looking sheepish.

"I don't understand. I blatantly disregarded your instructions," I say to him even though I'm still looking at her.

"I may have... ah... been a little overbearing with the scheduling," Sheng says then.

"A little," Mrs. Wang echoes and I can almost hear the correct application of sarcasm in her tone.

"But the schedules were meant for Mama's own good," he says in his own defense.

"I understand your concern for her well-being, sir. It's commendable, really. But scheduling out every minute of her every day, down to exactly what foods she eats and what clothes she wears is a little outrageous," I reply. I feel a little more free to speak my mind since it sounds like Mrs. Wang and Jie have already done their part to set him straight.

"The schedules were meant to be a help to you both. I want her to be happy here, and I thought keeping busy would help," he admits.

"She's capable of keeping busy all on her own. What do you think she did for all those months when she was living in her flat?" I ask. Mrs. Wang nods emphatically beside me, she's finally released my wrists from her grip.

"I happy," she says in English. Then she says something in Chinese where I hear the names "Moll-ee" and "Jas-par" so I know she's telling him the same thing she told me before, that as long as she has the people she loves that she is happy.

"Sheng, I know you love your mother. She loves you too, very much. But loving her and wanting the best for her are very different from commandeering her entire life. When you offered me this job, I told you that she didn't need a nurse and I still believe that. If she stays cooped up in the house all day every day, we're all going to go a little crazy," I add.

Sheng takes a deep breath and leans back against the wall, and I wonder what he's thinking. To be honest, I'm still a little hurt that he would think I would have done anything to put Mrs. Wang in danger. Not only is she my charge but she's my best friend and the very thought of hurting her in any way makes me sick to my stomach. It's offensive that Sheng would think or say otherwise, especially when he hired me for just this purpose.

"Yes, my wife and my mother have expressed the same sentiment. No more schedules," he says after a moment. "But you have to tell us where you're going."

"They did that already," Jie reminds him.

"Both of us. Just so that there's no confusion," he adds. I'm fine with this deal. While I had told Jie where we were going today, I kind of hadn't told Sheng on purpose. Even though I think his reaction might have been blown out of proportion, he was right to be concerned when he arrived home and couldn't find his mother and saw that she hadn't spent an hour writing letters to her friends back in China.

"Now, let's get ready for supper," Sheng says. The way he stands up and claps when he's done is exactly like his mother and it's easy to see where he gets it from. Mrs. Wang follows him out of the room and leaves me standing next to Jie silently. She offers me a weak smile.

"Thank you," I say. It seems like the right thing to do, especially since she had to speak up to her husband in a way that made her uncomfortable.

"Come in the kitchen and help me with the food?" she asks as a reply.

I haven't had any alone time with Jie since the night I first came over for dinner all those months ago. I didn't realize it was something I'd been missing until I'm invited to have more of it.

"How can I help you?" I ask her.

"Oh, I don't really need help. I just wanted an excuse to come in here and drink wine," she says coyly. "Would you like a glass?"

Before I can answer she hands me a goblet full of deep red

liquid and raises her own glass to my own.

"Cheers! Now, tell me about your dress!" she exclaims.

It had never crossed my mind that Mrs. Wang might not be the only member of the Wang household who didn't have friends or a life in London. I'd always seen Jie as this beautiful, stylish, successful, amazing woman - and while she is all of those things, I had always assumed that friendship came naturally to her. I never think about someone being beautiful, stylish, successful, amazing, and lonely.

I knew from Sheng that he and Jie had been married for eight years and they'd lived in London for seven and a half of those. He had made his new bride move halfway around the world when he'd been promoted at his Shanghai investment firm and was transferred to their London office. They had lived here ever since, only returning to China a handful of times to visit family. Jasper had been born here, their careers are here, practically their whole lives are here... except maybe for friendship.

And so, I sit in Jie's kitchen, sipping wine and telling her all about the dress I'm going to wear to Sam's gala, indulging her with all of the little details of my day and feeling happy that I have someone here who's on my side.

32.

Since Sheng has weekends mostly free, my time is my own, which is why I'm still in bed when my phone rings at nine on Saturday morning waking me from a comfortable slumber. It's the morning of the gala and I had had every intention of staying in bed for as long as possible.

"Hello?" I answer groggily without checking to see who was calling.

"Molly, don't hang up," Jake says on the other end. Now I'm awake. I sit up with a start, it's four in the morning back home, but given Jake's work schedule that's the least surprising element of this call.

"Mindy gave me your number," he continues when I don't respond. I'll kill her. I will actually kill her. What was she thinking?! This is the one thing I had made her promise not to do.

"I just... I really needed to talk to you."

I still haven't spoken. I don't know what to say. Jake hasn't had a word to say to me since he broke my heart in front of everyone in the world who mattered to me, so I'd be lying if I said I wasn't at least a little curious to hear what he suddenly has to say now.

"Jake, it's been almost a year. What could we possibly have to talk about now after all this time?" I ask him. Curious or not, this guy is a dirtbag.

"I made a huge mistake. Hurting you, thinking I'd be better off with Becca, I regret all of it," he says. Again, I'm silent. I could have told him that he'd regret it way back then, but I hadn't. Not that I would have taken him back if he'd expressed his regret sooner, but now it's all just a little too late.

"Okay, well thanks for letting me know," I say coolly. I can hear Mrs. Wang puttering about in the apartment and I wish that she'd come barging into my room without knocking again so that I'd have an excuse to end this phone call.

"Please don't hang up." He sounds softer, more vulnerable. There had only been a handful of occasions in our entire six-year relationship when I'd seen him that way. Once when his grandfather had died, twice after he couldn't save someone from a structure fire, once when the Indians lost the World Series, and once when we'd rented *Toy Story 3*. That was it. So hearing him this way now compels me to at least hear him out.

"I'm here," I say after a second.

"I'm so sorry, Molly, for everything. I was an absolute asshole to you, and I wouldn't blame you if you wanted to hate me forever."

That's good to know because hating him forever has been working out pretty well for me so far. Instead of saying this though, I just sit and wait for him to talk again.

"Becca and I are done. Not that that makes a difference to you, but we're over. It was a huge mistake. All she seemed to care about was hurting you, and after we saw you in London and she saw how well you were doing, she kind of… I don't know… lost her motivation to be with me, I guess."

This is more information than I'd had before, that it was Becca who had driven the whole thing. It was Becca who had gone after my fiancé, Becca who had made him fall in love with her, Becca who wanted to hurt me. But why? I had been nothing but loyal to Becca from the time we were five. I feel a knot rising in my chest. Why would she want to hurt me like that? A sob escapes my lips before I can stop it.

"Are you okay?" he asks. No, genius, obviously not.

"I don't understand…" I start.

"Why she did it?"

"Yeah. What the hell?" It feels like my entire life is flashing before my eyes, all the memories I have of Becca file through my mental Rolodex one right after the other: elementary school recess, our first school dance, getting our drivers licenses on the same day, high school graduation, college graduation... every piece of my life had involved Becca.

"I don't know, I think she was afraid," he says then, drawing me back out of my thoughts. Afraid of what? We'd promised to be together in the nursing home, what did she have to be afraid of?

"Afraid that you were going to get married and be happy and leave her behind," he adds, as if reading my thoughts, I wish he weren't able to do that. He's the last person that I want to have that connection with... or the second to last person.

"Would we have been happy, though? Really?" I ask.

"Ouch."

"Jake, let's not lie to ourselves. I meant what I said when you were here, you kind of did me a favor."

"I get it. You're still pissed at me."

"That's not it, Jake. I've had a lot of time to think about things. I wasn't happy, I don't think you were happy either. If you were happy, would you have gone running to Becca when she called? I don't think getting married would have made us happy, either. That's something you figured out before I did, I guess. But I've seen how things can be different now, how someone can make me feel; how someone SHOULD make me feel..."

"So, you're still with that guy then?" he cuts me off. He says "that guy" like the words are poison in his mouth.

"Sam," I say his name because I know that Jake won't. "Yes. For now. I don't know what will happen in the future, but I do know that I can't go back to the way it was in the past."

Jake doesn't say anything, I know he imagined this call going differently. Jake was always so full of confidence. With a more objective eye I've been able to see that it was often misplaced. It's likely that he genuinely believed that if he called me and apologized and told me that it was over with Becca that I'd be on the next flight back to Cleveland and we'd pick our lives right back up where we'd left off.

Even though I already know the answer, I ask, "Did you think I was going to want you back?"

He pauses for a few seconds before he answers, "I guess I hoped it might be possible."

It's a less confident answer than I would have expected from him, but then again, he is more vulnerable than I had ever seen him. It's tough to be vulnerable and confident at the same time.

"Jake, I'm sorry, but I can't."

It gets so quiet on the other end that I have to pull the phone away from my ear to see if we're still connected. He's there, so I just wait.

"You seem like you're doing real good," he says finally. He sounds dejected, like it's finally hitting him that I don't need him to be happy. I don't bother correcting his grammar, now is not the time for that.

"I am," I tell him, even though I only half believe it myself.

"Goodbye, Jake," I say as I hang up. I still feel like I could cry, but I've spent so many months crying over Jake, and I don't want to spend one second more on him. Although, I don't even know if I'd be crying over him anymore, really. If what he said is true, then it was Becca who orchestrated the whole thing to begin with. Becca who couldn't stand to see me happy. Becca who wanted everything I had all for herself. I have no reason to doubt Jake, it's exactly the kind of stunt that Becca would have pulled. I'd watched her do petty things for years, I just never thought she'd do them to me. But I can't cry over Becca anymore either. If what Jake said is true and she did screw me over like that, she doesn't deserve my tears. Instead, I shift my focus to a place where I can put my anger... Mindy.

It's way too early for me to call her, especially on a Saturday, but I need to strike while the iron is hot. Or while I am at least. Giving Jake my number was the one thing I'd asked her not to do. The only reason I'd let her have it in the first place was because she'd sworn to keep it to herself. Now I don't know what to do. She's the last member of my family that I even talk to at this point, I don't want to cut her off too. I hope I won't have to.

Mindy, we need to talk. You know why. I type and send the text before I can have second thoughts. Knowing my sister, I know she had good intentions. She probably thought that talking to Jake would give me closure. That hearing him apologize would make me feel better. That maybe I'd even decide that I should give him another chance and come back home. Why does everybody think that? Do they think that I'm so weak that I can't survive in this world on my own? Even if I did need a man to help get me through, why on earth would anyone think that man would be Jake?

I can't sleep anymore. All of my plans of staying in bed for as long as possible before taking my time in getting ready for tonight have been dashed by the anger fueled energy now coursing through my veins. Had Becca filled me with this much rage before? This is the second time since I've been in London that she has made me this angry, but I don't remember ever noticing it before. We'd fought over the years, sure, but we'd always made up. She'd never left me feeling anything other than love for her. Had I been that much of a fool? Had she been playing me the whole time? That's an extremely long game to play if so…

I can feel it running through my shoulders. It makes it so that I can't sit still, and I actually feel like going for a run. This is how you know something is wrong with me. I've always said that if you see me running, you should start running, too; because if I am running then something is definitely chasing me. That would be the only possible explanation for my taking a run, until now. Until Becca. In a way, it is sort of like Becca is chasing me, isn't it? Like she's chasing me from 3,000 miles away and I have to run just to get away from her. But that's a choice. I can choose not to run from her, not to let her keep chasing me. I don't have to understand her reasons in order to make that choice.

Instead, I shower and go through the motions of getting ready for the day. Of course, I don't know where I'm going or what I'm going to do when I get there, but that's not important at the moment. It's more about the action of just doing something with all of this emotion that matters. I carefully select my clothes and painstakingly curl my hair. I apply makeup as if I've watched a hundred YouTube tutorials. I take the time to give myself a manicure and paint my toenails to match. I figure it is all just a head start on tonight. When all of that is done and the feelings still linger, I finally head out the door.

The streets of Fitzrovia are bustling with weekend activity and as soon as I'm out in the hustle and bustle, it's easier to feel a little bit more like my problems don't matter as much. Out here I can blend in with the masses as they go about their holiday shopping and other menial tasks and feel like my world isn't continuing to implode, one thing after another. I'm just ascending the steps of the British Museum when my phone rings. Mindy.

"Hello," I say, because even with the advent of caller id, I still can't answer the phone any other way.

"Molly? I got your text, is everything okay?" she sounds panicked.

"Not really."

"What's wrong? What happened?"

"Jake called."

"Oh! Is that all? You had me worried there for a second." Seriously?

"I specifically asked you not to give out my number. Mindy, you promised me."

She doesn't say anything for a few seconds. "He told me that he and Becca broke up and that he wanted to talk to you so that he could apologize. Is that not what he did?"

"What he called about is beside the point, Min. I didn't want to talk to him, and you didn't give me the choice."

"I just thought…" she starts.

"You just thought that he'd call and apologize, and I'd be so happy to hear it that I'd take him back and be forced to move back to Cleveland," I finish for her. She's silent.

"The thought did cross my mind," she admits finally. I'm right, but this isn't one of those situations where that feels good.

I wish that I wasn't right about this, in fact. I wish that my sister cared more about my health and well-being than she did about whether or not I live in a world that makes sense to her (aka Cleveland, Ohio.)

"Mindy, I can't do this anymore," I tell her.

"Can't do what? Be in London? Do you need to come home?"

"No -- I can't talk to you anymore. At least not right now." Again, she is silent. I wait to see if she says anything else before saying my goodbyes, and I'm just about to when she finally speaks.

"What about Christmas?" she asks finally.

"I won't be there."

I'd been on the fence about whether I wanted to fly home for the holiday or not. On the one hand, being with family is literally what Christmas is about. On the other, I didn't know if I was ready to be back there just yet. Now, in this moment, I finally know the answer.

I have no idea what I'll do for the upcoming holidays, but I don't want Mindy to know that. What matters right now is that I won't be going home, not after everything that happened there this last year and especially not after what Mindy did today.

33.

My heart is broken. It goes without saying that I never make it inside the museum, after my call with Mindy I head right back home and crawl into bed. Mindy was the last thing I had left of my family and my old life. And now she's gone. She betrayed me, wholly and completely and right now it feels unforgivable. What's worse is that it was for her own selfish reasons, because she wanted me to come home. Maybe I was too quick to react, I could have tried to hear her out, but why do I have to be the one who is hearing people out all of the time? No. For now, I choose my heartbreak.

Almost instinctively I reach for Jane's locket which has taken pride of place right next to my bed. It's an absent-minded action, but it makes me feel closer to her. The knock on my door comes almost as soon as I let out the first sob. It's Mrs. Wang's familiar tap and I know she's heard me cry. I don't respond, but unlike the last time she found me crying in my bed, there's no lock on the door to keep her out.

"Moll-ee," she calls softly, I hear her feet shuffle across the carpeted floor. "You are okay?"

She places her body right in front of my face so that I have no choice but to look at her. I could rollover but that seems aggressive when I know she just wants to be there for me while I'm upset. Instead, I let her sit down on the edge of the bed and stroke my hair softly. It's comforting, but it also reminds me of how Mindy used to comfort me when we were children and I begin to cry even harder.

Was I this upset after the rehearsal dinner? I can't remember now. I think that night I was too stunned, almost numb. Mindy took me back to her house and tucked me into the guest bed and then went back downstairs to make some calls. I know now that they were the calls to tell people that the wedding the next day was off, but at the time I didn't realize that. I don't think that I cried that night. I didn't cry until the next day. I think ending things with my sister may hurt worse than being jilted the night before my wedding.

"What it is?" she asks. In any other circumstances, her sentence structure may have made me laugh. But today I can't muster the strength, it hurts too much.

When I don't respond, Mrs. Wang keeps prying. "It is Sam?" she asks.

"No. It's my sister," I say finally, more to get her to stop asking questions than because I want to talk about it.

"Okay?" she asks then. I know what she's asking – has something happened? Is everyone at home okay?

"She gave Jake my phone number after I specifically told her not to because she hoped that I'd hear from him and want to go back to my old life," I spew then. Mrs. Wang nods understandingly, but while her English has improved, I still have no idea if she understands. I find, though, that once I start talking about it, I can't stop, whether she understands or not.

"Family hard work," she says after I've run out of words. I smile for the first time all day. She could say that again.

It feels better to talk about my breakup with Mindy, but it doesn't change the ache I feel deep in my heart. I don't want to dwell on the sadness, though, not today. Today I have to be on and ready and happy to be on the arm of Sam Collins.

Ugh, that makes it sound like I'm not happy to be on his arm. I am... I think. It's all so complicated. I like Sam, a lot. But I have to decide if I want to live the kind of life that he lives; if I can have more days like today where I'm devastated this morning and pretending to be happy by nightfall. It's already exhausting, and I haven't lived it yet.

So far in London, when the going has gotten tough, I've relied on my old drama club experience. Today's performance, though, will stretch my limits far beyond anything I've ever done before, and I don't know if I'm up for the challenge today or tomorrow or any day after that. Now it's too late to cancel.

"I have to get dressed," I say suddenly, sitting upright in bed and knocking Mrs. Wang off balance. She and Jie had already agreed that they would help me get ready. At the time, I hadn't known I was going to need so much work, and now I'm a little worried that they won't be able to cover up my red eyes and that I'll be crying so hard that they won't be able to even attempt to apply eye makeup. Still, I don't have a choice.

That's not true. I'm sure that if I called Sam and explained the situation he'd be completely understanding and would probably excuse me from having to attend. But I'm not naïve enough to think that being Sam's date to the gala tonight means nothing. Until now, he's always brought his grandmother, which means that tonight is a test. It's a test to see how I do as I make my public debut on his arm. It's a test to see how I handle the pressure. I already know that I'm crumbling. But if I don't go tonight, I might not get another chance. I have to be there.

Mrs. Wang has gone off to fetch her daughter-in-law and all I can do while I wait is stare at my dress hanging on the outside of the wardrobe, clutching Jane's locket even more tightly in my fist. It really is a beautiful dress, perfect for the occasion just like the shop girl had said it would be and I'm lucky that I get to wear it. That's what I decide to focus on – I get to wear a pretty dress on a date with a handsome man. If that can't make me feel even a little bit happy, then nothing can.

"It's so lovely," Jie says. I hadn't noticed her come into the room but it's easy to see why her attention went straight to the dress and not to me sitting and staring at it.

"How are you? Mama Ting said you had a rough morning."

I let a laugh escape through my nose, calling my morning "rough" is the understatement of the century. This morning was the most traumatic that I've had in a long time, and that's saying something considering my history. But the word choice isn't Jie's fault. I shrug at her and offer a weak smile. "It wasn't great," I admit.

"Moll-ee, come. Sit," Mrs. Wang says as she enters, carrying a steaming mug of tea. She calls me toward the armchair that sits in the corner of my room. In the week I've been here, I've never used it though I had immediately liked the thought of having my own quiet place to sit. As soon as I sink into it, I make a mental note to spend more time there; it's heavenly, and with the hot cup of tea in my hand, I feel instantly comforted.

It's only then that I notice that Jie has brought down a treasure trove of makeup. When she opens the shiny silver case, it looks like a professional setup. It's funny considering she's always so fresh faced, usually wearing only a bit of mascara and lip-gloss.

"I'm a collector," she tells me. "You could call it my guilty pleasure."

She's a collector, alright. The case must be full of thousands of dollars' worth of product in every shade imaginable and she quickly sets about choosing exactly what will work for me. She even walks over to the dress a couple of times to compare the skirt to different pallets in her collection. The women in this family and their love for all things girly sure was squashed by those boys upstairs...

"Are you excited for tonight?" Jie asks when she finally gets started on my face. She dabs moisturizers and primers and foundations from the back of her hand with an applicator as if she's done this a million times.

"I wish I could say I was, but after this morning..." I start. I stop myself before I continue because I don't want to cry again and mess up all of Jie's work. Mrs. Wang is sitting on the ground beside my chair, and she squeezes my free hand gently, the other one still clutches the mug of tea.

"Do you want to talk about it?" Jie asks as she continues to work.

"Not really," I reply. Mrs. Wang lets go of my hand and reaches up to touch Jie's arm.

"You're right," she says to Mrs. Wang before turning back to me. "I'm sorry Molly, I didn't mean to overstep."

"You didn't. I'm just afraid that if I keep thinking about it and talking about it that I'll keep crying and then I'll be in no condition to drag myself out of here tonight." I try to sound light, friendly. Now that I know how much Jie needs a friend, I'm eager to be that for her and I don't want to shoot her down, but I also know my own limits.

We're all silent for a while after that as Jie does my makeup and I try my best to sip my tea without interrupting her. Since I'd given myself a manicure this morning while I tried to kill time before talking to Mindy, there's nothing for Mrs. Wang to do at the moment but sit with me. And, honestly, that's my favorite thing anyway.

It's hard, though, to stop my mind from wandering to Mindy. I imagine how she's probably out finishing her Christmas shopping, taking Teddy's gifts to my mom's house to hide them until Christmas because he has discovered every hiding place at their own home. I imagine how she'll stop for lunch when she's out and about and how she would have called me to see if I was free to join her, just like she'd been doing for years. And I wonder how she feels, too. Is she as devastated by the results of our conversation as I am? I'm sure she's confused. She probably feels blindsided. She wasn't expecting me to cut her off completely, even if I did get mad that she'd given Jake my number. But even as much as I think about it, I can't think of another outcome. No matter how much I want to, I don't regret how I ended it. Mindy wants me to step back into my old life as if nothing ever happened, and that's just not something that's possible any longer.

"Oh, Moll-ee," Mrs. Wang says then, she reaches up and wipes a tear from my eye. I hadn't even realized I'd begun to cry until then. That's exactly why I hadn't wanted to think about Mindy at all in the first place.

"I'm sorry..." I begin.

"It's okay! We can fix it! And the mascara... is waterproof!"

Jie says the last part like we're sharing a special secret and it makes me smile. It's weird to feel happy and sad at the same time especially when my head wants to feel happy so that I can make it through tonight and my heart wants to feel sad and mourn that I've lost my sister.

"I do hair," Mrs. Wang says then. I think it's her way of trying to keep me distracted and I appreciate the sentiment. She quickly hurries out of the room.

"You're in luck!" Jie exclaims. "Mama Ting used to be a hairstylist back in China when she was a young woman. You're getting a professional service for free!"

This is the most I've ever heard about Mrs. Wang's life before London and I'm immediately hungry for more. There wasn't anything in our time together that had given me any kind of indication that she'd had a career once, though maybe it was my own ignorance that I didn't assume she might have had a job in her old life.

"She did my hair for my wedding, I felt so special!" Jie continues. She swoops a brush over my face and it tickles my nose.

"What else was she like? When she was younger, I mean?"

Jie pauses for a moment, thinking. "I've only known her for about ten years, and she was done working by then. Sheng's father got cancer when Sheng was in university and Mama Ting started caring for him full-time. But Sheng always tells Jasper stories about what his childhood was like, how his parents loved singing and riding roller coasters and they'd travel all over Asia to ride the newest rides."

Huh, I never would have taken Mrs. Wang for a roller coaster enthusiast. The wildest ride she seemed to enjoy was the Underground. The love of singing didn't surprise me, but she only sang when she thought I wasn't listening. I guess I didn't know her that well, at least not the version of her who had had a life back in China. Just like she didn't know the version of me who had had a life back in Cleveland. We've given each other exactly what we needed for the life we have here, everything old is behind us.

"But, after her husband died, she stopped doing all the things that had made her happy before. She wasn't a thrill seeker anymore and she never went back to work - she started allowing Sheng to give her money. I think she lost the will to live for a while. That's why Sheng was so anxious to get her over here with us. Little did we know that it would be you who would do it," she continues.

"Me? Who would do what?"

"You who would bring her life back," Jie says just as Mrs. Wang comes back into the room loaded down with a basket full of hair styling supplies. Where had those even come from? I'd known her flat and now our shared bathroom pretty well and I'd never seen these things before.

"Moll-ee, you want up hair? Or down hair?" she asks, she makes a curling motion with her finger when she mentions down hair, apparently Tim hasn't taught her much about hair tools during their lessons.

"I loved the way you did it when I was trying on the dress. Do you remember?"

"Oh. Yes. So pretty," she says with a smile. I'd loved the way she did my hair the other day, but I'd had no idea that she knew exactly what she was doing when she had done it.

I haven't had anyone do my hair in ages, and I'd forgotten how relaxing it could be. I can't see Mrs. Wang working but I can feel her hands work expertly through my hair, which I can admit has gotten a little out of control. She handles my head and my hair with such tender care that I wonder what it must have been like to have been her client, I'm kind of sad to have missed the opportunity.

I haven't had anyone do my hair like this since the prom. For the wedding I was trying to save money and so Becca was going to do my hair, we'd spent weeks practicing different hairstyles, trying to get it just right. I hadn't even considered feeling special when Becca did my hair, maybe it's because she hadn't treated me like I was special the way that Mrs. Wang is doing.

"Okay, Molly, you're all done!" Jie says, calling me back into the moment. It's the first chance I have to realize that I wasn't thinking about Mindy and that feels like progress.

"Wow!" Mrs. Wang exclaims as she comes around to the front of the chair.

"How do I look?"

"So, pretty Moll-ee." She beams at me like I'm her own child.

"Let's get you into that dress," Jie adds.

This is what I had missed from the morning after Jake's announcement. I had missed being doted on as people worked on my hair and makeup. I had missed having my hand held as I slipped into my dress. I had missed having someone else put my shoes on for me. I didn't know that I had missed it, I didn't even know that it would make me feel any particular way. But now that I'm having the experience, I realize it's exactly what I needed.

"You look wonderful!" Jie exclaims with a gasp. I haven't looked in the mirror yet, but I feel wonderful so I'm sure she's right. As soon as I see myself, my breath catches in my throat.

"Wow, you ladies really did a great job!" I mean it, my face and hair look like they belong to a woman who attends galas in London with a local celebrity. I hardly look like me at all, and that's great because that's exactly how I have to feel to make it through this night in one piece.

34.

"Are you alright?" Sam asks when I teeter on my heels as I step toward his waiting car. He offers me his arm to steady myself and as I reach for it, I can't help but wonder if that's ever happened before. I don't think I've ever been the type of girl who got help from a man who was just being kind. Maybe that says more about men than it says about me, but still. It's shaped me into the woman that I am today... whoever she is.

I'd been afraid of these shoes as soon as I'd bought them, and the fact that I'm already struggling to stay upright doesn't bode well for the rest of the evening. If I'm being honest, though, I know Sam's not asking about the shoes. As much as I might look like a baby deer struggling to stand on the high heels, I look like a deer in the headlights even more.

"I'm great, it's just these shoes," I lie. I can see it in Sam's pause that he wants to press harder, to find out what's really bothering me that has nothing to do with my shoes. But I refuse to bring my drama into his night.

"Well, you look incredible," he decides finally. He offers me his megawatt smile and I melt. I don't know what it is about Sam: we've been on dates, spent hours on the phone, shared a lot of kisses, and even had sex and he still renders me completely hopeless and awkward whenever I see him.

He looks incredible too, in his perfectly tailored tuxedo that does nothing to stop the desire to reach out and grab his butt. I've never known the proper etiquette for complimenting men. Maybe that was Jake's fault, if I ever told him that he looked nice, he'd tell me that he didn't need compliments because he wasn't a pussy. Ugh, Jake. Thinking about him again puts a pit back in my stomach.

Something must change on my face, too, because Sam responds. "Are you sure you're alright?"

Am I the kind of girl who lies to the man she's seeing? It certainly seems like it would be easier to be that kind of girl. I could easily let my acting chops take over just like I'd planned. But I can't. Sam is looking at me with such earnestness and concern that I can feel the entire story getting ready to spill right out of me. If I lie, he's going to know.

"It was a tough morning. I'll tell you in the car. I don't want you to be late," I find myself saying. Mentally I'm kicking myself. This is supposed to be Sam's night. It's supposed to be about this cause he's passionate about and this gala that he's hosting. But I can't seem to shut my giant, American mouth.

"What happened?" he asks as soon as we're both safely in the back seat. And so, I tell him. Everything about Jake's call and then about my conversation with Mindy spills out of me. Sam listens intently. I keep waiting for him to chime in that I'm too emotional or that I need to suck it up for him tonight, but he doesn't. Instead, he nods and gasps in all the right places, offering me empathetic glances whenever they're appropriate.

"So that all happened today and it's a lot," I finish.

Sam's silent for a moment and I can't help feeling like I'm waiting for the other shoe to drop. I know I've already failed this test of being able to be Sam's date to an event like this and we haven't even made it to the event yet. He needs a trophy, not a basket case.

"How are you feeling now?"

"I'm not great," I admit. I turn away from him and look out the window, we're stuck in London traffic so nothing outside is going by quickly. I focus on a French Bulldog who has stopped along the side of the road to do its business.

"I considered telling you I couldn't make it tonight," I say to the dog, though that's not who I'm talking to. "But it was too late in the day and I…"

Seriously, Molly, stop talking. I don't know what it is, I like to think that I'm a pretty together person most of the time, this last year of my life notwithstanding. Maybe it's the weight of the day or the fact that Sam smells amazing and it's corrupting all of my brain cells. He reaches out and takes my hand in his.

"Thank you for coming."

The event is in the ballroom at The Dorchester, and it doesn't take long to figure out that the traffic we've been sitting in has been the line of cars just waiting to drop gala guests at the entrance. Of course, given the nature of the festivities, numerous attendees at tonight's event are in wheelchairs and need extra time and assistance to make their way inside. I've never done anything as grand as this. I remember watching all of the Hollywood awards shows with Becca over the years and how we'd comment on how glamorous it all must be. I can picture now the overhead shots that show the line of cars waiting to drop people off at those events, but I'd always ignored that image, choosing instead to think of the allure of a night like that. Now that it's me, I can confidently say that it's not that alluring at all.

"Ready?" Sam asks. It's finally our turn and I already see flashbulbs going off before our driver even makes it around to open the door.

"Yes?" It comes out more like a question and I know that neither Sam nor I believe it. He reaches for my hand and gives it a squeeze.

"It's alright. Take a deep breath, and just keep your eyes on me. Okay?" He's looking into my eyes with such sincerity that I couldn't possibly disagree. So, I nod almost imperceptibly and he leans in to give me a kiss just as the driver opens the door. Of course the cameras catch the whole thing, because they only ever seem to catch me kissing Sam whether I want them to or not.

He handles the whole thing like a pro, of course. He gets out of the car without letting go of my hand, then pauses to help me out. He stands tall and proud, buttoning his jacket with his free hand and pulling me closer to him at the same time, sliding his arm around my waist.

"Just breathe," he whispers into my ear before he places a chaste kiss on my temple.

I can do this. I can be this girl. I think to myself just as I hear one of the photographers call my name.

"Molly! Molly over here!" I can't place the speaker in the crowd.

"Molly, what do you say to those who have said you're just an opportunistic American sleeping her way to the top of the London social scene?"

I freeze but stop trying to look to identify the voice, it wouldn't matter even if I could find him. Who are those who think that? How do they know my name? I can feel the panic rising in my chest before I can do anything to stop it. It feels like the walls are closing in on me and I can't seem to take a breath. What am I supposed to do now? I can't breathe... I can't...

"I... have to go..." I say to Sam, dropping his hand before running through the nearest door. I can hear them calling after me, but I can't look back. I don't stop running until I hear only the faint muffled roar of their voices and find that I am standing in an industrial stairwell all alone. And barefoot.

Did I expect Sam to follow me? I guess maybe I did. A part of me wanted to be the damsel in distress and have my knight in shining armor come to my rescue. But I know why he didn't. He finally brought a girl to a public event, and she ran off on him at the first sight of attention. If I were him, I'd be beyond mortified and would do my best to carry on as best as I could. Heck, I had been him... all those months ago in Cleveland at my rehearsal dinner. I had been publicly humiliated by Jake just like I'd now done to Sam, and I know how well that turned out.

I thought that I could handle it. I thought that I could handle being this person who goes to fancy black tie galas and has their picture taken by prying paparazzi. But I can't. And if I can't handle being this person, then I can't handle being with Sam.

That's just the way it goes. I wonder how long I'll have to stay in this stairwell, though. I have no idea when the coast will be clear, and I could be here all night.

"Yes, in a stairwell just beyond the cloakroom," I hear the echo of his voice before I see him. He comes around the corner carrying my bag, the one Mrs. Wang had been so adamant about my needing, and my shoes. I'd hoped those had been abandoned forever, but I guess they're necessary if I ever plan to eventually leave this stairwell.

"Well, hello," he says with a smirk. He takes a seat on the ground beside me and hands me my bag. "You dropped this."

"I…" I start but he puts his hand on my knee, and I stop. I can't bring myself to look at his face, to see the shame that I'm certain is written there. I can't say for sure why he's not talking, but the silence that surrounds us feels like it lasts for hours.

"I should have prepared you for the cameras," he says at the exact same time that I say, "I'm sorry that I ruined this night."

What? How can he be blaming himself?

"After the kind of day you've had, I'm not surprised that question sent you running," he says thoughtfully. "This event draws a lot of celebrity support so there's always paparazzi posted up along the red carpet. They can be real wankers."

When he interlaces his fingers with mine, I practically lose it. "How are you not mad at me right now?"

"Why would I be mad at you?"

"Well, maybe because there are definitely pictures of me running away and abandoning you on the red carpet?"

"Oh, that. It's no big deal," he laughs.

"You don't have to lie to me to protect my feelings."

"Okay. It's a little bit of a big deal. But it will blow over. They'll have headlines for a couple of days and then some reality TV starlet will go topless on holiday in Thailand, and it'll be old news."

He says it so nonchalantly, like having your name and picture on the cover of tabloid newspapers is something that happens to people every day. He's an entertainment reporter, in his world that's EXACTLY the kind of thing that happens to people every day. But it doesn't happen in mine. This is the exact thing I was afraid of, having my life put out on public display like this. In a life like that I have to watch my every move and constantly be on my guard, I've already failed at that miserably... twice.

"I like you, Molly," he says then. It's like he knows exactly what I'm thinking. "I know my life is asking a lot of you. But know that it's not something I share with just anyone."

"I just don't know if I can be the kind of person who does this," I admit. "I'm more of a jeans and a t-shirt, drinking beer by the lake kind of a girl than a ball gown and high heels drinking champagne at a gala kind of a girl."

Sam laughs and I lean my head on his shoulder. "I like you, too. But I just feel like you need more."

"This isn't what my life is like, surely you know that by now," he says.

"This isn't the first time I've been in the tabloids," I retort without missing a beat.

"Touché."

We sit there like that for a while, neither of us saying a word. I'm still not convinced that I can be the kind of woman that Sam needs. But I also hear him telling me that that's not the person he expects me to be. It doesn't add up in my head, and yet he is here; sitting with me in this back stairwell while I have a panic attack instead of being out on the red carpet, beginning his hosting duties. I'm not used to people choosing me. I'm always the one doing the choosing, the one being there to support the people I care about. That's how it had been with Mindy and Becca and Jake. Not a single one of them would have followed me into this stairwell. They each would have waited until I emerged on my own and demanded that I pull myself together.

Before we have a chance to continue our conversation, a very familiar five-year-old superhero comes flying through the stairwell. He's followed by his parents and Mrs. Wang, who hurries quickly to me and sits down on my other side. I don't know why they're here or how they got here so quickly, considering the traffic. But as soon as I see them, I realize they're exactly the people I want to see right now.

"Hello, Moll-ee," Mrs. Wang says to me. I would have expected that when she met Sam for the first time, she would have been lavishing all of her attention on him but instead she keeps her focus on me. "You are okay?"

"Oh, I know you!" Linda says suddenly. She's clutching Daisy's arm as they come to meet us. Linda looks beautiful in a long-sleeved black velvet dress. Her hair has been curled and styled and she's even wearing a bit of makeup.

"What is going on?" I ask, unable to hide my confusion.

"Your phone was in your bag when you dropped it and I made a call. And we left a seat open for Granny in case she was feeling well enough to attend tonight," Sam says matter-of-factly.

"But why?"

"I thought that after the day you had, you should be reminded of who your family is now," he says. My eyes fill with tears, and I try to will myself not to cry.

"It's okay, the mascara… is waterproof!" Jie cheers, echoing her words from earlier.

"My friend Janie always used to say that sometimes the best family you can have are the people you choose for yourself," Linda says with a knowing smile.

"We're always here for you, Molly. After everything you've done for Mama, you're family," Sheng says. Mrs. Wang raises my hand to her lips and kisses it softly.

"Look, Molly, I like you," Sam says. "But if we don't end up together romantically, that's okay. Because what I'm really offering you, what we're all really offering you, is more than that. What we're offering you is a family. We may not look like much, but we're all yours. This is a life of your own making, and we're here for you no matter what."

I don't know what to say. My heart is full, in the same way it was when Linda remembered my name or when I learned that Mrs. Wang called me "My Molly." I had left my entire life behind in America because I wanted to run away from my broken heart, and I hadn't known what I was running to. Sam is right, though, the people in this room have become my family. They don't always have their words or their memories, but that's what makes me love them so much. Not to mention the fact that they all dropped everything to come find me in a stairwell at a hotel in London in the middle of December simply because I needed them. That's the thing that means the most. They chose me.

"Mr. Collins?" a voice calls from just inside the door. "Erm, you're needed on the red carpet, sir. We want to get a few good shots before the event begins."

I feel Sam's whole body heave when he sighs. He stands and dusts himself off before turning to face me. "I guess it's time to get back out there and try this again. What do you say?"

I can't believe he still wants me out there with him, posing for pictures after everything that just happened. I can't believe that he didn't take his chance to break clean away from me once and for all. I can't believe he went through the trouble to get everyone I love in one room when I was having a crisis. I can't believe that when Linda told me I should meet her grandson, this is who she meant.

I know what it means to choose to go with Sam, too. It means more than choosing Sam and his lifestyle. It means choosing all of these people who have come through for me tonight. It means choosing this life that I've started in London and letting the life I'd left behind finally die. It means so much more than just agreeing to go back to the red carpet with him.

I look at him with a smile, placing my hand in his outstretched one.

"I say yes."

ACKNOWLEDGEMENT

Thank you! The fact that you have finished reading my novel is the greatest gift in the world to me. When I was nine years old, locking myself in my bedroom to write the "Great American Novel," I couldn't even begin to imagine you. So, thank you.

Everything Old came to me in its entirety for the very first time in my writing career, but getting it out into the world has not been easy. I want to thank every person who has been beside me on this journey. Thank you to every person who rejected this book for giving me the drive to keep going on my own. To my proof-readers and friends who gave me honest feedback: Erin, Sam (thanks for feeling honored that I gave a boy your name), Claire (who read it in multiple draft formats), and Cara (aka Mom). Also, thank you to my husband, Allen, who found the real-life Jake racing us to the door at Leoda's Pie Shop in Maui (cargo shorts, sunglasses, and all).

And, lastly, thank you to Anna. Everything I do is for you. I hope you will always chase your own dreams.

ABOUT THE AUTHOR

Lindsey Brunette

Lindsey Brunette is a Los Angeles based writer with a passion for telling the stories of real women starting over. Her memoir  Being Here: Reflections on Life, Love, Faith, and Turning Thirty was published in 2018 and tells her own story of choosing to give up the life that she knew in order to have the life she deserved. Lindsey lives with her husband and toddler daughter as well as their Boston Terrier puppy and a flock of backyard chickens. You can visit her online at LindseyBrunette.com